"Some are born great, some achieve greatness, and some have greatness thrust upon them."

—*William Shakespeare*

View the author's website at www.arsenex.com

Visit the author's Facebook page at www.facebook.com/stephenarseneault10

Follow on Twitter @SteveArseneault

Ask a question or leave a comment at comments@arsenex.com

Cover Art by Kaare Berg at:

bergone.deviantart.com and bitdivision.no

Cover Design by Elizabeth Mackey at:

www.elizabethmackey.com

Copyright 2016-2017 Stephen Arseneault. All Rights Reserved.

All rights reserved. No part of this book may be used, reproduced or transmitted in any form or by any means, electronic or mechanical, including photocopying, recording, or by any information storage or retrieval system, without the written permission of the publisher, except where permitted by law, or in the case of brief quotations embodied in critical articles and reviews.

This book is a work of fiction. Names, characters, businesses, organizations, places, events, and incidents either are the product of the author's imagination or are used fictitiously. Any resemblance to actual persons, living or dead, events, or locales is entirely coincidental.

Novels written by Stephen Arseneault

SODIUM Series (six novels)

A six-book series that takes Man from his first encounter with aliens all the way to a fight for our all-out survival. Do we have what it takes to rule the galaxy?

AMP Series (eight novels)

Cast a thousand years into the future beyond SODIUM. This eight-book series chronicles the struggles of Don Grange, a simple package deliveryman, who is thrust into an unimaginable role in the fight against our enemies. Can we win peace and freedom after a thousand years of war?

OMEGA Series (eight novels)

Cast two thousand years into the future beyond AMP. The Alliance is crumbling. When corruption and politics threaten to throw the allied galaxies into chaos, Knog Beutcher gets caught in the middle. Follow along as our hero is thrust into roles that he never expected nor sought. Espionage, intrigue, political assassinations, rebellions and full-on revolutions, they are all coming to Knog Beutcher's world!

HADRON Series (eight novels)

HADRON is a modern day story unrelated to the SODIUM-AMP-OMEGA trilogy series. After scientists using the Large Hadron Collider discover dark matter, the world is plunged into chaos. Massive waves of electromagnetic interference take out all grid power and forms of communication the world over. Cities go dark, food and water supplies are quickly used up, and marauders rule the highways. Months after the mayhem begins, and after mass starvation has taken its toll, a benevolent alien species arrives from the stars. Only, are they really so benevolent? Find out in HADRON as Man faces his first real challenge to his dominance of Earth!

ARMS Series (eight novels)

ARMS is cast in one possible future, where Earth was nearing an apocalyptic event. Two competing colony ships were built, taking five million inhabitants each through a wormhole to a pair of newly discovered planets. The planets were settled and not long after the colonies looked to the surrounding star systems for ownership and expansion, which led to a centuries-long war between them. A truce was declared after the aggressor side began to lose ground.

Tawnish Freely and Harris Gruberg are genetically engineered Biomarines. Their lives have been dedicated to fighting the war. With a truce declared, they find themselves struggling to find work among a population that fears them. Work is found only by delving into the delivery of illegal arms to the outer colonies. Things go awry when they discover their illicit dealings may just be the catalyst that brings back the Great War. They are determined to prevent that from happening.

FREEDOM Series (eight novels)

After a period of domination over the lesser alien species of the galaxy, humanity finds itself enslaved for nearly five hundred generations. A highly addictive drug called Shackle has made Humans little more than drone workers. They are abused, sold, traded, and hunted, valued only in credits. But a mysterious virus is sweeping through the Human population, altering gut bacteria, making them immune to the drug that subjugates them. Humans are becoming aware of their condition. They will fight for their freedom.

Find them all at www.arsenex.com

ARMS

(Vol. 1)

War for Eden

Chapter 1

Tawnish Freely, a former Biomarine with the Domicile Defense Force, stood behind the transparent blast-wall with her hand on the grip of her plasma pistol. She gazed down the docking tube as her captain, Bax, attempted to conduct the sale of small arms to a trader from the outer colonies. The trade was not going as smoothly as planned.

Working as a grunt on a personal cargo ship was far from the future Tawn had envisioned when the Great War ended in a truce, two years prior. Regulars, as was her captain, rarely hired Bios, but for whatever reason, Baxter Rumford had made an exception. For that, Tawn was grateful.

The *Fargo* sat docked with the *Blazer* in an uninhabited system in the truce zone. The tall, thin, redheaded captain was working a sale to Bryce Porter, a trader from the Geldon colony, who would in turn try to sell the merchandise to the settlers in the outer free colonies. It was Tawn's first time out. She was nervous over the exchange, but confident in her ability to act should there be trouble.

"I take precautions, because you can't earn a living if you're dead," the buyer said as he stood blocking the open airlock.

Bryce wore a white, clean, neatly pressed tunic. The docking hatch, as was the surrounding cabin of his ship, was bright and shiny, almost glistening. He stood in a defiant stance, his feet positioned shoulder-width apart, his arms crossed and his chin held high in the air. "Show me the goods!"

Baxter Rumford's fists dug into her hips. Her blaster pistol and short deck-sword hung on the belt-clips to her sides, the sword also strapped to her thigh. The captain of the *Fargo*, sporting the face and body of a model, spat on the deck. "Show me the credits, moron."

Bryce returned an angry glare, raising his voice. "You can't just spit like that! This is my ship! *My home!*" He took a step

2

back, opening a cabinet. A cleaning cloth was retrieved. He knelt and began the process of wiping up the affront to his property.

"Don't care." Bax growled. "I have better things to do than to argue with some obsessively hygienic moron out here in the dead of space. Now show me I'm not wasting my time."

"You're an abomination to all things civil, Miss Rumford. Bring the merchandise over and I'll transfer your precious credits to your account. But until that freight is in my hold you aren't seeing anything. You imperious little space tart."

"Space tart?" Bax again spat. She glared at the kneeling Bryce Porter, her face flushed red with anger. With her right hand, she reached down to grasp the handle of the blade strapped to her left thigh. "You're lucky I don't pull this pig sticker and gut you right here and now."

"Again with the barbaric behavior." Bryce shook his head as he wiped. "The recorders on this ship say you aren't going to gut anyone."

"Slug!" Bax yelled down the docking tube as she looked over her shoulder. "Drag those containers over here!"

Tawn secured her pistol before coming from behind the transparent security wall. Seconds later, the containers in question were on the move.

Bryce continued to polish his floor with a scowl.

As Bax stared down, the corner of the wipe-cloth was pinned to the floor with the glossy, red heel of her high-legged boot. "Look Porter— I don't like you. And you ever wanna buy from me again— you need to show respect."

Jerking the cloth from her hold, Bryce stood and walked to the cabinet. The cloth was neatly folded and dropped into a dirty-clothes bin. "Fine by me. There are plenty of other suppliers out there selling your numbers."

Three containers of weapons were dragged across the docking tube by the new hire. She returned for a fourth marked "Plasma Charges".

A proximity alarm sounded on the trader's ship. *"Alert. Alert. Vessel approaching."*

Bryce glanced back at his console display before turning again to face the seller. "What is this? You brought others? Are you robbing me?"

Bax stared over his shoulder with a look of shock. "That's a New Earth warship!" She grabbed his forearm, reaching for the account store on his wrist. "Give me my credits!"

Bryce jerked away. "You brought Earthers? Are you insane!"

The struggle momentarily stopped as a voice came over the general comm. *"This is the New Earth destroyer Hemlock. Power down your drives and prepare to be boarded."*

Tawn dropped the container of charges in the buyer's hold. "Two more boxes of residuals. What do I do?"

Bax again reached for the account bracelet on Bryce's wrist. "Give me my payment!"

Bryce covered the store with his other hand as he refused. "Two more boxes!"

Bax spun, taking her assistant by the shoulder and shoving her toward the docking tube before breaking into a run. As they entered the *Fargo*, she slapped the airlock button to close the hatch. A sharp cut to the right and a further sprint had the nervous arms-dealer at the pilot's console.

The docking tube retracted. The *Fargo* began to pull away. Bryce Porter turned his ship in the opposite direction. The New Earth destroyer continued to close.

An angry Bryce came over a comm. "You will pay for this Rumford! No trader on the station will do business with you once this gets out!"

As the *Blazer* accelerated, four pulses from a plasma cannon saw to the end of the Geldon trader, Bryce Porter. His ship half disintegrated in a bright flash, the remainder shattering into a thousand pieces. Tawn took the seat beside her boss.

Bax slowly shook her head as she pulled back the throttle. "Can't outrun those."

"What do we do?"

The *Fargo* came to a stop.

"We do whatever they want."

Seconds later, the *Hemlock* pulled alongside. A docking tube extended with a boarding party of New Earth Marines moving onto the *Fargo*. The sale of illegal arms was over. Baxter Rumford was taken across the tube to the New Earth warship as Tawn was confined to her chair. After two years of struggling to find work, her first job with the potential to earn a living... was seemingly ending in disaster.

***

Seven weeks later

Bax spat on the deck.

Tawn frowned. "You know, some wouldn't consider that a very lady-like act."

"They teach you that in warfare charm school?" Bax said with a huff.

"Nope. Just saying. You get drunk and talk about meeting a good man and then you act like an orangutan— scratching your ass and smelling your finger. Not very attractive."

Bax flipped her head from side to side. Her relatively short, bright red hair whirled out around her head as if from a televised shampoo commercial. "If my butt itches, I scratch it, OK? Why should a slug care?"

Tawn sighed. "I care because I have to see it. Look, you've got the body and the face to make a play on just about any guy on the station. Why do you keep picking those seedy losers at the bar? You know, a guy with a chiseled face and a handful of credits isn't everything."

"Says the crewman who can't even breed. And who can't pay her bills, so she spends her time off-world, helping her captain sell illegal arms to the scum eking out a living in the outer colonies. Taking love advice from a slug is about the last thing I'll be doing."

"You sure can be harsh, but I can't argue with any of that. You're the only one who's given me a chance since the war ended. And I'm thankful— at least I will be if I ever get paid. And you should be glad to have me. Who else can handle and has fired half the weapons you're pushing out here?"

Bax tilted her head and scoffed. "Wasn't me who called an end to the war with New Earth. What a dumb name— New Earth. What moron came up with that?"

"Like ours is much better?" Tawn said as she snorted a laugh. "Domicile. Why not just call it House?"

Bax checked the nav display for approaching ships. "No one here yet. You have that manifest ready? I want us to be in and out on this one."

Tawn nodded as she looked over the info on her console. "Fifteen repeating plasma rifles. You do know those are highly illegal, right? We get caught and it's execution time. Not like the standard plasma unit, which is illegal enough."

"And the twenty-six zappers?" Bax asked.

"I wish you wouldn't call 'em that. It's not good for business. Anyone who knows weapons calls them by their name, Fox-40s, not the sound they make when fired."

"Fox-40." Bax scowled. "Another dumb name. Who came up with that? Some zookeeper?"

Tawn took in a deep breath. "No. The F designation is for firearm. The 40 is the unit number. It's the standard issue sidearm for—"

Bax raised her hand. "Yada, yada, for the Domicile Defense Force and you Biomarines. I know the story. You've told me at least twenty times now."

"Yet you still call them zappers."

"They are what they are."

The short, tank-like first mate turned to face her console display. "Here we go. We have an inbound cargo ship on the sensor array. Ten minutes and we'll be docked. The nav ID shows it to be the... *Gulward*."

6

Bax smiled. "Good. Now— read off the rest of that manifest to me..."

***

Tawn edged the *Fargo* in close, pressing the console button that allowed the auto-docking computer to take charge. "We'll connect with the *Gulward* in thirty seconds."

"I've got a good feeling about this one." Bax leaned back in her seat with a smile.

The Biomarine scowled at the rickety excuse for a ship on her display. "Why is every other vessel we dock with such a turd?"

"If you haven't guessed it already, we're mostly dealing with maggots in this business. Bryce Porter, even though an idiot, was an anomaly."

Tawn stood and walked toward the cargo hold hatch. "Cletus Dodger. That name sound legit to you? I'll bet he hasn't had a bath in a month."

"Don't care what his name is or what he looks or smells like so long as he has the credits." Bax reached for the airlock door button. "You know this buy lets me pay you for last month, right?"

Tawn smiled as she moved behind the transparent blast wall. "I know it. And I hope this goes as smoothly as our last two. And just so you know, if it's anything like that Geldon deal, you best be getting your ass back here without arguing over credits. This slug wants to keep breathing. We lucked out with all that contraband having been moved to the *Blazer*. They probably only let us go because there was no evidence of arms dealing."

"Yeah, well, you can't win them all. Just follow my lead and we'll be in and out of here."

"Ready."

Bax stood five meters across a docking through-way from her buyer. "You Cletus?"

6

A heavyweight man in a tattered trenchcoat replied, "You don't look like a Baxter."

"You got a problem with it, track down my derelict parents and take it up with them."

Cletus looked down the tube at a ready and armed Tawn. "You can tell your slug to relax. I'm unarmed. But Farker has a nasty bite if he feels I'm being threatened."

A mechanical pet trotted into view behind its owner.

Bax laughed. "Farker? What is that, a robotic dog? And who named him that?"

Cletus shrugged as he clomped forward. "Real ones kept dying on me. When Farker dies, I just plug him in for a bit and he's good as new. Ain't that right, boy? And I call him Farker because his bark sounds more like a fark than a bark. Even if I knew how to fix his programming for that I wouldn't. I like his — fark."

The unusual pet offered a very mechanical wag of its short tail.

Bax frowned as she checked the time on her bracelet. "Pathetic. OK then. Let's get this deal done. You have the fifty-six hundred forty-two credits?"

"After I see the goods I'll be happy to make the transfer."

Bax held up her hand, stopping Cletus at the end of the docking tube. "Show me— before you step on this ship. I need to see proof."

Cletus held up a wrist bracelet displaying a universal account and the credits waiting to be transferred. "Happy?"

"Right through here, Mr. Dodger. Your purchases await." She flipped a latch and opened a container.

Cletus picked up a plasma rifle. "Charges?"

Bax pointed to another case. "Four hundred, as ordered. And we won't be bringing them close to any of these rifles while we're docked. I don't like it when things get messy. And a loaded plasma rifle has messy written all over it."

"I must insist that you open the container so I can inspect its contents."

"Fine." Bax huffed. "Put the rifle back and I'll be happy to open her up."

Cletus looked the redhead up and down as he placed the weapon back in its case. "I would never have taken you for an arms dealer, Miss Rumford. That goon behind the blast wall—she's more what I'd expect."

Tawn scowled. "Can I frag him now?"

The captain shook her head. "Not 'til after the credit transfer's complete."

Cletus stared at Tawn as Bax opened the case full of plasma charges. "I like her spunk. Would you be willing to trade her for Farker?"

Bax smirked. "Does he moan and complain all the time?"

"Never." Cletus smiled as Tawn returned an angry glare.

Bax glanced at Farker who was now sniffing around Tawn's feet. "Yeah... no. I think I'll keep her. Sometimes you get attached and they're hard to part with, you know?"

The robotic dog went flying against the docking tube wall as Tawn kicked it with a heavy boot. Following several simulated yelps, the companion of Cletus Dodger scampered back to its own ship.

"What was that for?" Cletus gave an angry glare. "You always abuse innocent animals? He's only following his friendship programming."

Tawn spat on the deck. "Contraption tried to hump my leg. Nobody humps my leg without my consent!"

"I'll bet. And that spitting... not very lady-like... even for a slug."

Bax chuckled before looking at the time on her bracelet. "OK. Let's get this finished before a new war gets started. Satisfied with the charges? We have other business to get to."

"They appear to be in order."

Bax cracked open another container as Tawn scowled at a robotic dog that was now poking its head back into the far end of the docking tube. "Here's your zappers."

Cletus looked up. "Zappers? I'll have to advise you to not call them that. These are weapons... powerful and deadly weapons. Many a colonist would grimace at their only means of defense against a wild bogler being called a zapper. It's called the Fox-40 and is revered by its owners. Each of these will fetch a premium price."

"Premium, you say?" Bax grinned.

Cletus sighed. "Our terms are not open for negotiation, if that's what you're implying."

Bax smacked the heavy buyer on the back of his stained overcoat, pulling her hand back in regret as something gooey clung to her palm. "Hmm. Not a problem. The 40s are all here."

The container was further opened, revealing the preferred defensive weapon of the outer colonies.

"These two crates have the other items you requested." Bax frowned as she swung her hand in an attempt to liberate the goo. "I threw in an extra shock stick as a bonus. Something to keep you motivated for doing business with me. What is this?"

She stared at the glob in the center of her palm before attempting to wipe it off on a nearby wall. "Slug. Help the man load his goods. Mr. Dodger, I believe payment is due."

Tawn slapped her Fox-40 onto her hip-clip and stepped out from behind the blast wall. Picking up the first crate of residual items, she began to muscle it through the docking tube to the *Gulward*.

Cletus Dodger transferred the credits to a grinning Baxter Rumford.

As the transfer completed, a loud voice could be heard coming through the docking tube. "Somebody better get their robotic menace off my leg before it gets disintegrated!"

Cletus scurried into the tube to rescue his pet.

An alert came on the *Fargo*'s comm system. *Approaching vessel. Approaching vessel.*

Bax raced toward the *Fargo*'s cockpit as she yelled. "Dump the crate and get your ass moving, Slug! Mr. Dodger, I'll meet you here same time tomorrow to deliver the rest!"

Cletus yelled back as he hurried toward his own controls. "Agreed! Nice doing business with you!"

Tawn hustled back through the tube, slapping the button that closed the airlock. The robotic dog Farker chased his new friend onto the *Fargo*.

As the docking tube collapsed into the *Fargo*'s hull, a voice came over the general comm. "*This is New Earth Destroyer Hemlock. Power down your engines and prepare to be boarded.*"

Tawn sat in the copilot's chair, flipping her display to the defensive console. "Shields are online... crap! We have weapons fire!"

Powerful plasma beams shot past as the *Fargo*'s engines pushed her toward her one-sixteenth light-speed maximum. Bax piloted the small ship into a nearby asteroid field, their safe-lane for an escape should something go wrong. The jump engine worked to come online.

Tawn yelled, "Thirty seconds to jump!"

Bax maneuvered the *Fargo* behind a large asteroid as they continued to speed away.

The first mate zoomed in on the *Gulward* as it remained in place. "Fool isn't moving!"

"What's a New Earth destroyer doing out here again?" Bax asked with an annoyed look. "This whole system is supposed to be off limits."

"Probably up to no good just like we are. We aren't exactly being legal here. I'm sure they take violations of the truce seriously. Can't say I would want the outer colonies armed either."

Tawn glanced down to her left. "What the... that stupid dog followed me over!"

Two more plasma beams slipped past the fleeing craft as a third was targeted at the *Gulward*. A violent explosion saw the end of Cletus Dodger.

Tawn said, "They mean business... hit that button!"

"One sec. We jump now and we pull half those rocks out of their orbit. I'd rather not move around in junked up space if it's all the same to you, Miss Leg-Humpee."

"Nice. Thanks for bringing that up just before we die."

Bax laughed as her hand hovered over the jump button. "First... we aren't gonna die. And second... I'm gonna bring that up every chance I get. That's like the most action you've had since you started with me, isn't it? Hahaha!"

"Why did I know this was going to be a bad day?" Tawn shook her head.

The button was pressed and the *Fargo* slipped through a wormhole to empty space, two hours' travel from Domicile.

"Relax." Bax grinned. "We're safe. And we just made a big haul."

"How you figure?"

Bax held up her bracelet. "The credit transfer cleared, and Mr. Dodger is no longer in need of his merchandise. You will be the recipient of double your expected pay when we sell this cargo. I told you this gig was gonna pay you for last month. Bada-bing, bada-boom."

Tawn returned an uneasy look. "He must have next of kin or something the cargo would go to."

"Right. Next of kin." Bax laughed. "It's illegal. This is the real world, Freely. We're keeping it. And it looks like you just picked up a new pet."

Tawn scowled as she looked down at the mechanical menace which was now wagging its tail. "We still have to find another buyer."

"Already taken care of. I have someone waiting in Chicago Port. And he has 5 percent more credits than poor old Cletus back there."

Bax glared at her still sticky palm. "What is this?"

"What is what?"

Bax held up her hand. "I touched Cletus' coat and came back with this."

Tawn laughed. "Aren't you the one who said to never touch the clients?"

"Probably. And here's hard evidence as to why."

Tawn powered down the defensive shields. "Who's this prearranged buyer?"

Bax frowned in disgust as she wiped her palm with an alcohol towelette. "His name's Harris Gruberg. I call him Goober. He's one of you... a stump... a Biomarine. He served in the DD as a lifer like you. Got discharged about the same time you did.

"Flies a bucket of bolts I wouldn't fly planetside, much less out here. Cletus is... was... a better potential client. Sad he had to go like that. This guy is making deep runs to the newest colonies on Grendig and Farmingdale. Probably uses all his profits just to pay for fuel. You see, that's why I only take the near runs to the traders. Much better margins and I don't deal directly with colonists."

Tawn looked out the viewport at the approaching Chicago Port Station. "A DD lifer and a stump. I like him already."

"Don't show him that face, he'll be humping your leg."

Tawn shook her head as she made a nasty face at Farker, whose mechanical jowls turned up at each corner offering an unnatural smile. "Seeing me humped by a robotic dog. That must make you all giddy inside."

Bax grinned, "It does. And I'll be bringing it up every chance I get so long as I still have oxygen in my lungs."

Chapter 2

Chicago Port Station was the main stop before going planetside. All commerce coming to and from Domicile traveled through the station. A population of nearly a hundred thousand residents brought with it the need for shopping, restaurants, sporting venues and parks. The main deck of the station was called the promenade. Harris Gruberg was sitting on a bench along the promenade as Baxter Rumford and Tawnish Freely approached.

Bax put her right foot up on the bench beside Harris, her short shorts exposing her fleshy white leg. "You still want that deal, Goober?"

Harris grinned at the display. "It's Gruberg... and it depends on what you're selling this time."

Bax returned a look of disgust as she pulled her foot back to the floor. "That all you stumps think about?"

Harris leaned forward. "When they genetically engineered us, it included our brains. We were built to be aggressive."

Bax crossed her arms. "Well get any thought of that out of your genetic... brain. The only deal I have for you is the weapons deal we arranged before... minus one crate of residuals. Price is the same though."

Harris replied, "Doesn't seem quite fair. We agreed to terms."

Bax shrugged. "I have the goods... you want the goods... other traders want the goods. You want them? Or do I go somewhere else?"

Tawn stepped up. "You won't find better."

Harris pulled back and held up a hand. "Whoa. Didn't know you were gonna sick your dog on me."

Tawn scowled.

Bax laughed at Tawn's expense. "Look. The deal is available if you want it. I'll even let you hump my dog's leg if you agree."

Tawn returned an almost hurt look. "I'm not your dog."

Bax turned. "Then don't stick your nose in my business."

Harris looked over the hardened DD Biomarine who stood just behind Bax. "I'll take the deal. You keep the mutt. When do you want to do this? I have buyers waiting that are eager for their merchandise."

Bax held out her hand with a slip of paper. "We have the goods ready to go. Meet us at these coordinates in six hours. You miss the time and I talk to my friend at the trade commission about pulling your dealer license. And my friend is a good friend if you know what I mean."

Bax placed her foot back on the bench, exposing her leg and emphasizing her possible pull with the commissioner in question.

Harris Gruberg stood and scowled as he took the paper. "I'll be there. And just so you know. You do me wrong and I won't hesitate to put a plasma round right there between your pretty little eyes. And you'll never see it coming."

Bax smiled. "We'll be waiting."

***

The *Fargo* docked with the *Bangor*.

Bax shook her head. "*Bangor*. Dumb name. Who came up with that?"

Harris replied, "Was on there when I bought it. How about *Fargo*? You dream that up yourself?"

Bax made an ugly face.

Harris chuckled as he glanced up at Tawn standing behind the blast wall with her hand on her Fox-40. "Brought your dog I see, very trusting."

Farker bounded up to his new owner, sitting back on his haunches as his stubby tail moved back and forth. Tawn attempted to kick him away.

"And your dog has a dog. Nice."

Tawn replied, "We know our stumps. And this dog will rip your face off if you try anything."

Harris looked down, Farker returned his unnatural grin. "That's just weird."

Bax said, "You got the credits?"

Harris looked over the containers. "I do. Looks good. Grab that side and let's get this over with."

Bax hesitated as she glanced at the time on her bracelet. "You don't want to inspect the merchandise?"

Harris shook his head. "I've already told you the penalty for doing me wrong. And I'd rather not be out in this area longer than necessary. Too many ships have been disappearing. I had a friend who—"

Bax held up her hand. "Save it. Slug... get over here and help the man. Residuals first."

Harris picked up his half of the plasma rifle container. "Rifles first. I have limited room and need to stack them in order."

Bax huffed and put a heeled boot on top of the container. "Payment first."

Harris set his end of the box down and began the transfer of credits into the account of Baxter Rumford. The rifle container was lifted and moved through the tube. Farker followed.

An alert sounded over the *Fargo*'s comm. *Vessel approaching. Vessel approaching.*

Bax ran toward the cockpit yelling as Tawn hustled back through. "Will deliver at the same time tomorrow! Be here or forfeit your assets!"

Harris yelled back. "I'll be here. And what about your dog?"

The airlocks closed and the docking tube retracted. Harris pushed his throttle to full as plasma beams began to be fired in his direction.

16

A voice came over the general comm. "This is the New Earth Destroyer *Hemlock*. Power down your engines and prepare to be boarded."

Harris shook his head as a wormhole opened in front of his ship. "Not today, Earther. Harris has left the building."

The *Bangor* sped through to safety and the wormhole closed.

Baxter Rumford and Tawnish Freely escaped through the asteroid field before jumping through a wormhole of their own.

Tawn flipped off the defense shield. "Twice in a row? We need to pick a new spot for the drops."

Bax brushed it off. "Coincidence. Did you notice the flash of a ship being destroyed?"

Tawn looked over the sensors. "Don't see one... wait... I have a wormhole. Gruberg jumped through a wormhole. He made it out."

Bax scowled. "We'll get him tomorrow."

Tawn tilted her head in question. "What?"

Bax gave a fake smile. "Nothing. We got paid. You'll get your cut."

***

Harris Gruberg sat on his usual bench on the Chicago Port Station promenade with Farker laying beside his feet. Both were ogling the passersby. Tawn approached, stopping directly in front of him and jacking her foot up to prop on the bench beside him in an attempt to be provocative.

Harris frowned. "Doesn't really work for you, Bulldog. Slugs and stumps weren't designed to be attractive."

Tawn withdrew her foot with a scowl. "Shut your blowhole. I'm here doing you a favor."

Harris chuckled. "You have my guns?"

16

Tawn shook her head. "I don't. And I think my captain is running a scam. That's three times a New Earth destroyer has shown up. The last guy wasn't so lucky."

Harris shrugged. "It's free space. Everybody knows they have patrols out there. Goes with the job."

Tawn replied, "Yeah, look, as a fellow Biomarine, I'm trying to clue you in. Semper Fi you know. I think my boss is setting you up. Good for me as I keep getting paid for the same cargo, but very bad for you. Were you friends with Cletus Dodger? That was his dog."

Harris shrugged. "I'm a competitor of Cletus Dodger. Wouldn't really call him a friend."

Tawn shook her head. "You're not a competitor anymore. That same destroyer turned him into space dust a few days ago. Exact same time as our transaction... and that destroyer just happens to show again? I don't think so. And we've snuck away twice now without taking a hit.

"Any destroyer gunner I've ever heard about would not have missed with that many shots from that close. Especially not twice."

Harris thought for a moment. "You trying to tell me Red works for New Earth?"

Tawn looked around before replying, "I can't say. We had a deal that went similarly bad a couple months ago. An Earther destroyer grabbed us. They talked to her for several hours before sending us on. And they didn't ask me a single question.

"I was just happy to be let go, so I didn't press her for details, and she didn't volunteer any. I asked around. Mr. Dodger was the third trader to go missing in six weeks. You wanna keep your atoms together, you might want to steer clear of Baxter Rumford."

Harris returned a sly smile. "Nice. She sends out her dog to try to scare me away from my pickup. I see the scam. You can tell her I'll be there today to get my rightful property."

Tawn scowled. "Idiot. I tried. Guess you'll get what's coming to you."

Harris grinned. "Tell her I'll be there... and thanks for caring."

Tawn slowly shook her head as she turned to walk away.

Harris said, "You don't want your dog?"

Tawn kept walking. "Keep him. He's yours."

Harris reached down to scratch the simulated fur head of his new friend as he threw a smile and a wink at a passing lady. The smile was not returned.

***

Later that day, the *Bangor* was sitting in wait as the *Fargo* approached. Ten minutes after contact was made, Harris Gruberg was walking through the docking tube with a happy Farker at his heals. The robotic dog began to squeal and vibrate when he saw Tawn moving to behind the blast wall. The excited behavior was not returned.

Bax stood waiting at her end of the tube. "Glad you were able to slip away. How'd you know to have your wormhole drive up and charged? That's a mighty expensive thing to keep running."

Harris replied, "I take precautions when I think they're necessary. Now let's get this moved."

Bax crossed her arms as she stepped back. "Sure you don't want to check that the merchandise is still there? I could be ripping you off."

Harris stopped inches from her face. "And I could be tracking you down and plugging your forehead. You gonna help with this or what?"

Bax stepped back. "Our deal was yesterday. I should be charging you for fuel and storage."

Harris smirked. "Yeah right. And no trader would do business with you again. Slug, grab that box."

Tawn shook her head. "I've been told I'm off the clock. Those are your goods. Move them yourself."

Harris scowled as he reached down, taking the handles of a container and hoisting it up to his waist with a strain on his face. "Thanks, ladies."

As the fourth container was moved and stowed, a grinning Bax stuck her head in the docking tube. "Enjoy the ride to Farmingdale, Stump."

Harris yelled back. "I'm sure I will."

Farker scrambled back across the tube as Bax reached for the airlock button, stating under her breath, "Always check your cargo, dumbass."

Tawn asked as she returned a concerned look. "What? What'd you just say?"

Bax smiled. "I wished him well. Let's get back to port. I have to get another deal in the works if we want to be eating next month."

The *Bangor* moved away without incident as Baxter Rumford fired up the wormhole drive of the *Fargo*. Two hours later the two women were pulling into Bay 22 of Chicago Port Station.

***

Bax and Tawn walked from the bay into the main hallway heading back to port central. A five minute stroll past the warehouse area had them entering the promenade.

Bax turned. "You're on your own, Slug. Check back in two days, four hours and I should be ready for a new deal."

Tawn said, "Aren't you forgetting something?"

Bax returned a blank stare.

"Pay?" Tawn added.

"Oh. Fine. Hold up your store."

A transfer was made.

Tawn looked at her account. "Uh, what about yesterday's deal? We got paid. Where's my cut?"

Bax smiled. "Sorry. Didn't you read the fine print of our contract? It says net thirty, which won't be for a month. And it also says transfers are made at the convenience of the paymaster. I'm the paymaster. Next month seems more convenient."

Tawn scowled. "I do have bills, you know."

Bax turned to walk away. "You have two free days. You're a strong girl. Go make yourself some money."

Tawn stood with her fists on her wide hips, staring down the promenade at the tall, slender Baxter Rumford as she sauntered away. She glanced down at her heel expecting to see a gleeful Farker. As much as she despised the mechanical pet, she now somehow felt she missed him.

Spinning on her heels in the other direction, she walked toward the nearest pilot's hangout... a place where she hoped to pick up extra work.

***

Six hours had passed before Harris Gruberg entered Trader Mike's Lounge. Tawn Freely was seated in a corner booth with a half empty ale on the table in front of her. Harris sat across from her with an angered expression on his face.

Tawn gestured. "Sure. Have a seat, Stump."

Harris scowled. "I have a shocker aimed at your gut right now. You're gonna tell me where your boss is or I'm gonna light you up with more volts than even *your* bioframe can handle."

Tawn smirked. "Sure you do. Nobody brings a weapon on the station. Fastest way to get spaced."

Harris lifted his hand carefully, exposing the top section of the charged pistol. "Nobody but me. You see, I'm willing to take the risk if it means getting to waste Earther spies like you. And I would bank on the prosecutors not charging me seeing as how I'm doing DD intel business. Now where's your boss?"

Tawn leaned forward. "You find something out? She's dirty, right? Just like I said?"

Harris returned a confused expression. "You do realize I'm arresting you here, right?"

Tawn pulled back. "Me? What for? I tried to warn you!"

Harris nodded. "And I'll make the prosecutors aware of that."

Tawn let out a sigh. "You're a cop... we sold you illegal arms. I knew this job was bad news."

Harris stressed, "Where... is... Baxter... Rumford?"

Tawn leaned forward. "I... don't... know. She took off to drum up new business. She won't let me near her contacts. Thinks I'll steal them and strike out on my own. And just how would I do that? I have forty-nine credits in my account and I'm past due on my rent. Heck. I'll be lucky not to have been evicted already when I get home. I almost don't want to go."

Harris looked at her in disbelief. "I don't think you're grasping what's going on here. You tried to kill an officer of the DD intel force. You might get spaced for this yourself. And if it was up to me, I'd walk you to the nearest airlock right now."

Tawn smirked. "Yeah, right. Look, I know what we're selling. They don't space you for that. Even with those repeaters I'm looking at six years at the most. I know the law says execution, but that's reserved for treasonous acts. Selling a handful of weapons to the outer colonists is hardly treason."

Harris growled, "You stuck a transmitter in that cargo! I nearly got blasted three separate times before I got wise and dumped it. Sure enough, ten minutes after I purged, that destroyer was sniffing all around it. That tells me you and Red are both working for New Earth."

Tawn half frowned. "I don't know anything about a transmitter. I'm just the grunt help. She uses me for protection until a credit transfer is made and I move cargo once that's done. That's all I do... which is why I have forty-nine credits to my name."

"Where's your boss?"

"I... don't... know. I already told you. And I don't know anything about any transmitter, or where she gets her guns, or anything else. Wait... I can tell you this... about two months ago we had a deal going in that same spot where we made the trade. It was my first run with her and we got tagged by that same destroyer. We had transferred the cargo to the buyer's ship and the destroyer vaporized him when he tried to run.

"They questioned her for two hours before releasing us. I assumed it was because there was no evidence left, which got destroyed when they toasted the buyer. So they must have either turned her right then or she was working for them before we met."

Harris slowly shook his head. "You think I'm an idiot because I'm a stump?"

Tawn crossed her arms. "You think I'm an idiot because I'm a slug? You think I want to be spending my days in places like this trying to find whatever grunt-work I can? I gave sixteen years of hard combat to the DDF. This is my world.

"And even though they seem to distrust us, these are my people. I would never in a million standard years do work for the Earthers. You know how many of my friends they killed with that insane war? Cut a fellow Bio some slack. You know how hard we have it out here."

Harris slowly lowered his shocker, slipping it back beneath his leather vest. "You really don't have a clue, do you?"

"Not about anything to do with New Earth... no, I don't. I'm just trying to keep myself fed out here. A year and a half down on the surface and not a single job prospect. Nobody wants to take a chance on a slug."

Harris scratched his left ear as he scowled in thought. "They really did screw us, didn't they? Designed us for war. Made us mean and ugly for the sole purpose of scaring the enemy. OK, look, are you still working for her or did she dump you?"

"She'll be back in... forty-six hours. I'm to meet her at the ship for another deal. You say you're working for DD intel? They need slugs?"

Harris said, "Let me see your left hand."

Tawn held it out across the table. Harris slapped a tracking bracelet on her wrist and shoved her hand back.

Tawn asked. "What's that for? Am I being deputized?"

Harris chuckled. "Are you that dumb? I just arrested you. You're my prisoner until I get my hands on Red. That's a tracker."

"And after that?"

Harris smiled. "After that you're the DDI's business. What they do with you from there is up to them."

Tawn sighed. "When you have a prisoner, are they at least allowed to eat?"

Harris shrugged. "Help yourself."

"Prisoners don't get fed? Aren't I your responsibility now? I would think they'd reimburse you for any expense."

Harris drew in a long breath. "You know, you're starting to become a pain in the ass."

Tawn replied, "Hey, girl's gotta eat. And I'm sure I've got some kind of prisoner's rights to food or something. And I could use a shower if we have a chance."

"You think this is some kind of all expense paid holiday you're on or something? You've just been nabbed for treason. I'd be more worried about contacting a lawyer than getting a shower."

"Do I get food or not?"

Harris stared back at the pug-nosed Biomarine for several seconds. "Fine. But keep it under five credits. Order what you want."

Tawn gave a mimicking reply in a deep voice. "Fine. Order what you want. And five credits? What am I supposed to get with that? A roll?"

Harris flipped open the menu. "Right here. Potato soup. A staple that's been with us for five thousand years. Came with our ancestors from Earth. You can thank me later."

Chapter 3

Tawn ordered the potato soup, nodding to the waitress as she collected the menu. "You still have my dog?"

Harris replied, "Thought you said it belonged to Cletus Dodger. You laying claim to it now?"

"Maybe. You have him?"

Harris whistled into his wrist comm. The mechanical dog raced into the pub and slid to a stop in front of his new master.

A manager approached the table. "No pets allowed in here."

Harris flashed his DDI badge. "It's robotic. And bring me an ale."

The manager returned an indignant look before walking back to place the order. The DDI were not to be trifled with. More than once a business had been shuttered for an investigation and the manager was not interested in being out of a job... even if only temporarily.

Tawn grinned. "I want me one of those badges."

Harris shook his head. "You need to offer a special skill before they'll give you one. You do anything special besides rolling over for Red and playing spy?"

Tawn shrugged. "I'm a level four marksman. Or at least I was."

Harris looked up with interest. "Level four? That makes you probably one of about thirty in the entire Corps. Impressive if true."

Tawn half smiled. "And it's twenty-eight now. Two of the others were lost in the Helm Engagement just before the truce."

Harris asked, "How'd you manage a level four? I thought those only went to snipers."

Tawn again shrugged. "Just aimed and pulled the trigger like everyone else. I did my last year and a half as a sniper."

"Hmm. I never heard of a slug or a stump getting sniper duty. We're the ones they like to throw in the meatgrinder for hand to hand."

Tawn scooped up a fresh spoon of the soup. "Don't I know it. Eight hundred ninety-six kills. Mostly on or around Baross IV. Can I see that badge again?"

Harris shook his head. "It's only to be pulled for official business."

Tawn laughed. "Like having your robotic dog in an eating establishment and ordering an ale?"

Harris replied, "I just placed a treason suspect under arrest. I'd say that qualifies."

The potato soup and ale were finished and the prisoner marched back to the docking bay where they would wait just out of sight for Baxter Rumford.

Tawn looked down at the dog from the bench where she sat. "You give him a name yet?"

Harris replied, "Thought his name was Farker?"

Tawn nodded. "It was. You want to keep that now that he's yours?"

Harris shrugged. "Sure. Just as good as any."

Tawn looked around the bay. "We really gonna wait here for another forty-something hours?"

Harris leaned back on the bench, crossing his powerful arms. "What would you suggest?"

Tawn returned a blank stare. "You aren't much of a planner, are you?"

"I do what's needed."

"You don't have a place where we can sit in comfort for the next day and a half?"

Harris thought before standing. "OK. Come on. We have the *Bangor* in slip 27. Best I can give you is a cot."

Tawn sighed. "Sadly, I sleep on a cot at my place. Don't have much for furniture."

Harris smirked. "Old habits, huh? I slept on a cot for five months after getting out. The beds in all those flop houses were no better than sleeping on the floor. Would still prefer a bunk on a troop carrier. I slept through half the Helm engagement in one, while half our hull was being filled with holes."

Tawn nodded. "I looked for several months to try to find one in surplus. When they drydocked those ships they shredded all the mattresses. Can't say I was happy about that."

"Hmm. Wish I'd thought of that early on. The bunks in the *Bangor* would have fit one of those perfect."

Tawn asked as they walked, "How'd you get hooked up with the DDI?"

"Truth is... I got bagged trying to do just what you're doing. Only on a smaller scale. I acquired two Fox-40s in a card game and I was attempting to sell them when I got grabbed."

Tawn held up a hand. "Whoa. You had a couple 40s here on the station?"

Harris laughed. "Goodness, no. That was planetside. But the guns were registered as stolen, so they had me on possession. One thing led to another and they offered me a job tracking down dealers. They're wanting to keep an eye on the outer colonies, and specifically on any weapons heading to Eden."

Tawn winced. "Eden? They should have called that place Hades. What do they care about Eden?"

Harris leaned in. "Not many people know this, but the Truce of Beckland was only signed because the New Earthers were out of titanium for their ship hulls. Their planet is almost devoid of the stuff. No titanium for hull alloys means inferior ships or no ships. And as it turns out, Eden is rich in titanium."

Tawn asked, "So why don't they just go take Eden?"

Harris reached up, scratching his neck. "They can't do that without violating the truce. That would bring back war, which they need the titanium for beforehand. Right now Eden's government has no interest in selling titanium to New Earth. They're pacifists who migrated there thinking nobody would bother them on the desert planet. DDI thinks the New Earthers are trying to arm an insurgency on Eden, so they hired me to find out what's going on."

They arrived at the *Bangor*. After boarding they sat across from each other on a pair of benches in the cabin.

Tawn scowled. "Where'd you get these benches? The license registration bureau? These are horrid."

Harris replied, "Hey, they came with the ship. If you'd rather you can sit on the deck."

Tawn shook her head. "I would assume the DDI told you not to tell anybody about what you're doing, right?"

Harris thought for a moment. "Well... yeah. If word got out the DDI was watching, the Earthers might take all their efforts underground."

Tawn smirked. "Anyone ever tell you you're a moron?"

"That's been said before. Why?"

"Because you just told me about the DDI's secret investigation. What if I told that to someone who then told it to a New Earth sympathizer? Your operation would be blown. Are you so dense you don't see that?"

Harris scratched the back of his head. "I guess that wasn't the smartest move, huh? OK, forget about everything I told you."

Tawn laughed. "I can't forget that. But I tell you what... you take off this tracker and get me a job with the DDI and it won't matter. I'd love to be smashing the heads of anyone interested in giving New Earth war materials."

Harris stood, pacing back and forth in front of the bench where Tawn was seated. "OK, look, I made that all up."

Tawn squinted her eyes. "What are you talking about?"

Harris stopped, returning to the hard bench with a sigh. "That tracking bracelet... it's just a cheap credit store, nothing more. I'm not an agent of the DDI, and the whole Eden deal... that's a rumor I heard from a drunk. I just want my guns. I need those. I have bills just like you, only worse. I kind of borrowed money from the wrong people. If I don't pay them in a week they'll come to collect the *Bangor* and break my kneecaps."

Tawn crossed her arms as she chuckled. "You're in as much of a mess as I am... or maybe worse."

Harris replied, "What you said back there about slugs and stumps... you were right. The people don't trust us. Nobody fought harder for their freedom, but we're different physically. We were bred to fight and there's no more fighting, making us obsolete."

Tawn chuckled. "OK, stop it. Now you're just bringing me down. We just have to find a place where we fit."

"War is where we fit."

Tawn asked, "Show me that DDI badge."

A black leather fold was retrieved from a pocket. Tawn opened it to reveal the badge.

"The Sheriff Dry-cleaners?"

Harris smiled. "It was nicely embossed with gold leaf. And they give me a 5 percent veteran's discount. Just wish I had something to dry-clean."

Tawn laughed out-loud. "This is rich. I'm not saying it didn't work, but tell me you haven't used that elsewhere."

Harris shrugged. "I have. A couple times now."

"And nobody questioned it?"

"They were too terrified to ask. Who wants to question the DDI?"

Tawn returned a concerned look. "They are out there... DDI agents. They bust you trying to pull that scam and they'll burn you."

"I'm just trying to survive out here like you. You're running illegal arms to the outer colonies. How's that any worse?"

"It's not. And we'd both probably be doing OK at it if it wasn't for Baxter Rumford. You aren't in need of a first mate are you?"

Harris returned a stare before breaking into a chuckle. "The two of us working together? We can't even feed ourselves. How are we gonna pull off any kind of business venture?"

Tawn smiled. "We're gonna stick it to Bax, that's how. She owes you and she owes me. If we work as a team maybe we can at least get our pay."

"What are you suggesting we do?"

Tawn leaned forward, placing her chin on her fist as she thought, rising up when she had an answer. "How about this... she'll be back tomorrow, hopefully with more weapons to sell. You set up a deal with her. Tell her you have a buyer on Eden. When she shows to deliver the goods, I'll turn my Fox on her and we leave with the cargo."

"So your plan is that we rob her?"

Tawn shrugged. "Not like she doesn't owe us. And if she's been turning traders over to the Earthers for execution, she deserves a good kick in the gut."

"And how do we deal with her afterwards?"

Tawn smiled. "You think she's gonna go up against a stump and a slug when she owed them already?"

"Sounds like a half baked plan."

Tawn laughed. "We got anything else in the oven?"

"We don't even have anything else to put in the oven. If we do this, how do I know you aren't gonna hang me out to dry just to get paid by her?"

Tawn shook her head. "Robbing you does me no good. You've got nothing to take. You don't own your ship and your credit store is as empty as mine. No... we take her down. You'll have your arms to sell and I get half when we're done.

"After that, we go looking for a legit dealer. Not legit – legit, because this is still illegal, but you know what I mean. There are colonists out there with money and goods to trade. And there are weapons down on the surface to be purchased and sold."

Harris looked on with a scowl. "Working with a slug... not where I thought I would end up."

Tawn took off the bogus tracking device, handing it back. "This is yours."

Harris said, "Keep it."

Tawn looked it over for a brief second. "Doesn't even work, does it?"

Harris smirked. "Nope. Works great as a phony tracking device, though."

Tawn shrugged as she placed it back on her left wrist. "Maybe I'll keep it then."

"You have any food at your place?"

Tawn laughed. "Yeah... no. You hungry now?"

Harris winced. "That ale today is all I've had since yesterday. And you owe me a potato soup."

"You didn't pay for that. You scammed the guy out of it... and your ale. With your phony badge. Say... if that badge worked once, it could work again. I'll play the prisoner if you can get us a comped meal. I'm thinking the buffet at the Emporium."

Harris thought for a moment. "I am hungry. That buffet's like eighteen credits each, plus beverages."

Tawn grinned. "Yeah, but it has everything. And if we aren't paying for it, who cares what it costs. Come on. We have a day and a half to kill. Let's get us a free meal."

A short walk had them standing in line to get into the Grand Emporium Buffet.

The attendant at the register asked, "Two?"

Harris said, "Two for the Grand Buffet please. And two beverages, premium."

The attendant smiled. "Someone is eating well today. That's forty-four credits."

Harris flashed his fake badge. "DDI investigator."

The attendant replied, "We need a credit deposit anyway. Sorry. The manager will comp you at the end, but our policy requires the deposit."

Harris looked at Tawn. "Give her the credits."

Tawn returned and angry stare. "Put the deposit on your account."

Harris leaned in with a low voice. "Just hold up your store. There's people waiting behind us."

Tawn shook her head. "No. Use yours."

"I don't have enough."

Tawn asked, "What?"

Harris held up his store. "I don't have enough."

He turned to the attendant. "Payday tomorrow."

The attendant smiled. "I need the deposit if you want to go in."

Tawn held out her wrist. Forty-four credits in her account were marked as a deposit. The attendant waved them through.

Tawn stopped. "You have four credits to your name?"

Harris frowned. "I spent it all on those arms. Was expecting to get paid for them."

He glanced back at a staring Tawn before turning back toward the buffet. "Look at all that food. You ever see anything so beautiful?"

Tawn sniffed the air as she looked over the fifteen meter long premium buffet line. Her mouth began to water. Harris hurried to the front of the line, grabbing three plates. A variety of steaks and various carved meats were available. Sauces ranged from traditional, to spicy, to insanely hot.

Slugs and stumps were heavy eaters when they had the chance. Their metabolisms were slower than the average human, and they could easily consume twice as much. While at war, meals were often not convenient and more often not available. The two bio-engineered humans tore into their high stacked plates like ravenous animals. Several families having their meals at the tables beside them got up to move.

Both returned for seconds with their plates piled high with more meats and desserts. Proteins and carbs were the staple diet of a Biomarine. Harris and Tawn feasted as they also consumed a dozen premium ales each. When the feeding frenzy was over, there were two full bellies protruding under the table.

Harris leaned back with a satisfied look on his face. "I could get used to eating like that. I'd weigh five hundred kilos in three months, but it would be so worth it."

Tawn released a loud burp, driving another disgusted couple from a nearby table. "Yeah. That hit the spot. Any more and I think I'd split open. Go ahead and call the manager over. I don't like the hold being placed on my credits."

Harris nodded, waving over a busboy and asking for a manager. Just under a minute later, a young man, neatly dressed and barely out of primary school, came to their table.

"Can I help you?"

Harris pulled his leather fold, flashing his phony badge. "Consider our meal a contribution to the DDI for your safety and security."

The manager smiled. "I'll need to see some credentials."

Harris sat back, putting his arm up on the back of his chair. "I just showed you my badge."

The manager shook his head as he gestured toward his neatly pressed shirt. "You just showed my your discount card for the Sheriff's Dry-cleaners. I go there too. This establishment has no problem comping the meal in support of our global defense, but I need to see some real ID."

The snarky young man leaned in with a grin. "There are those who would try to scam us, which is why we require a deposit. Please, sir, show me your credentials and we can all be on our way."

Harris stood with a scowl. "This is the last time I eat here. And if this station gets invaded, I'll be standing outside laughing as this place burns to the ground!"

The stump turned and walked quickly toward the exit door. Tawn looked up at the manager with a pursed smile. Standing, she hurried after Harris as he exited going out into the promenade.

Tawn glowered. "What the heck? I just paid forty-four credits for that!"

Harris replied, "It was *your* hare-brained scheme. And that's why I always keep my requests under ten credits. Nobody cares to question that amount."

Tawn sighed as she looked at her account. "This is just great. I now have five credits to my name."

Harris laughed. "Look on the bright side. You have a full belly and more credits than me. I have a grand total of four. Had I made my sale yesterday, that number would be sitting at over eight thousand."

Tawn pulled back. "You make that much from a trade?"

"Well... no, not really. There was the cost of the goods, about fifty-eight hundred in this case. And the cost of the regular and the jump fuel, about eighteen hundred there. That was gonna leave about eight hundred credits when I was done. That's half a ship payment every month. Only have to do that twice a month for the next twenty years."

Tawn reached up, rubbing her forehead. "So my haul after we do this is gonna be about four hundred credits? For robbing someone?"

"Now wait a minute. I never agreed to those terms. I'm the one who took all the financial risk here. You're just getting paid for... well turning on your boss. I was thinking something more like ninety – ten. I need those credits to pay my debts."

"So do I. Look. This deal doesn't work without me. If I don't roll over on her, you don't get your merchandise. Why would I risk prison or possibly death over eighty credits? She would already be paying me sixty."

"Death? From that bag of bones? You're a slug, I'm a stump. We were born to fight. She doesn't stand a chance against either one of us, let alone two. I tell you what... I'll go fifteen."

Tawn laughed. "You'll go fifty or the deal's off. There won't be any negotiating. You screwed up and didn't check your cargo last time. I shouldn't have to pay for that. We're either partners or I just go back to her and do my job. And besides, you owe me a Grand Buffet with a premium beverage. That's twenty-two credits by itself."

Harris stood in silent denial for most of a minute before returning a response. "Fine. Equal shares."

Holding up a finger he pointed. "But we split costs. And that meal we just finished... consider that your buy-in to the partnership."

Tawn took in a deep breath as she scowled while thinking it over. "Agreed. Equal shares and I'll forgive the meal."

Farker began to emit a tone that he was running low on charge. Harris reached up under his chin, flipping the power switch to off.

Tawn asked, "You aren't gonna charge him?"

Harris replied, "Not here. They charge a premium for the power used while docked."

Tawn laughed. "What's that cost you a credit? Can't even afford to power your dog?"

"Yep. That's 25 percent of what I currently have. I'll hook him up when I'm on ship's power. It's cheaper."

Tawn looked around the cramped cabin of the *Bangor*. "So what do we do now?"

Harris replied, "We wait. It's all we can afford."

Chapter 4

During the forty hours that followed, two eating establishments were scammed out of exactly eighteen credits, not including the stiffed tips. Tawn returned to the docking slip two hours early to wait for her boss. Harris camped out just around a near corner, watching the incoming board for the *Fargo* to arrive.

The Manten Yards produced trading ship pulled into port. The outer hatch opened. Baxter Rumford stepped out.

Tawn was waiting. "You get cargo?"

Bax nodded. "More than last time. And I have a buyer on the hook."

Harris rounded a corner, catching Bax off-gaurd. "Hello, Red."

Bax looked on nervously, not having expected ever to see Harris Gruberg again. "Goober? You want something?"

Harris replied, "I do. I want more of what you're selling. And I'll pay a 10 percent premium this time. That last cargo went fast and my buyers are itching for more."

Bax thought for a moment. "Wasn't expecting you back here. Didn't think you liked me."

Harris smiled. "What's not to like? Oh, and you'll want to be careful out there. I got chased by a New Earth destroyer, ditched them three times before I slipped away for good.

"Anyway, the payday was excellent and I could move as much cargo as you can provide, one trip at a time, of course. I won't tell you what colonies or who the buyers are, but they're eager for more."

Bax raised her chin. "I could go 15 percent. I'll have to pay my current buyer a residual for canceling. Just good business, you know."

"I can go fifteen." He looked around. "Although I would prefer we make our arrangements someplace else. These docking bays have eyes and ears."

Bax gave a furtive glance. "You meet me in the same place as last time, six hours from now and you'll have your goods."

"I'll be there." Harris smiled before spinning on his heels as he began to walk away.

Bax turned to Tawn with a grin. "Idiot."

Tawn stared out toward her future accomplice in crime. "How much cargo do we have?"

"Maybe three times the last haul." Bax smirked. "This goes down and I might feel generous enough to pay you for last month already."

"I could get aboard with that." Tawn nodded. "Wasn't able to find anything while you were gone. There was one gig as a bouncer, but it only paid eight credits for an eight hour shift. Free booze though."

Bax looked her up and down. "Hope you didn't drink them dry. You look like you put on a couple pounds. Come on. I'm feeling generous. I'll buy you a beer at the Emporium. I need some lunch."

"Yeah," Tawn hesitated. "Thanks but they asked me to not come back there for a while. There was a bit of a ruckus, so I'll have to pass. I can wait here at the ship for you."

Bax scowled as she turned. "Suit yourself. Don't expect such a generous offer next time."

***

The docking computer took over and the *Bangor* was soon connected with the *Fargo*.

Bax stood in the docking tube. "Before you come over I need to see proof of your credits."

Harris stood in his airlock. "What... you don't trust me? After all we've been through?"

"Just show me the credits, Stump. I don't have time to fart around with the likes of you."

Tawn pressed the blaster tip of her Fox-40 into the small of Baxter's back. "You have time today."

Bax turned her head slowly to look down at the weapon. "What is this?"

Harris walked forward. "This is payback for you adding a transmitter to that last cargo. I had to dump it before I got vaporized. The way I see it, you owe me this. Any excess, I'll be happy to pay you the fair market value for, just not until after I've sold it."

"This is robbery, plain and simple." Bax scowled.

Harris laughed. "Who you gonna report us to? The trade commissioner? I don't think so. I should zap you right here and now for setting me up. All I'd have to do with this ship is aim it at that nearest star, letting nature take its course. We'd walk away free and clear. Doubt there's anyone back there that would miss you."

Bax put on a pouty face. "My elderly mother depends on me. If I don't go back, she starves."

"That the same mother you said was a thug?" Tawn spat. "Used to beat you every day? I'm thinking your mother probably disowned you decades ago."

Bax shook her head. "I have friends. They'll catch you."

Harris replied as he placed the tip of his own Fox-40 onto her forehead. "Your friends, which I doubt you have any of anyhow, don't know where you are, who you're with, or what you're doing. That would be sloppy business on your part given what we do. And I don't take you as being that sloppy.

"So here's what's happening. I'm gonna take that 'pig sticker', as you call it, off your hands. Then you're gonna start dragging boxes over to the *Bangor*."

"I don't carry boxes." Bax huffed. "That's what I got the slug for."

Tawn pressed with her weapon as she leaned in close. "In case you didn't pick up on it before, the slug doesn't work for

38

you anymore. Now get your skinny ass over there and start moving those containers!"

Tawn Freely and Harris Gruberg held grins for fifteen minutes as Baxter Rumford struggled with each and every package. By the time the last container was in transition, beads of sweat dripped from Bax's forehead.

Tawn said, "You're gonna need a shower after this. You aren't smelling so fresh. Hey, Harris, aren't you glad we were engineered not to stink? I can go for a week without putting off B.O. Doesn't seem to work that way for our lady-friend here."

Harris nodded. "Can't say how many times I was disgusted by that from the regulars in the service. You non-bios have some major drawbacks."

Bax stopped, taking in several deep breaths as she placed her hands on her hips. "At least my face doesn't look like somebody hit it with a concussion round."

Tawn laughed, "You might even have to buy yourself a new outfit when you get back. Those yellow pit-stains... those aren't gonna go over well while you're parading yourself up and down the promenade."

The last of the containers was moved and stacked. An out of breath Baxter Rumford leaned over on one hand.

"Go," Harris said. "Get off my ship. You're stinking the place up."

Bax passed a grinning Tawn as she stomped her way through the docking tube. Without a further word spoken, the airlock was closed, the docking tube retracted, and the ships separated.

***

A wormhole opened with a jump being made to the free space surrounding Chicago Port Station.

Tawn asked, "I'm looking over the manifest. This is way more than we had last time. A hundred fifty-two repeaters. Two

38

hundred twelve Foxes. Fifteen hundred charges. This is a gold mine. Who's the buyer?"

Harris half frowned, replying in a low voice. "We don't have one."

Tawn asked, "What? What'd you say?"

"I said we don't have one. Last time out I was planning to freelance."

Tawn looked on in disbelief. "It'll take us three months to move this stuff one at a time."

Harris scratched his bald head. "Best I've got is the rumor about Eden."

Tawn held up a hand. "Given what you said about the titanium and all, no way do I want to get involved in that."

"Not suggesting we do. Besides, that was just a rumor. I tell you what... I was heading to Farmingdale before. We might just jump out there to see what we can find."

"Hold on." Tawn thought for a moment. "The first deal we had that went bad was with a Geldon trader. Wasn't anything near this size, but we might be able to move a good chunk if nobody else has filled that hole. He must have had buyers ready."

"And then there's Cletus Dodger. I want to say he was heading to the colony on Bella III. Might be some ready-made sales there too."

Harris smiled. "I like the sound of both of those. You know, you just might make a decent partner after all."

"I'll be the brains and... I'll be the brawn."

Harris replied, "I like that. Yeah." He paused. "No... wait."

***

The *Bangor* buffeted as it entered the atmosphere of the planet Geldon. The single colony, Rumidon, located in the higher, temperate latitudes, was named after the probe that discovered the habitable area of the planet. Geldon space was on the edge of where a jump drive could reach from Domicile.

Many of the more than twelve thousand colonists who inhabited the rocky surface were miners, hoping to make a big find of a rare mineral. The only mines turning a profit were powerstripping bauxite, a mineral that was also plentiful on New Earth.

The Truce of Beckland had taken the bottom out of the bauxite market, with cargoes becoming available for trade from a much closer New Earth. The population on Geldon had dropped by half in the two years since the signing of the accord. The rumor was that tourists interested in sport hunting had recently become a new revenue stream.

Tawn held the arm of the copilot's chair. "This ship... who's the maker? I don't recognize it."

Harris nodded. "There's only about a half dozen left that are spaceworthy. It's a Zwicker. The military stopped surplussing them about two centuries ago. When the jump drive fails you can't get parts to repair it. So they wind up planetside in whatever system the drive died in. Not good for much other than hauling manure when in atmosphere. They're heavy and hard to control."

Tawn tapped on the near wall. "What's this beast made of?"

Harris gripped the joystick tightly as the ship rocked and jerked. "Before the titanium alloy and electronic shields of today, they used a mix of depleted uranium and metallic carbide. The armor was made thick back then because the weapons they used were projectile.

"Lots of railguns, I've been told. This ship has two of them. Haven't worked in a couple hundred years though. Not that they would be legal anyway. Even if we wanted to bring them online, parts aren't available for repairs."

Tawn smiled. "Railguns... now that would be something to have."

"As a consequence of this armor, she can take about a half dozen plasma rounds before her hull cracks. At least in theory she can. In practice, I know she can take at least four. She kept me alive when that destroyer was on my tail. That and making jumps. Her drive spins up almost instantly."

"Wait." Tawn sat with her jaw dropped. "You took a plasma round from that destroyer in this?"

Harris grinned as his thick neck did its best to hold his big head steady in the turbulence. "Four hits. Direct ones too. This box ain't exactly spry when you're trying to run. You'll see it's even less so when we have to head into Rumidon Port. In the thick of the atmosphere, she flies like she has a hundred head of bogler stampeding around inside her. But she'll get us there."

The buffeting stopped and the *Bangor* began to drop like a stone. Harris enabled the retrojets and the flying refrigerator-shaped ship jerked and then briefly stabilized.

Tawn had a nervous look on her face. "How many trips in atmosphere have you made in her?"

Harris replied as he pulled back and pushed forward on the joystick. "One, if you count the trip up from Domicile. I just picked her up last month."

"So this will be your first time landing her?"

Harris pushed several buttons on the console in front of him as he continued with seemingly violent adjustments of the joystick. "You might want to stop distracting me with talk until I have this barge on the ground. I'm having a bit of a tough time managing her."

Tawn closed her mouth as she looked out the viewport to take in the scenery of the area surrounding Rumidon. High, snow capped mountains were dotted with the occasional green valley. A lack of tilt and an almost perfect circle orbit left the planet seasonless. After a quick glance over the console in front of her, Tawn pressed the autopilot button. The violent ride ended as the *Bangor* quickly stabilized.

Harris looked up in anger. "Now what'd you do that for?"

Tawn shook her head. "So we don't die?"

"We weren't gonna die, and I need practice flying this thing manually. What if we get attacked? What good is autopilot gonna do us?"

Tawn took in a deep breath before slowly letting it out. "Look. I'm not opposed to practice. And when we get on the ground, you're welcome to take her up for all the practice you want. I might even do the same.

"But we don't have to do it with a full load of cargo banging around back there. Those containers are rugged enough, but I wouldn't necessarily put my faith in whoever packed them. I'm sure they weren't intending for them to be going for a ride like this."

Harris held up his hands before crossing his arms. "Fine. We'll be on the ground in ten minutes. Never knew a slug to be so scared."

Tawn returned a dirty look. "Just don't like taking a beating when it's not necessary, that's all."

Her gaze returned to looking out the viewport. "So the Geldons... miners and sportsman? That what you said? Doesn't seem like a good mix. One works hard all day while the other plays hard. And I'm thinking not having credits versus having too many."

"The miners like protection. Protecting their families and their property. I've been told to expect the occasional offer of a gemstone instead of credits. I expect them to be after the Foxes.

"The sportsmen... they love to shoot. They'll want to shoot anything and everything. I expect them to jump on the repeaters. You can't shoot those back home. Out here? Nobody cares."

A yellow diamond appeared just over the horizon on the nav display. "Here we go. Two minutes."

A voice came over the general comm. "Approaching craft. Please identify yourself so customs registration work can begin."

Harris accepted the comm. "This is the trader ship *Bangor* out of Chicago Port Station. We have miscellaneous items for trade and sale."

The voice replied, "Welcome, *Bangor*. Your visit has been logged. See the detailer at slip fourteen when you arrive. You'll find fourteen at the north end of the field. Be advised we're expecting storms within the standard hour. And please adjust your clocks as necessary for Geldon time. We hope you enjoy your stay."

Tawn nodded. "That was easy."

"I'm told some of the colonies aren't so friendly."

Tawn leaned back in her chair with her arms crossed. "So my partner has yet to visit any of these places. This is his first time dropping down through the atmosphere in this ship. And his first time selling arms. You have sales experience before this, right?"

"It's arms." Harris shrugged. "I know arms. How hard could it be?"

Tawn smacked herself on the forehead. "Doing sales is like this whole world unto itself. You know the merchandise, which is great, but you have to know how to convince the buyers this is something they're in desperate need of. They can't live without one, or five. They aren't safe just walking down the street unless they have a Fox-40 strapped to their hip."

"Sounds like I have my salesman right here."

Tawn pointed to herself. "Me? If you're relying on this face to bring in the buyers, you're pushing your luck." Tawn shook her head. "A stump and a slug are the face of our business. This should be good."

"If this was all bugging you, why didn't you bring it up before? We could have grabbed some slick-mouthed kid out of a retailer back there at the promenade to be our face."

Tawn mumbled in a low voice. "Didn't think about it."

Harris asked, "What? What'd you say?"

"I said I didn't think about it, OK?"

"That's what I thought. Look, we've been in combat. We're genetically stronger and faster than these people. We can handle this."

The *Bangor* landed with a short skid on the concrete in the space marked with the number fourteen. Twenty minutes later, they were through customs and walking into the terminal. They exited through the terminal door and were left looking down a road toward the town a half a mile away.

Tawn said, "What do we do now?"

"We walk."

Chapter 5

The Rumidon colony came with a main drag and two parallel side streets. It covered two scant square kilometers. Wheeled vehicles appeared to be the primary mode of local transportation. Personal flyers dotted the side streets as the bulk of the population on Geldon lived well outside of town.

As the edge of town was come to, Tawn and Harris received odd looks from two old men sitting in front of an assayer's office.

Harris walked up to the men. "Is there a meeting hall or trading post here in town?"

One of the men pointed. "Other end."

Tawn asked, "What about transportation?"

The other man laughed. "If ya didn't bring your own you're hoofing it."

"I love small towns." Tawn nodded thanks. "The folks are honest and friendly."

A vehicle came zipping up the street, pulling to a stop beside the travelers. "Need a ride?"

Harris asked, "How much to the other end of town?"

"Two credits."

Harris laughed. "Now that's funny. We can walk that in a few minutes."

The driver looked up toward the nearby mountain and shrugged. "Suit yourself."

The wheels of the vehicle chirped as the driver pulled away. The two old men stood and hurried into the assayer's office.

Harris looked at Tawn. "Honest and friendly, are they?"

Tawn pointed at the horizon over his shoulder. "The guy at the terminal mentioned a storm. You think that's it?"

A white swirling cloud obscured the view of the mountain the vehicle driver had been looking at.

Harris grabbed Tawn by the shoulder. "From the looks of that wind I'd say we better get our asses off the street!"

An attempt was made to enter the assayers office. The door was locked and the two old men stood grinning, shaking their heads, just on the other side of the thick tempered glass.

Tawn glanced back at the port terminal. "We aren't making that."

The pair sprinted down the street, trying the handle of every door they came to. The winds began to pick up, an extreme gust nearly knocking Harris from his sturdy feet. The old men in the assayers office had their faces planted against the glass as they attempted to watch the two visiting fools caught out in the vicious storm that was now turning the street white with blowing snow.

The temperature dropped forty degrees in two minutes' time as Harris and Tawn continued their sprint. A second violent gust blew Harris over forward. Several tumbles had him back on his feet and still running. Tawn opened the door to the town's only restaurant, nearly tearing it from its hinges as she held it open, yelling at her partner.

"In here! Come on!"

The bartender-owner raced to the door, attempting to pull it shut as the winds forced Harris further away. "Close that door you dang fool!"

Tawn gestured toward Harris with her head. "What about him?"

The bartender pulled the door shut just as a third heavy gust swept down the street. "If he survives the next five minutes he's welcome back. Until then, this stays shut!"

The door was locked.

Tawn's face was pressed against the glass window as the wind and snow howled by. Harris, attempting to force his way back, continued to be bowled over by fierce gusts, again tumbling before coming back upright on his feet. The storm then ended as suddenly as it had begun, the winds dying down within seconds.

The bartender unlocked the door. "You can go fetch him now."

Tawn raced out into the meter deep snow, calling out for her friend and partner. "Stump? Where you at?"

Fifty meters down the road, a snowdrift began to move. Harris emerged with a handful of scrapes on his shoulders and elbows. After shaking off the snow like a dog, he cut through the drift to a waiting Tawn.

"That was something."

Harris replied, "You made it inside. Way to leave your partner stranded."

"You're a big boy." Tawn laughed. "Can't handle a little breeze?"

"Never seen anything like it. Now I know why there are no signs or benches up and down this street."

Doors opened and people walked out, returning to their lives. Hundreds filled the streets as they made their way back to their vehicles or the business they were tending to. The restaurant owner stood looking over his strained door with a scowl.

Tawn trudged past the stump who was still attempting to get his wit together. "Come on. We have business to do."

At the end of town both the meeting hall and trading post were closed. A young boy, curious about the two oversize visitors, rode up on a scooter.

Harris asked, "What are you looking at?"

"You're big, mister. What you doing here? Store is closed."

"Why?"

"Probably all up at the mine from the cave-in." The kid shrugged. "The Duke, store owner, he went to help."

Tawn asked, "Where's this mine?"

The kid pointed. "Straight out, two kilometers, up on a hill to your left. They said Mr. Tombo found a vein of silver in his mine. At least that's the rumor. He tried some blasting and went back in after. That's when the main shaft collapsed. Hey, you're shoulders and elbows are bleeding. What happened?"

Harris replied, "None of your business, Kid. Now scram."

The electric scooter's engine whirred as the kid rode off toward the other end of town.

Tawn said, "We could use a couple of those scooters."

Harris chuckled. "Yeah, like that thing would have enough power to move your big ass."

Tawn glanced back and then looked at Harris. "It ain't no bigger than yours."

Harris gestured toward the location of the mine. "It's two kilometers, let's just run it. We could use the exercise."

A fast paced jog through the rapidly melting snow had the two standing at the mine entrance several minutes later. A small crowd was gathered outside.

Tawn stepped forward. "Any way we can help?"

One of the townsfolk replied, "Not unless you can dig. We're waiting on the equipment to get here."

"Can I take a look?"

The towny stepped back. "Have at it."

Tawn stopped, picking up a large pair of gloves from a fold-out table sitting to the side of the crowd. "I'll return these when I'm done."

"What are you doing?" Harris asked.

"I'm gonna move rock, if I can. Grab a pair. Make yourself useful."

Harris entered the shaft behind her as he pulled on a pair of workgloves. They stood for most of a minute looking over the rubble that blocked the passage about twenty meters in.

Tawn inspected the ceiling just above their heads. "Seems solid enough here. I say we start moving rock."

"You think you're gonna dig through that by hand?"

Tawn stopped and stared. "There's people trapped in there. You don't want to help, then go back and hang out with the locals." The Biomarine slug picked up the first of hundreds of small boulders to be moved. "Either carry or get out of my way."

Harris shook his head. "We're arms dealers... not rescuers."

Tawn stopped beside him with a ninety kilogram piece of rock in her grasp. "Rumor was they found silver. Silver buys guns. We manage to free these people and goodwill will get us an audience. Now grab a rock and get moving."

Harris picked up the nearest loose rock, a much smaller piece of stone.

After dumping hers outside, Tawn returned for another, chiding her partner as she passed. "Oh, big man... don't strain yourself."

Harris glanced at his shoulder. "I'm bleeding. This won't help it heal."

Once outside, the kid with the scooter was standing in observance of the big visitor. "That's it? The one the lady had was like four times that size."

Harris scowled. "Beat it, kid. You're not helping."

An hour later a third of the rock blocking the passage had been moved. A personal workcraft, the flying equivalent of a wheeled truck, settled next to the mine entrance. Three miners hopped out, pulling equipment from the bed in back.

A pair of laser cutters were soon at work breaking the larger of the boulders down to size. Two hours after the effort had begun, a breakthrough was made. Another ten minutes of digging had a passage large enough for one of the miners to slip through.

The miner returned several minutes later. "Nope. Didn't make it."

The trading post owner, Duke Fizel, stood with a dejected look on his face.

Tawn removed her gloves and patted his back. "We did what we could. I'm sorry."

Duke shook his head. "It was brand new. Took two months to get and they're now on back order."

Duke turned. "Tombo, you're paying for this!"

The miner named Tombo held up his hands. "Sorry, Duke. That was an act of God. I followed your instructions to the tee."

Tawn turned. "Wait... you're Tombo? I thought you were trapped in there?"

"Who told you that?"

"Well, what were we digging for?"

Duke replied, "My ground penetrating radar equipment. It let's you see about eight meters back into the walls of your mine. Twenty-six hundred credits and it took two months to order and get shipped here. That's five hundred credits a month of rentals down the crapper."

Duke looked at the miner who had slipped through to get status. "Any chance of a repair?"

The miner slowly shook his head. "Not unless you're a miracle worker. Smashed flat."

Duke scowled at Tombo. "If I had a blaster I'd blow your head off right now."

Harris stepped forward. "You need weapons? We have some for trade."

Tawn rolled her eyes.

Duke stared at the genetically engineered Human standing beside him. "I was speaking figuratively. Tombo is my brother. Who are you?"

Tawn nudged her way in with a hand outstretched. "Sorry for my partner's suggestion. We're traders, we just arrived. We were looking for you in town."

Duke looked Tawn up and down. "You a slug?"

"I am." Tawn nodded. "Just out here trying to make a living."

"What is it you have for sale or trade?"

Harris replied, "Personal firearms. Repeating plasma rifles, Fox-40s, shock sticks and a variety of other gear."

Duke scowled. "You'll be having to take your contraband elsewhere. We don't need any weapons here."

"No wild animals about? I thought there were sportsman adventurers coming out here."

Tombo stepped forward. "The animals here are docile. They might as well have been hunting cows. The hunters were nothing but trouble, even mistakenly took a shot at one of our miners."

Duke said, "We ran the last of them off about three weeks ago."

Harris frowned. "No need of personal protection, then, I suppose."

Duke shook his head. "We take care of our own."

Tawn placed her hand on an unscraped portion of Harris' shoulder. "Come on. Let's see if we can hit the diner for some grub before heading out."

After a fifteen minute walk, service at the restaurant was refused by a still angry owner. Another five minutes had the pair stepping back aboard the *Bangor*.

Tawn plopped down in the copilot's chair. "Well that was a bust. Sounds like we should be in the ground penetrating radar business instead."

"We'll do better. We have Grendig, Farmingdale and Bella III still to go."

Tawn tapped her fingers on the console in front of her. "We visit a mining colony we should be pushing mining gear. I wonder if the weapons trade has dried up following that truce."

Harris reached for his lap belt to strap himself in. "Domicile has enough crime to support a healthy gun trade. People want to protect themselves."

Tawn asked, "You aren't planning on flying us out of here manually are you?"

"I was."

Tawn scowled. "Maybe I'll just grab one of those repeaters for myself and stay here. Ever thought about mining?"

Harris laughed. "With a repeater? No."

"Hey... wait a second." Tawn smirked at the thought. "Give me fifteen minutes?"

"What's on your mind?"

Tawn smiled. "Just sit. I'll be right back."

A repeating plasma rifle and a charge were extracted from the cargo hold. Tawn Freely hopped out onto the tarmac and hustled across the concrete to a rocky outcropping several hundred meters away before disappearing behind it. The rumbles of plasma fire could be felt for several minutes. Tawn returned, stepping up into the cabin with a grin.

"What?"

"I just blasted a two meter hole in the bare rock out there. These plasma rifles, they're designed so that any explosive effect doesn't come directly back at you. I used it to drill a passage I could stand upright in. You could cut twenty meters into solid rock with a single charge. That's twenty credits worth of resource to go twenty meters. Leaves a fine gravel on the floor too, something easily removed by these miners."

Harris rubbed his head. "What are you suggesting?"

"I'm suggesting we try to sell these repeaters to the miners, you moron. For about six hundred fifty credits they could drill a hundred meter shaft in less than a day. That proposition has gotta have some value to it."

"So you wanna go back and see if they bite?"

"I do." Tawn nodded. "And think about this... we find someone to repackage this thing so it doesn't look like a rifle and we could make a fortune selling them as mining gear. Think about all the charges we could sell on a regular supplier basis."

Harris released his belt. "Well let's go give it a try."

Two hours were spent with the trading post owner and his brother, demonstrating the benefits of the repeating rifle as a mining tool. A single rifle and five charges were purchased for a special deposit price of three hundred credits, close to their cost. Another hour was spent conducting a test going deep into a nearby rock wall.

At ten meters the passage collapsed due to the vibrations from the plasma rounds. The explosions caused microfractures that ran deep into the rock in every direction. Duke Fizel handed the rifle back, demanding his deposit be returned. A disheartened Tawn Freely released the hold on the funds.

After returning to the *Bangor*, Harris strapped himself in. "Who's the moron now? We're down two charges and we have a used repeater to sell."

"Really thought we had one there."

Harris looked over with a grin as he tightened his lap belt. "You might want to snap that together and cinch it tight. I'm feeling the need for some practice about now."

"This punishment?"

Harris flipped on the retrojets as he continued his grin. "Take it however you want."

The ride back to open space was not for the faint of heart. As the dark of space was reached, and the planet put ten minutes behind, a wormhole was opened to the colony of Grendig.

Chapter 6

Grendig housed forty-two thousand colonists, all living in a single structure. It was an ice planet with a liquid ocean just under the surface. Other than fishing, there was nothing much else to do. The harsh temperatures, rarely reaching zero degrees on the Celsius scale, left most inhabitants staying indoors.

A fifty-meter-wide hole had been drilled through the thick ice. Submersible fishing vessels with long nets were sent out daily. A cargo ship coming from Domicile twice a month, to pick up the catch they had for sale, was the only interaction with home.

Again, the locals were less than friendly and in no need of weapons. Harris' effort to sell a repeating rifle as a drill to dig through the ice fell on deaf ears. Tawn suffered through another round of atmospheric practice as the *Bangor* made its way back to free space. The next jump would be made to Farmingdale.

***

The ride down to the surface, and on to Farmingdale Colony #1, was bumpy but tolerable. Harris was getting command of his ship. Tawn was still not impressed. The boxy freight-shuttle settled on the tarmac next to two other small ships. A courtesy vehicle was waiting to take them the five kilometers into Colony #1.

Twelve colonies dotted the otherwise largely flat plains of the southern hemisphere of the small planet. Reduced gravity made walking without having a hop in your step difficult. The Biomarine duo entered the local supply store. The lone clerk stood with a pursed smile on her face.

Tawn bounced up to the counter. "Who would we talk to here about selling some personal firearms to?"

The clerk's eye's grew wide. "Nobody here in town. You'll have to go up to Colony #13 in the mountains. They do hunting and such up there. Down here we have no need."

Tawn sighed. "Can you offer the coordinates to Colony #13?"

The clerk replied, "It's the only mountain range on this continent. The colony is on the east end. You can't miss it."

Tawn rapped her knuckles on the counter. "Thanks."

The *Bangor* was piloted toward the mountain colony. Farm after farm stretched out for kilometers as the craft moved over the plains. Upon arrival, five small concrete buildings made up Colony #13. The *Bangor* hovered and then dropped down to a grass field with a ship marker.

Tawn scowled. "Not looking promising, is it?"

A short walk had the two entering a meeting hall, where twenty of the colonists had gathered.

Tawn apologized for the interruption. "Sorry."

A man standing at a podium spoke. "You come in for the migration?"

Harris asked, "The migration?"

The man gestured toward the outside. "The herds of boglers that will be through here in a couple hours. It's a biannual event. Millions of those beasts will be charging right down through this valley and out onto the plains. That's why all those farms are to the south. You had to have flown over the separation wall coming out here."

Harris nodded. "We did. Was kind of curious as to what it was for."

The man walked out from his podium. "In about ten days we'll be taking down every bogler we can. Feeds us and gives us meat and fur to trade with the farmers. When the herd has passed we'll spend the next thirty days skinning, drying and packing the meat. You interested in some work? If so, you came at just the right time."

Tawn asked, "There's five buildings out here. How many of you are there?"

The man glanced around the room. "This is it. Except for one on lookout for the herd. We'll spend the next forty days right here in town, and then head back to our cabins in the mountains. There's plenty of space out here if you want to homestead. You look like a sturdy couple; it can be rough living at times, but I'm sure you'd do fine."

Tawn scowled. "Oh, we're not a couple. We're business partners."

The man nodded. "Yeah, well, call it what you want. If you want the work, it's coming this way. If not, you'll want to move that ship. Of course I guess you'll want to move that ship anyway. There's a rock outcropping about two kilometers south of here. You could park it there."

Harris replied, "We saw it."

Tawn said, "We're here to sell personal arms. Any of you have a need?"

Four hands were raised.

Harris asked, "What can we sell you?"

One of the men stepped forward with a sewn up sleeve. "I need a right arm."

The other hunters laughed.

Harris shook his head. "Can't help you there. We're selling firearms. I have repeating plasma rifles... ideal for hunting bogler. Or we have standard plasma rifles and Fox-40s."

One of the men raised a hand. "You mean zappers?"

Tawn stood silent for several seconds. "Some people call them that. You need one?"

The man asked. "How many kilos?"

"How many kilos what? What are you asking?"

"How many kilograms of bogler meat? I could use me one of those zappers for the strays during the summer."

Harris raised a hand. "You don't have credits?"

The man chuckled. "Mister, everything on Farmingdale is barter. I'd be willing to trade two hundred fifty kilos of dried and packed bogler beef for a zapper."

Tawn asked, "Does anyone have credits? Or do the farmers trade credits for meat?"

The men in the room looked around at each other. None were wearing the common account bracelet seen on Domicile and the other colonies.

The lookout raced into the door. "They're coming early!"

The door to the building was pulled shut and locked.

Harris moved toward the exit. "If you let us out, we'll come back after."

The man shook his head. "Sorry, too late. This door opens and we all die."

The walls began to shake as the sound of hooves grew from a low rumble to a violent torrent of stampeding chaos.

The speaker grimaced. "Sorry about your ship. We usually have at least an hour's notice."

The lookout said, "They didn't pool in the upper pasture this year. They just came racing down. I barely made it in here."

Tawn asked, "So what do we do? How do we get out of here?"

The speaker replied, "You don't. Not until it's on the wane, which is usually eight to ten days."

"What are we supposed to eat and drink in the meantime?" Tawn asked.

"These buildings are connected by tunnels. We'll move over to the dining hall in a few hours, unless you need food this instant for some reason."

Harris looked around the room at the burly mountain men and four husky women who were now their mates for the next eight or so days. "I don't suppose there's a deck on top of this building, is there?"

The speaker nodded. "Right over here. I'm Noff, by the way. Toby, put the ladder up for us."

The lookout cut through the others, propping a wooden ladder against a wall that led up to a hatch. A quick climb had him through and standing on the roof.

Noff gestured toward the ladder. "Go on up if you're curious as to what so many beasts look like. Might even be able to see what's left of your ship."

Harris was the first up the ladder, followed by Tawn and then Noff. A sea of gray-furred boglers covered the previously grassy valley floor that surrounded the five buildings. Colony #13 had become five tiny concrete islands in a matter of a few minutes. Coming over a rise from the west the grand herd streamed down into town. On the east, the torrent of boglers was quickly spreading out onto the plains. The *Bangor*, now upside down, sat a hundred meters from its prior location.

Harris shook his head. "That ship weighs tons."

"Holding up pretty well so far." Noff nodded. "What's she made of?"

"Depleted uranium and metallic carbide. She's dense and heavy."

"Well, if she survives, you're likely to have a long walk to get to her. They got her rolling pretty good there."

One of the colonists stepped close up behind Tawn. "You look pretty and you smell good, my name's Hobb."

Tawn took a whiff, scrunching up her face. "I'm a slug and you're a skunk. Sorry, the two don't really mix."

Tawn looked back to see three more sets of overly friendly eyes ogling her sturdy body. "Sorry fellas. Not gonna happen. I'm a city girl."

Harris laughed. "City girl? Since when?"

Tawn returned a vicious gaze. "Mind your own business, please. Now Mr. Noff, we mentioned that we have guns for sale. Is there an exchange on this planet where we could trade that meat for credits?"

Noff thought. "We only trade with the farmers. If there's any type of banking system here on Farmingdale, you'll have to go ask them."

Harris looked back at the others who were now crowding the roof. "So what do you guys do for ten days when this is going on?"

"We tell stories from the past year," Noff replied. "Most of us haven't seen another person during that time, except the few of us that have wives. Janeal, my wife, is the sister of Mardo over there, he has a wife. And Baka and Handy have wives. The rest of us are loners.

"But I could tell you what's been going on with just about any of these fellas over the last ten years. Except this past year. Haven't heard those stories yet.

Noff crossed his arms. "Mardo and I live across the valley from each other. I see him and my sister-in-law Willia out roaming their side of the valley once every few weeks. Other than that I think this year I saw at least three others once. We never talk though as it would leave us with nothing to say during the migration."

Noff gestured to the others. "Come on. Let's head over to the lounge. We can get started with the stories."

The settlers of Colony #13 began to climb down the ladder.

Tawn asked, "Are the women here?"

Noff nodded. "Over in the bath house. We give them their privacy before the migration. They'll join us in the lounge shortly I'm sure. They offer some of the best stories every year. My wife, Janeal, is an excellent storyteller. If you'd like a bath, you're welcome to join them."

"I think I'll pass, thanks."

The group gathered in the lounge. Three dozen individual chairs made a semicircle around a single highchair. The speaker, when given the main chair, would stay for up to a day, depending on the stories they had and their ability to tell them.

Noff, the elected chieftain of Colony #13, had the honor of being the first to speak. The group settled as the four women came through a hatch door from a tunnel, taking their places with their men.

"Well, we packed our meat from the last migration on our sleds and began to drag it back to our cabin. You all saw us leave. Anyway, we hadn't gone two hundred meters and our sled broke. We had to stop to fix it. Used the twine we got... I think two migrations ago. Yep. We traded the farmers five kilos of meat for it. Still got enough for another three or four migrations. Just in case we need it."

Tawn strained to listen over the rumble of bogler hooves as Noff droned on for two hours about every little detail of his trip carrying the meat from the colony back to his cabin. There would no doubt be an equally as boring version coming from his wife when her turn came to the speaking chair.

The slug sat with her jaw dropped slightly while attempting to keep from rudely falling asleep. A glance at Harris yielded an image of a Biomarine slumped in his chair, eyes closed, and drool coming from the corner of his mouth. The mountaineer sitting beside him watched it curiously, waiting for the latest string of spittle to separate and drop. Tawn stopped to rub her tired eyes as Noff interrupted a particularly boring story about patching a hole in his roof. It was time for a dinner break.

Tawn shook Harris. "Stump. Get your ass up. Dinner time. And clean your mouth. You look disgusting."

Harris checked and wiped the wet corner of his mouth with his forearm. "What'd I miss?"

Tawn returned a scowling stare. "Did you hear about his fall into the ravine? Or about the wall of the storehouse collapsing after a heavy rain?"

Harris shook his head. "I must have been out by then."

Tawn replied sarcastically, "I'll make sure he tells them to you personally. They were screamers."

The dinner consisted of year-old, dried bogler strips with a home brewed beer that had an extra kick to it. The mostly quiet colonists were soon chatting away, with laughter and singing breaking out shortly after. The feast was followed by a ritualistic walk back to the lounge in complete silence.

As everyone took their seats, Tawn raised her hand. "Sorry to interrupt, but are we allowed to speak?"

Noff stood from the speaking chair. "How rude of us! Of course! You must have new stories from years and years worth of living. I'm certain the others would be equally as fascinated to hear them."

Nods and agreeing mumbles went around the room.

Noff moved to the side of the chair. "Please. Come take the floor. We would be honored."

Harris chuckled. "You gonna tell them about how Red was ripping you off? We took an oath about the war."

"Maybe. Or maybe I have a story or two in me. You know. Both of us fought as Biomarines for sixteen years. And if you read your release papers you'd have seen that they negated all oaths and pledges. We're free and they don't want us back. Anyway, gotta be a few experiences to talk about from that."

Harris sat back in his chair. "Didn't realize they took the mufflers off us. This could get interesting."

Tawn sat in the highchair, making herself comfortable. "OK. Who here knows what a slug and a stump are?"

Several hands were raised.

Tawn shook her head. "I'm not talking about the slimy little animal or the cutoff trunk of a tree. I'm talking about the war with the New Earthers."

The hands dropped.

Tawn smiled. "We have to roll the clock back about fifty years. On Domicile, the war had been at a stalemate for almost a hundred fifty years. The DD, Domicile Defense, would destroy a half dozen New Earth ships in a battle and six months later they would do the same to us.

"The colonies out here... if they had leanings or dealings with one world or the other they would periodically get raided. I'm sure you heard about Farmingdale getting completely wiped out twice."

Several eyes grew large.

"No? Well I'll have to come back to that. You see, our scientists and leaders decided they needed to work on a super-soldier of sorts. Due to a plethora of spies on both sides, our weapons were equal, and our ships were equal, leaving only our fighters to monkey around with.

"Mr. Gruberg there and myself are the result of that monkeying around. We're what you would call Biomarines. Genetically altered Humans.

"We were taken as donor sperm and eggs and fiddled with until the genetic traits the military was looking for came out. We're strong and agile. We can run fast and have great endurance. Our metabolism is slow so we don't have to eat as much, but we do.

"Our blood holds a slightly higher oxygen content, so we can fight in an atmosphere with about 20 percent less oxygen and still function at peak. Basically, they took a bunch of the good genes and crammed them into us. We number about ten thousand, and I believe we were part of the reason the truce was signed.

"Now, as you can see, with all that design and manipulation being geared toward war, they left off those genes that would have made us attractive to other humans. I'm referred to as a slug. I have the body of a bulldog with this flat pug face. The slug name came about during our psychological training where we were called pretty much every name in the book. Slug stuck."

One of the colonists raised his hand. "I think you're pretty."

Tawn replied, "Thank you, Hobb. Might be because you only have one eye. You and I mixing would be something like trying to cross a cuddly male kitten with one of those boglers out there. Not gonna work on any level.

"Anyway. The male version, Mr. Gruberg there, he's called a stump. All you have to do is look at him to know why. He's got that bulbous head with a thick short neck. He's as deep front to back as he is side to side. Again, we were bred for war."

Tawn shifted in her chair, taking a relaxed posture as her story would be long. "So what was life like as a young slug? Well, as early as I can remember I was in combat training. Making war, combat, it's like second nature to me. I was made, and trained, to be a killing machine.

"Not what I chose, but what was chosen for me. Same with my partner over there. We each saw our first combat when we were thirteen. They told us it was a training mission and then dropped us in the thick of an actual battle to evaluate us. We excelled.

"So they made more of us. I think Harris was division eight. I was division six. I believe two hundred forty of us came out that first year.

"Half are dead, and probably half again are missing this limb or that or this organ or that. But we persevered. We survived. We overcame the obstacles they put before us, and we stand here before you today in spite of the hardships we faced."

Hobb held up a hand. "What was your fiercest battle?"

Tawn thought for a moment. You know what? Let me think on that for a few minutes. We'll bring Mr. Gruberg up here to tell you about his. I'd be curious to hear that one myself."

Harris stood and moved to the chair. "Gentleman... ladies... you better fasten your lap belts..."

Chapter 7

Harris gave a synopsis of several of the battles that preceded the fight called the Helm Engagement. Transport fleets had dropped thousands of soldiers on a rocky world with a thin atmosphere. It was similar in size to Domicile and New Earth, but with no vegetation to speak of because of a 7 percent humidity level. Helm was bone dry.

Both sides had a limited number of plasma charges for their weapons. The fleets, after dumping the soldiers, fought a fierce battle to the last ship, abandoning the ground troops with both sides fearing to commit more ships. Twenty thousand Earther regulars had been placed against six thousand Domer regulars and four hundred slugs and stumps.

Harris said, "We sat for three days just staring across a rock strewn field that separated our lines, each force tucked behind a hillside. I was given a night watch. Stump vision is 20/12 as compared to most. We can see more detail. And it's better in the dark than standard.

"Anyway, I was watching these two Earther mooks who were watching me when the head of a guy just to my left exploded. Brains and skull were everywhere. It was a mess. Then the same thing happened just to my right. That's when I saw the faintest muzzle flash coming from a hilltop behind the enemy. Someone was picking us off from nearly three kilometers distance.

"I pinpointed the sniper using a laser-scope, and a guided mortar saw to it they didn't pick off anyone else. Of course that sniper was not the only one. Turned out there were a dozen, and they were the elites of the Earther forces. Our colonel called on three slugs to take them out. Unfortunately he also called on us to move back over the hill out of sight.

"The Earthers used that mistake to mount an assault. They were coming up the front of our hill before the alarm sounded.

We held for a while, mostly in the center where the slugs and stumps were positioned. That turned out to be our colonel's second mistake. Both ends were overrun and our support in the back got wiped out and our supplies destroyed.

"In a bold move, our major, a slug, called for our force to charge down the front of the hill. Five hundred regulars and half of our Biomarines made the break while an equal-size force held that hilltop. I was in the force that charged out.

"After diving into a cluster of Earther Marines, I drew my sword and started to hack and slash. It was bloody, body parts were flying everywhere. The screams were horrific. Soldiers and Marines were dying to my right and to my left... up and down what we later called Slaughter Hill.

"My platoon broke free through the enemy lines and raced across the rock-covered field in the darkness. The rest of our breakout force was slowly pushed back up the hill, at great expense to the Earthers. Thirty-six of us, all slugs and stumps, charged up the opposing hill.

"The Earther lookouts were all watching the battle unfold on the other hilltop when we came upon them. Using our swords so as not to alert their support troops we were coming, we hacked them down one by one.

"When we descended on their encampment, they were in complete chaos. I shot, and hacked, and shot, and hacked, for what seemed like a couple hours. Turned out later we mopped them up in forty standard minutes. The three slugs that had been sent after the snipers completed their mission and joined us on that hilltop. We had captured two cases of those sniper rifles.

"Over the next three hours, the thirty-nine of us were credited with just over four thousand kills. The total would have been higher, but we ran out of rounds for those rifles. Our troops on the other hill fought valiantly, but their survival wasn't to be. When the last man fell, the twenty-thousand-man Earther force had been chopped down to just under three thousand. Those three thousand then turned their sights on us.

"We blew up their remaining supplies, before using our plasma rifles to kill hundreds more as they crossed that field.

Our major called for us to retreat, taking refuge on the hill behind us, which was steep and tall, preventing any type of an all-out charge coming up. But they tried anyway.

"Eight hundred men were sacrificed trying to force their way up that harsh terrain. Another hundred lost their lives trying to come around behind us, which was nearly impossible. The back of the hillside was a two hundred meter sheer rock cliff. Several more attempts to breach the hill from the back failed miserably.

"After that, we settled into a game of whack-a-mole. Somebody showed a head and they lost it. They told us twenty-nine hundred fifty-six New Earth regulars had survived the taking of our hill. Two days later we had their number reduced to just over eight hundred. And we still had our thirty-nine.

"Had they not destroyed our supplies when they overran us initially, they would have been able to mortar us off that hill. As it turned out, a lack of water is what finished them off.

"Our Biomarine bodies are efficient at cooling themselves internally. We don't sweat much. As a consequence, the dry Helm air didn't knock us down like it did them. That and the fact that the first night, our colonel ordered the roundup of any surviving Earther soldiers who were lying around us. If they still had heartbeats, they were put to use.

"It was grisly, but we were ordered to slit their wrists and to drain, filter, and drink their blood while preserving what water we had. The poor sap I grabbed kept me hydrated for two days.

"Our packs contained a small pump filter that took the toxic amounts of iron out of the blood. Drinking blood otherwise would make you sick. Anyway, we used the handful of survivors who had first charged up that hill as our personal water-bags. Our major was one of the few of us who had an above-average IQ. And she was all about taking every step she could to keep us alive.

"By the sixth day, we walked down that hill and offed those soldiers who were still breathing... one by one. Thirty-nine of us, out of more than twenty-six thousand soldiers who were dumped on Helm, claimed that planet for Domicile and all her citizens."

Harris looked around the room to see nothing but wide eyes.

Tawn said, "Wow. You, sir, are to be commended. Didn't know you were one of the thirty-nine. That was the premier fight of the Biomarines, and was the beginning of the push that saw four other planets liberated before the truce was called."

Harris nodded. "Lost a lot of friends that day. The next fight, the Battle of Bloody Moon, the major took a plasma round in the neck. No offense to you, Freely, but she was the best slug I ever knew."

Noff said, "We like to think our lives out here are a struggle, Mr. Gruberg. You have given us new perspective. Miss Freely? You have a similar experience? Compared to our mundane lives, you two have intriguing histories."

Tawn took the highchair. "My first story wasn't quite like that. I was the member of a squad that was sent in to clear a city block in the Durant Colony of Haterra. The main Earther force was in retreat. We were given the task of cleaning out the ones who wouldn't leave.

"Mind you, many of these were the actual homeowners who thought they were just defending their property. Of course, two years before, these same people had butchered the Domicile settlers who had been there for centuries. So we didn't have much sympathy for their cause.

"Anyway, my teammate and I entered one of these houses. It was like most of the homes on Haterra, a concrete slab and concrete walls. Similar to this very building, but with two windows. We swept the main rooms, three of them on the first floor, and found them to be clear. Wanda, my teammate, as she moved to the stairs going up, the inhabitants tossed a grenade down.

"I managed to duck behind a counter, but Wanda was caught in the open. The frag split the back of her right thigh wide open in three places. At that same moment, the whole family, four in all, came charging down the stairs with their weapons firing.

Before I could move, Wanda took three rounds from a Bartlet-3, the Earther equivalent of our Fox-40s.

"One round entered her left forearm from the inside edge, taking half the meat and muscle off the back. Another struck her in that same shoulder, shredding her shoulder blade as it came out the back. A third entered her right leg, causing further injury to what had already been mangled by the grenade.

"From my vantage point I still couldn't see them on the stairs, but Wanda could. She pulled her sword with her right hand and charged right up into them, taking out the mother first, followed by the two teens. They fired repeated rounds at Wanda as she charged up the steps. Don't know how they missed her, but they did. Their cowardly father was coming down last.

"As I moved across the floor to help my teammate, two heads and then the lower half of a torso tumbled down in front of me. The father came skidding down on his chest a few seconds later, terror in his eyes. Wanda rolled down behind him, stopping on her good leg before driving her blade through the back of his skull. Had they just given up, they'd have been returned to the Earthers for relocation.

"I did my best to give Wanda emergency aid until the medic team got there, but they were too late. As she died in my arms, I swore to myself that one day I would be as good a Marine as Wanda was. Even with all my training, that episode left me a bit out of it. When the cleaning of Durant was finished, I got sent back for an evaluation.

"During that trip, I paid a visit to the marksman range to try to take out some frustration. One of the instructors took an interest. Two weeks later I joined an elite team of snipers. I finished the war without ever getting close to another Earther soldier."

Harris said, "I'm sure there were other experts well before our time, but she was one of only thirty snipers to ever be certified as level four. And the only slug so far as I know. We were the foot soldiers, the building stormers and the sewer rats. Slugs and stumps got the dirty jobs, and the most difficult ones."

Noff asked, "Do you fault the military for who you are?"

Tawn replied, "Fault? Are you kidding? I like who and what I am. While a part of me does wish they had focused a bit more on appearance, I wouldn't trade my body or my life for anyone else's."

Noff glanced at Harris, who answered as well. "Just like everyone in this room, there are parts of it I'd love to swap out, but overall... I'm with her. What about your lives here? Any adventures? Hardships you've had to overcome? Or even stories you've heard over the years? We've got a lot of time to still cover before that herd passes."

Hobb held up his hand. "I had a pet bogler once. Raised it from a calf. Shot it when it ate my cat."

The room erupted in laughter.

Hobb crossed his arms with a huff. "I loved that cat! You can't get them out here."

Other stories of survival began to emerge from the mountain men and women who occupied the lounge at Colony #13. Harris and Tawn were called upon repeatedly to tell more tales of the war.

Harris was deeply involved in a harrowing engagement when the lookout came down from the roof. "Herd has passed! Time to clean up the strays!"

The men and women rose quickly, hustling to a storage locker that contained their crude but effective weapons. The remainder of the day saw a hundred eighty-four strays taken down.

The forth building in the colony was their butchery where the women ruled the day. Carcasses were stripped and cleaned, meat sliced for packing in salt and hides stacked for tanning. The event continued for thirty hours straight until the fifth building, used for storage, was completely full.

Harris and Tawn made their way out onto the plain. The *Bangor* was found, scratched and beaten, lying on its port side.

The stampeding herd had pushed the twenty-ton craft more than a kilometer from its landing location. Harris used the ship's retrojets to right her, before a quick flight had them back at Colony #13.

Harris asked Noff, who was busily stacking the hides for the tanning that would come in the days that followed, "So if I go back to the farmers, how many kilos of meat are you looking to trade? How many weapons do you need?"

Noff sighed. "I'm sorry, Mr. Gruberg. We have to finish this and I'm on the verge of collapse. We'll be sleeping for a day when this is done. Come see me after that and I'll give a full accounting of what we might want from you."

Noff turned to continue his work as Tawn smacked Harris on the shoulder. "They're feeding us. We aren't burning any fuel. One more day won't kill us."

Harris replied with a growl. "If we don't make a sale soon the stress might."

Tawn said, "Well, let's do some preliminary math. How much can the *Bangor* haul?"

Harris replied, "Three tons, give or take."

Tawn rubbed her chin. "If we go with the two hundred fifty kilos per weapon Noff offered, that's a dozen sales. Last I knew bogler or similar beef fetched a couple credits a pound. Three tons would be six thousand credits. Sounds like a haul to me. We just take the meat straight back to Domicile. Heck, we could dump the guns and just make beef runs as far as that goes."

Harris laughed. "First off, two credits is retail, for wholesale you'd have to cut that in half. And whose gonna buy three tons of meat that hasn't been professionally slaughtered, packed, and inspected according to government regs?

"The farmers might, but not for any premium price. We'd be lucky to get a credit for ten pounds of this stuff. Wouldn't be enough to pay for our jump fuel. And I have no desire to be in the meat-hauling business. I think this whole deal is gonna be another bust."

Tawn sighed. "Maybe robbing Bax wasn't such a good idea. I thought you already had buyers out here. You think she'd be willing to give us a quarter on the credit for what that cargo is worth?"

Harris shook his head. "She'd spit in our faces. We can sell it. We just have to find the right buyers."

Two days later, the Colony #13 mountain men returned from their rest. A price of three hundred kilos of preserved and packaged bogler meat was agreed upon... if that meat could be converted to sufficient credits at the farming colonies.

The *Bangor* lifted off the grassy plain just east of the mountain colony. A short flight had her again setting down at the spaceport for Colony #1. A tour of the handful of buildings in town would yield no interest in the bogler from the traders. All necessary supplies would be had over the course of the year from the mountain men.

Harris shook his head in disgust as the *Bangor* shot up through the atmosphere. Jump coordinates were set to the colony on Bella III and a wormhole initiated. Upon arrival, the centuries-old ship was manually piloted down through the atmosphere and was soon landing at the spaceport of the colony city named Baddington. After receiving direction to sit tight for a customs inspection, the genetically altered duo waited.

A figure riding a small tracked vehicle approached and stood just outside as the hatch opened. "Mr. Gruberg?"

Harris nodded. "Come on in. She has the manifest ready for you and the cargo is over there."

Tawn held out a tablet displaying the goods to be made available for trade.

"You got a name?" Harris said.

"Plymouth Vontmier."

Tawn asked, "These are all classified as personal weapons. I don't suppose you'd know what the market for such weapons is here on Bella would you?"

Plymouth rocked his head back and forth as he counted containers. "Mmm. It comes and goes. There's a big hunting tournament coming up next month in Blackwood. You might do well with that. How much would you estimate your cargo is worth?"

Harris asked, "You talking retail or replacement cost for us?"

"Sure, retail." Plymouth replied.

Harris shrugged. "I suppose anywhere from twelve to twenty thousand credits. Why?"

Plymouth entered several numbers into his own electronic tablet. "We have an import tax on Bella. It comes to 10% of sales."

Harris scowled. "10 percent retail? Kind of steep don't you think?"

Plymouth replied, "I don't make the rules or laws, Mr. Gruberg. I do however have some autonomy in this situation. I would be willing to use the lower of the two figures you provided, should say... one of those repeaters fall from its case and into my possession?"

Tawn stepped forward. "A shakedown. Do you know what a slug is, Mr. Vontmier?"

Plymouth returned an uneasy look. "I do."

Tawn nodded. "Then you're familiar with their temperament?"

"Well, not generally, no."

"They can be very nasty, easily brought to anger, if they feel threatened or abused. That generally goes for cheated or mistreated as well. And given that you confessed to having some autonomy, a statement we have recorded here on our ship's system, I'd say you might fall into the cheated category. And just so you understand my meaning, I'm a slug."

Plymouth took in a deep breath and held up a hand. "I'm sorry, perhaps there was a misunderstanding. What did you estimate your replacement cost to be?"

Tawn shook her head. "No. I think we're going to go a different route. Seeing as how we don't yet have a buyer for any or all of our cargo, I think there won't be any import taxes taken out until such time as we go to leave. At that time, an inventory can be conducted, and taxes paid on the items sold, at the retail minus cost price. I would think that to be standard practice in all the colonies. Is that something you can work with, Mr. Vontmier?"

Plymouth hesitantly nodded. "We've had similar arrangements with other trading partners. I believe the agreement papers can be drawn up to accommodate that."

Harris cut into the conversation, pushing Tawn back a step. "Mr. Vontmier, I apologize for my partner's forward behavior. And if you're willing to expedite the agreement, I might be willing to shake one of those repeaters loose from its container. Call it a thank-you and a gentleman's agreement that we would be treated in a preferred manner should we again come to Bella III."

Plymouth's demeanor changed from one of fear to a smile. "I'll have that to you in a few moment's, Mr. Gruberg."

The customs agent scowled at Tawn as he walked back to his tracked vehicle, calling into his command.

Tawn shook her head. "You just gave away four or five hundred credits."

"Call it greasing the skids for future business. Thanks, by the way, for loosening him up. I was half expecting a call to be placed to their local police and a wagon to be sent out to collect us for threatening a government official."

Tawn looked out at Plymouth Vontmier. "How do you know he's not doing that right now?"

Harris glanced at the containers of weapons. "What guy doesn't want a repeating plasma rifle? And I'll bet he's willing to pay the forty credit price for a plasma charge for it. Might even buy several."

"Charges are twenty credits."

Harris laughed. "I knew slugs were slow, but you're giving them a bad name."

Tawn thought. "OK. Got it. We should make him buy five at that price."

Plymouth returned with his tablet held out. "Tap to accept the agreement. And I reduced the taxable rate to 8 percent. A preferred rate."

Harris opened a container and retrieved the used repeating plasma rifle. "As we agreed to, unofficially of course. And I'm certain you will be wanting to buy plasma charges for your new weapon. These are full power, military grade, if you will. They're forty credits apiece. At a quarter power setting, which is preferred for target shooting as well as for most game, you can expect to get a thousand rounds from each charge. How many would you like?"

Plymouth grinned as he held and looked over the ultrapowerful personal weapon. I think five... no... seven. I can make that price back by charging my friends to fire a repeater. Thank you, Mr. Gruberg... and Miss whatever-your-name-is. Thank you both. I'll send out a taxi for you to take into town. My treat."

A transfer of two hundred eighty credits was conducted. Plymouth Vontmier stepped down from the *Bangor*, almost tripping over his own feet as his concentration was centered on his newest acquisition.

Harris turned to face Tawn. "Our first sale. I've got a good feeling about this place."

Tawn nodded sarcastically. "Yeah. A repeater and seven charges for two hundred eighty credits... the way I read it, we're already swimming in loss."

Chapter 8

Harris closed and locked the container before walking to the door. "Weather looks good. Wonder why Mr. Vontmier drives a tracked truck?"

Tawn replied as she reached for Harris' arm, "Did you not read any of the climate data on this planet before we got here? And let me see your store. Half those credits are mine."

Harris pulled back. "Ahh, no. Our agreement stated *after costs*. Seeing as how you just said this was a loss, I believe you owe me a few credits."

Tawn scowled. "You're gonna make this relationship hard, aren't you?"

Harris laughed. "You have the psychological training to cope with tough situations. I'm sure you can handle it."

Tawn crossed her arms. "I'm sure I'd snap your stump neck if you actually had one."

A flying taxi approached, landing up close to the *Bangor*. A door swung open to its passenger compartment.

An unusually skinny old man said, "Get in if you would. You're costing me oxygen."

The two hopped in, and the door closed as the craft lifted.

Harris asked, "Costing you oxygen?"

The old man nodded. "Bella is light on the stuff. Government claims 17 percent. Most say it's closer to 16. Anyway, all of our vehicles and buildings have oxygen generators so we don't all end up dumb. Generating costs fuel, which I pay for myself. Where you headed exactly?"

"There a trading post or a gun club or anything similar in town? We have personal firearms for sale and we're here looking for a market."

The old man frowned. "Hate to tell you, but we have a regular supplier we've been dealing with for several years. Everybody likes him, so you might find business slow here."

Tawn asked, "You wouldn't be talking about Cletus Dodger, would you?"

The old man lit up. "Yeah, you know him? He's a friendly sot... and a good tipper."

Tawn placed her big hand on the old man's shoulder, swallowing it in her palm. "Unfortunately, Mr. Dodger is no longer with us. He got caught in the middle of a trade by a New Earth destroyer. They fired on him, destroying his ship."

The old man glanced back with a sad look. "No kidding? They got Cletus? That's a sad day. He was sweet man. And his dog... what a hoot."

Tawn chuckled. "You talking about Farker?"

The old man nodded. "Yeah. What a sweet animal."

Tawn gestured back toward the *Bangor*. "We have him on the ship. Cletus kind of left him to me."

"Farker? He would never have got rid of that dog. How'd you say you got it again?"

Harris interrupted. "She worked for a trader who was doing a deal with Cletus. They got caught by the Earthers and just as the ships went to undock the dog ran across to her ship. Cletus didn't make it out. She couldn't care for the dog, so she left him with me. I believe she was tired of him humping her leg."

The old man laughed. "That's Farker. All part of his friendly programming, you know. Cletus said he was one of a kind. Claims to have found him roaming on... Delin? Deadland? Midland? Or something like that. Some uninhabited planet. Said he was hanging around some abandoned building by himself.

"Anyway, I'd love to see Farker when you make a run back to the ship. Give me call, I'll be happy to take you whenever you're ready."

A comm channel was exchanged. The taxi landed in a lot beside a building with a sign showing it to be *Bella Sports, Inc.* Harris tipped the old man two credits and sent him on his way.

"Miss Freely, may I follow you inside?"

Tawn replied, "You expecting them to be shooting or what?"

Harris smirked. "No. But now that you mention it, I'm gonna be following you a lot."

Four men and two women were browsing the aisles as Tawn and Harris walked up to an unattended counter.

"He'll be back in a few minutes," One of the customers said. "Back in the crapper."

The store owner, Bonn Herrik, came from the back, fastening his pants. "Sorry, business. How can I help you?"

Harris said, "You familiar with Cletus Dodger?"

Bonn smiled as he looked behind them. "He here? Finally... was expecting him a few weeks ago."

Tawn leaned on the counter. "I guess we're the bringers of bad news today. Mr. Dodger passed away. We're here in hopes of picking up his clients. He left me his dog before he passed."

Bonn winced. "Farker?"

Harris nodded. "Yes. Farker. And she couldn't care for him so now he's mine. Sweet dog."

Tawn scowled.

Bonn nodded. "Yes. Yes he is. And who are you?"

Harris held out a hand. "Harris Gruberg. This is my associate, Tawn Freely. We're out here with the hopes of supplying Mr. Dodger's former clients with personal firearms."

Bonn replied, "I see. And how exactly did Cletus pass?"

Tawn bumped Harris to the side. "He got caught in a trade for the weapons he planned on delivering here. A New Earth destroyer did him in before he could plead his case or make a run."

Bonn frowned as he shook his head. "Same thing happened to his competitor a month before. He always said it was a dangerous business."

Tawn took a deep breath. "Very. Both New Earth and Domicile think traders like us are trying to arm the outer colonies for war. Domicile tends to be a little more judicious should they catch you in the act of not going through the proper channels. It usually results in a fine and possible prison time, at least that's what I've been told. The Earthers? They just blast you to oblivion."

Tawn made an explosive gesture with her hand, causing Bonn Herrik to take a step back.

"So you say you have weapons to trade?"

Harris nodded. "Repeaters, Fox-40s, charges for both, and a number of difficult to acquire accessories."

Bonn tilted his head. "Scopes?"

Tawn again leaned forward with a smile. "We have a dozen of the latest models."

Bonn came out from behind the counter. "I recommend an auction. I conducted four such auctions with Cletus and all went very well. The colonists of Bella III are hungry for weapons, whether they be for hunting or sport or self defense. And they are willing to pay a premium."

Harris grinned. "What kind of premium are we talking? Say... for a repeater?"

"Repeaters, of course we only had two last time around and the bidding got almost out of hand, they went for fifteen hundred credits each. How many do you have?"

Tawn said, "A hundred fifty-one. And two hundred twelve Fox-40s."

Bonn's eyes lit up. "Outstanding! And I think we can sell every one! The bidding won't be fifteen hundred credits, but seven hundred is not out of the question. And the Foxes, I believe we'll be able to get five hundred each for those. How many charges do you have?"

Tawn replied, "Roughly fifteen hundred. All military grade."

Bonn rubbed his hands together. "Spectacular!"

Walking back behind the counter, Bonn turned. "I'll begin organizing the event at once. If you have interest, that is."

Harris said, "We have interest. And this auction, can I assume you'll be taking a cut? If so, how much?"

Bonn rolled his eyes in thought. "I believe a fair cut for an auctioneer is 10 percent. Given the quantity here, I would be willing to go 8. And you won't have to do anything but provide the items to be sold. I will do all of our marketing to ensure we have the largest available crowd. And I'll host the event here at the store. Will you be able to provide samples for potential customers to look over?"

Harris nodded. "I think we can do that. When would you want them by?"

"Immediate if possible. Look behind you."

Harris turned. Each of the customers who had been browsing the store at their arrival was now standing behind them. Listening for details of the upcoming auction.

"And I believe we'll have the same response from the entire community. We do have our annual competition hunt coming up next month. This could not be better timing."

Tawn patted Harris on the back. "I think we need go get some samples."

Harris glanced back at the storekeeper. "Could you call us a taxi back to the spaceport?"

Bonn reached behind his counter, picking up a set of keys. "Are you familiar with a flyerlight?"

Harris replied, "That's like a flying truck, isn't it?"

Bonn nodded. "Have you piloted one before?"

"I've driven just about everything at one time or another. Military training had us piloting tanks, trucks, ships, scooters, flyers... you name it. Even if I don't know the model I can figure it out."

"Behind this building. Please be careful. Repairs out here in the colonies can take months." Bonn tossed the keys.

Tawn snatched them from the air. "I'll drive."

Harris followed her out of the store and around the building. "Seven hundred apiece for the repeaters. Even with his fee we're gonna come out of this with better than twenty thousand credits to our names. Of course we'll have to divvy out all the costs before splitting, but I think we're gonna be in great shape."

Tawn's expression turned to one of confusion. "Wait... seven hundred a piece and we have a hundred fifty one to sell? This can't be right... that's over a hundred thousand credits!"

Harris laughed. "What? No. That's..."

Tawn could almost hear gears turning in the stump's head.

Harris looked out the window and then at his partner as the flyerlight lifted from the ground. "How'd we screw that up? The Foxes are gonna bring in a similar amount. And the charges at least half that again. Are we talking a quarter million credits?"

Tawn nodded with a smug grin on her face. "I think we are, Mr. Gruberg. We could be sitting on over a hundred thousand credits each!"

A half dozen samples were collected and returned to Bonn Herrik at Bella Sports, Inc. Within days a line of prospective buyers wanting a look at the merchandise stretched out the door. Tawn stood at the ready giving demonstrations.

"This is the Saxon Repeating plasma rifle. Model ML-DX2. The same weapon used in the war by yours truly, and by Mr. Gruberg over there. He used this very weapon at the Helm Engagement. Any of you familiar with the Helm Engagement?"

Blank stares and several head shakes of *no* were returned.

"At the battle for Helm, more than twenty-six thousand soldiers from both sides were dropped in for a fight to claim the planet. Mr. Gruberg there was one of those twenty-six thousand. The fighting was over in about ten days. Thirty-nine Biomarines were the only living beings who walked away from that fight. Mr. Gruberg was one of those thirty-nine. And he was carrying one of these... the Saxon Repeating model ML-DX2.

"This is the weapon that won that fierce battle. It's ideal for home defense, sport, or on the lowest settings, game hunting. Now, come up and have a look. We have six lines for the six samples. When you're done there, we have another six lines for the Fox-40s. Take your time at looking them over, but please be courteous, as others want to have a look too."

Harris said, "You sure you didn't do sales before? That even had me wanting one."

Bonn leaned in. "Keep making that speech to each new group. That alone might drive the price up by another hundred credits. Look at them. They're excited. I'm excited."

Tawn grinned.

Bonn said, "We have close to a million colonists here on Bella. And most of them are outdoors types. I expected a good response, but nothing like this. Those repeaters might fetch a thousand credits each. Even the plasma charges could be bringing in fifty. Is there any way to acquire more of those? The supply we are providing is tight."

"It's not illegal to transport a plasma charge," Tawn replied. "Don't know that we'll be able to get any more of the military grade ones, but standard charges? Those can be had for five credits all day long on Domicile. And that's retail. We could be back in a day with a full cargo of those. Probably what? Fifty thousand units?"

Harris slowly nodded. "Possibly."

Bonn asked, "Any way to make that happen before the auction? We could sell out a load like that alongside these weapons."

Tawn rubbed her chin. "What we gonna do with the weapons in the meantime? Is there an ultrasecure vault around here we could rent?"

Bonn replied, "You could store them right here. I have room. And I'd be willing to provide around-the-clock security. They'd probably be more secure than they are sitting out there at the spaceport."

Harris let out a deep breath. "You sure you can keep them safe?"

82

Bonn nodded. "I'll see to it myself. Go... bring as many charges as you can. Take the flyerlight to the spaceport right now. I'll handle the crowd here."

Harris frowned. "We have one big problem with that scenario. I need jump fuel. A full tank. I have enough to make it home, but not enough credits in my account to purchase more. Or to purchase the charges for that matter."

Bonn asked, "How much is a full tank for your ship?"

"Roughly eighteen hundred credits."

Bonn held up his account bracelet. "Here's a three hundred thousand credit advance. You'll need that for the inventory."

Harris stared at his account as it filled with more credits than he had ever seen in one place. "Whoa. That's insane. Almost makes me uncomfortable carrying that much."

Bonn smiled. "If this goes off as I think it will, you'll both have that in your accounts when it's over. Now go. Make this happen!"

***

Harris emerged from the wholesaler on Domicile with a grin on his face. "Three and a half credits each. And we have seventy thousand of them. I tested the quality on a couple, they were decent."

Tawn said, "I just hope Mr. Herrik can move that many. Might kill off our pricing for the military grade units."

Harris nodded. "I was thinking the same, but even if we only get ten credits each for these that's... close to half a million credits. These are the outer colonies, charges will be hard to get. I think we'll do better than ten."

The happy duo returned to the city spaceport to await delivery of the goods.

Tawn sat at bar in the terminal, sipping on a premium beverage. "I was just thinking about Bax. She was gonna sell that first batch of weapons for about fifty-five hundred credits.

82

I just did the math basing the cost on what we could have gotten some of those for from the wholesaler here. That cargo should have been close to fifty thousand in cost. Something doesn't add up. You think they were stolen?"

Harris shrugged. "Couldn't say. With the wars over and the politicians looking for cash I heard they were auctioning surplus military hardware for ten kilos a credit. Could be somebody lucked into that cache of weapons with a bid and she was moving it for them."

Tawn shook her head. "I don't know. Anybody who had those must have known their value."

Harris chuckled. "We didn't. Maybe she ripped off some other dumbass slug and stump. Had we walked away from this at the start with a thousand credits in our pockets, who's to say we wouldn't have been happy and never questioned it? Other than the illegal aspect to it. Seems like easy enough money."

Tawn nodded. "Maybe. Hey, you still have all those unspent credits in your account. Might not be a bad idea to wait out the cargo on the *Bangor*. This deal and the monies that are involved are making me nervous."

Four hours of sitting around in the cockpit discussing the recent events saw delivery of the seventy thousand plasma charges. The *Bangor* lifted from the city spaceport on its way back to Bella III. The auction would go off in two days. Tawn grew increasingly excited with anticipation.

Chapter 9

Bonn stood at a podium with a gavel. "Ladies and gentleman... let the auction begin! All bidders should have received your digital packets. Credit deposits should now be in place and awaiting acceptance. If not, you will be shut off from participation in approximately three minutes.

"The bids will go as follows. A base price will show on your auction tablet display. You may accept that bid or enter one of your own. So long as your bid is valid, the value on your display will show as green. Should another outbid you, that value will turn yellow. You will not be allowed to bid more than your deposit amounts.

"The process is simple and straightforward, and it should conclude within ten to fifteen minutes' time. We will be beginning with the Saxon Repeating rifles, which will now each be bundled with a single military grade plasma charge. Select Accept or enter a value to begin. Should anyone become upset or unruly for any reason, they will be immediately escorted out of the building and will not be allowed to return or to bid further. We are adults here. Please act accordingly. And good hunting to all."

The warehouse area that had been cleared for the auction was jam-packed with bidders. The minimum price of the repeaters quickly climbed from the six hundred credit mark to just over a thousand. Five minutes in, the bidding price had surpassed fifteen hundred credits, the high previously achieved by Cletus Dodger. When the last of the bidders declined to raise their bids, the price sat at twenty-two hundred fourteen credits.

The Fox-40s saw a similar run, coming in at just over a thousand credits each. They, too, included a bundled military grade charge. Following those were standard plasma rifles, two hundred sixty-two of them, bringing in seven hundred twenty credits when bundled with a standard plasma charge. When the auction of the final products was finished, the auction total sat at just over one-point-six million credits. All purchases were delivered, and all buyers left with grins on their faces.

Bonn patted a stunned Harris Gruberg on the back. "That went well. I think we let the buyers settle for a few weeks and we might be able to do this all over again. After that we may have to wait until next year. Don't want to saturate our market."

Tawn looked at the total. "You get 8 percent. That's just over a hundred thousand credits. And you did all the work. Almost doesn't seem fair."

Bonn smiled. "Are you kidding? This was a marketing bonanza. I've sold half the store's inventory in the last two days alone. Would have taken me nine months to turn over that kind of stock.

"If you can provide similar hardware for us to do this again in a few weeks, I might just be able to sell the whole store and retire afterward. Probably everyone on this planet knows and is talking about the auction at Bella Sports. My competitors are all squirming with envy about now."

Tawn asked, "Do we have to wait for transactions to clear the banks?"

"Not with held deposits. The credits are in my account. Give me a moment and I'll have the transfer ready for you. Minus the three hundred thousand advance of course. And my fee. Let's see. Your total is just over one and a quarter million credits. And here you are."

Harris stared as the credits in his account soared.

When the transaction was complete, Tawn had her account bracelet held out. "Fill her up. And I'm feeling generous today. Let's just round down to the nearest hundred thousand. That should give you more than enough to cover any costs, and a little extra for your troubles."

Harris held up his bracelet. "You're OK with six hundred thousand even?"

Tawn laughed. "Who wouldn't be? I can buy my own ship with that."

The credits moved across to a grinning, genetically-enhanced, Biomarine. "How much did you give for the *Bangor*? She's not a bad ship."

Harris continued to stare at his account. "Around a quarter mil. But it's spread over twenty years. Probably double what it's worth."

Tawn replied, "I don't know. Has a decent cargo hold. Simple to operate. You had to do any maintenance?"

"None. And she flies like crap. She has a jump drive that has been prone to failure in this model. And there's a smell to her that I can't quite place. Oh, and she's about as ugly a ship as was ever built."

Tawn thought about his statements. "I don't know. I kind of like her. I'll give you a quarter mill for her. Kind of seems like something a slug or a stump would own."

Harris looked up at his partner for several seconds. "Uh, no. She's not for sale."

Tawn laughed. "I thought you just said you paid twice what she's worth? I'm willing to make that decision right. Sell me the *Bangor*."

"No. Can't do it. She's got sentimental value. If I sold her, Farker would be heartbroken. He's become very attached to it."

Tawn chuckled. "That dog has been powered down for a couple weeks now. His only attachment to that ship is an electric cord. But that's OK, I understand. Probably not a good time for either of us to make rash decisions with our new-found wealth."

Tawn sighed as she gazed at her bracelet. "Six hundred thousand credits. Looks like dumping Bax was definitely the right thing to do."

"You know we can never tell her about what transpired here. And we're probably gonna get a fight from her about how much she's gonna get."

"I think we have more than enough now to buy her silence."

Harris replied, "I'm not giving her a dime more than agreed to. Remember, she tried to have me killed."

Tawn landed the flyerlight on the tarmac beside the *Bangor*. "Look. We have a ready market here on Bella. She's the only supplier we know. If we try to go legit we'll be having to get tangled up in all the government red tape. Maybe we cut her a sweet deal on another load? If she gets credits in her pocket she's gonna come away happy. And we can make her happy. I think."

Harris boarded the ship and went straight for the robotic dog. The button under his chin was pressed and the mechanical pet came to life. He was eager to see his owner as always. Tawn sat in the copilot's chair as the *Bangor*'s retrojets came to life. Her steel and faux-fur friend attached himself to her leg.

"Why have I not seen him do that to anyone else?"

Harris laughed. "You know animals have a sense about them. Maybe he sees you as needy."

Tawn scowled. "Yeah. Right. It's mechanical with a programmed brain. It doesn't have a sense of anything it's not been told to know."

Tawn pushed the dog gently away with a finger pointing scold. "No more. I've had enough. You do that again and you won't be my friend."

The dog laid flat on the deck with two sad eyes looking upward. He then rolled over on his back, curling his front paws down in a submissive gesture.

Harris looked at Tawn. "I don't know who did the programming for that pet, but that is just perfect. It knows enough to take your scold and turn it around on you. You look like the bad guy here."

Tawn crossed her arms as the *Bangor* jumped through to Domicile space.

$$***$$

The two Biomarines sat in a bar on Chicago Port Station. Farker was nestled on the floor beneath them. Harris checked out the ladies in the crowds moving past the bar as he looked out a front window. One of them pulled up short, standing in front of the glass with her hands on her hips.

Baxter Rumford stomped into the bar. "Where's my merchandise?"

Harris replied, "Sold it. Won't say where. But I have your credits. I did a few calculations, and I'm being generous here, I have eight thousand one hundred fifty-nine credits for you."

Bax huffed. "That cargo was probably worth thirty times that much."

Harris shrugged. "Not if you don't have buyers. And if it was worth that much, why not cut out the middleman and sell it yourself?"

Bax flipped her hair, offering her best smile. "So really, where's my cargo?"

Tawn leaned forward onto the bar to look around Harris. "Sold. And it's not coming back. Too bad you don't have more of it. We could sell that too."

Bax sat on a stool beside Harris. "Maybe I do have more. What's in it for me?"

"Triple what we paid for that. If you can provide us with a similarly sized load," Harris replied.

Bax tapped her fingernails on the edge of the bar. "Let's just say I did have a similar number of weapons available. Name me a fixed firm price."

Harris leaned closer. "Thirty thousand credits?"

Bax laughed. "Ha! I could get fifty without leaving this bar."

Harris looked over at Tawn. "Would you be willing to part with fifty thousand credits for another delivery?"

Tawn nodded. "I could get behind that. When could you have them ready?"

Bax looked down the bar toward the docking area of the station. "I have almost the exact same load waiting right now. If you want it, though, you're gonna be moving it over yourself. I'm not dragging anything again. Destroyed my nails."

Harris replied, "We'll take it, but we get to pick the transfer point."

Bax shrugged. "Fine. But I need to see proof of the credits before we leave here."

Harris lifted his bracelet, tapping away on the control buttons before showing it to his repeat supplier. "Fifty thousand, on hold, assigned to Baxter Rumford to collect within twenty-four standard hours."

Bax looked at the empty bottles on the bar in front of the two Biomarines. "Someone celebrating? You must have done well."

Tawn nodded. "We got paid, so yeah, we done well."

Bax stood. "See me at my slip with coordinates and we'll make the trade. And if this works out I might have another, even bigger one for you. With buyers and all. I'd do it myself but I'd just rather not deal with colonists."

Harris asked, "Where you getting all this stuff? Mil surplus?"

Bax thought for a moment. "Yep. Surplus. But don't be asking around or trying to break into my business. That would mean all-out war between us."

Baxter Rumford stood and sashayed across the floor and out onto the promenade, waving with the fingers on one hand as she passed the window.

Tawn turned up the remainder of a beer before setting the bottle back on the bar. "That was too easy. I don't trust her."

Harris replied, "She said mil surplus, which was what we suspected. She got over the first deal. And she's looking to move her merchandise. What's to be suspicious of?"

"She didn't even ask for her eight thousand credits. Coming from her I call that highly suspicious."

Bax placed her hand with her long slender fingers on Harris' shoulder. "About that. I do need my credits."

Tawn said, "How many of you are there walking around here? I just watched you go by."

"I turned back when I remembered."

Harris held up his store. "Credits should be in your account."

Bax turned. "See you at the slip."

Tawn watched as she paraded out onto the promenade walk and then again past the window. "I'm still suspicious."

Harris laughed. "Suspicious enough for another round?"

Tawn rapped her knuckles on the bar. "If that requires suspicion, then yes. Hit me again."

Two additional hours of drinking passed.

Harris took a swig of his new beer. "Now this brings back memories. Having a few credits to your name and the time to just sit back and chill on R&R. If this deal works out as sweet as the last one, we might just be set for life. What would you do with a million credits in your store?"

Tawn rubbed her forehead. "Not sure. I heard there's a colony of us settling in on a planet in the Rabid system. Maybe I'll buy a ship and check it out."

"Rabid." Harris chuckled. "Perfect name for a colony of slugs and stumps. Where'd you hear that rumor from?"

Tawn gestured toward the planet Domicile as seen through the skylight above them. "Heard it from a couple other slugs down on the surface. Mostly just talk I think. But I'd go check it out if I had a ship."

Harris set his beer on the bar. "Fifteen each. I think we've had our quota. I think I'll go back to the ship to nap for a bit."

Tawn shook her head. "Not me. I'm heading to the Waldorf. Gonna get a nice hot shower and then hit their spa for a massage. Some lucky masseuse is gonna be rubbing his hands all over this."

Harris returned a scowl. "Lucky, huh? Call it what you want. I'll be at the *Bangor*. Come collect me and Farker when you're ready to face Red."

Harris nudged his robotic pet to life, left a generous tip, and stumbled toward the door before collecting himself. A calm walk out and toward the docks proceeded.

Tawn stood and winked at the bartender before turning to make her way toward the Waldorf. A hot shower was something she was in desperate need of. Fifteen minutes later the warm water was cascading from her hair onto her shoulders. A smile was on her pug-shaped face.

***

Farker farked with delight as Tawn Freely came aboard the ship. "Where's the stump at, boy?"

The dog turned to face the partially open door to the bunkroom. Tawn glanced in and then turned away in disgust. She banged her fist on the wall out in the cabin.

"Harris! Get up! We've got business to take care of! And for Pete's sake... cover yourself up!"

A groggy Harris Gruberg stumbled to the door poking his head out with one eye open. "Sorry you had to see that. What have I been asleep for? Two hours?"

Tawn shook her head. "Try four. What's the matter? Stump can't hold his beer anymore?"

Harris grimaced as he moved to close the door to wash his face. "Apparently not. I used to be immune to that stuff."

Tawn laughed. "We're getting old. Might be time to ease back on the throttle a bit. Release day was the last time I had that many beers and I kind of felt like this, now that I remember. And you need to get yourself together. Bax is no fool. If she's pushing this merchandise on us for that cheap there has to be a reason. I need you to be sharp out there."

Harris cracked open the door as he dried his face with a towel. "We'll be fine. If she tries something we'll see it before it happens. That's what they trained us for."

"So I can guess you've kept up on your training? Don't you start losing muscle memory after a few months on the bench? And please. Pull up your drawers or put on a belt or something. Nobody wants to see the crack of your—"

Baxter Rumford stood in the doorway behind Tawn. "You two gonna do this thing or what? Have I been sitting over there wasting my time on a couple morons? I have places to go and people to see."

Tawn replied, "Hold your horses. Harris has to put on his makeup and do his hair."

Bax winced. "He doesn't have any hair."

Harris stepped out of his bunkroom as he pulled a tight shirt over his tree-trunk-like abdomen. "You ladies aren't gonna start fighting over me, are you?"

Bax frowned. "Only if one of us is forced to stay here with you. And it looks like the slug already drew the short straw."

Coordinates were given for an exchange and the transfer was made. The *Bangor* jumped to Bella III as the *Fargo* returned to Chicago Port Station. Instead of having to wait for another auction, Bonn Herrik purchased the entire cargo for a cool million credits outright. An offer for more stock was put forth with a similar payout promised.

Chapter 10

The *Bangor* and her Biomarine crew made five additional runs over the course of a week. Each time paying fifty thousand credits to Baxter Rumford and receiving a million in return. Bonn Herrick had handled each of the transactions on Bella III, leaving Harris and Tawn to only deliver the goods.

Harris had his feet propped up on his console as the box shaped ship made its way toward Chicago Port Station. "Can't believe how my luck has turned since acquiring this ship."

Tawn turned up a cold beverage. "Yeah, the easy money is making me nervous, though. This might be my last run. I know Bonn said Bella was a big market, but we've delivered a thousand repeaters. Just over a million people... I know they're outdoorsy and all, but that's enough to start a small war out there. I thought he was worried about saturating the market?"

"All I know is the credit transfers are going through. He must be selling to other dealers there now or something. And what do we care so long as we're getting paid?"

***

Bax was waiting at her slip. "Just wanted to let you know, I had someone talk to your buyer."

Tawn returned an angry stare. "You try to go around us I'll slit you from top to bottom."

"Relax slug," Bax said as she turned to face Harris. "Can you put her back on her chain for a minute?"

Harris replied, "Just tell us what you have to say."

"As I was trying to say, my associate talked to your buyer and they sized the market potential now that word has gotten out. I've rented a larger ship. You'll be hauling twenty-five hundred of each weapon along with half a million military grade charges out there. It's all prearranged. You still get your generous cuts at the same rates. You two are probably gonna be the richest pair of Bios on Domicile. Mr. Herrik is willing to pay ten million credits for delivery. You know the drill to get through customs there and to get them delivered. I've already taken an advance from him to cover my portion."

Tawn returned a half scowl. "I don't get it. Why give us so much when you could hire your own delivery grunts for a fraction of the take?"

Bax shrugged. "As much as I dislike the two of you, you've shown you can be trusted. I was miffed when you stole that first load, but you came back and paid me for it. And I haven't had a single issue since. My suppliers are moving the merchandise they want. I'm being paid, you're being paid, Mr. Herrik's being paid. And the end buyers are getting the personal defense weapons they want. Sounds like a win for everyone.

Bax crossed her arms. "Now... what I really want to know is... what are you gonna do with all those credits?"

Tawn replied, "We'll figure something out."

Harris asked, "Where's this rented ship?"

Bax held out a slip of paper. "You'll find it parked at these coordinates. Use this entry code and she's yours."

Tawn slowly shook her head. "This is too big a deal to be this easy. Are we gonna find an Earther destroyer waiting there for us?"

Bax sighed. "Not unless you brought it. Look, you'll be flying to those coordinates in the *Bangor*. If anything looks off, just fly yourselves out of there. One of you will be flying the rented ship and the other your own ship. When you get to Bella all you have to do is deliver the security code for the rented ship to Mr. Herrik. He'll take care of the return. You collect your credits when he gets the code and you're then free to go."

Tawn scowled as she looked at Baxter Rumford.

Bax held out her hands with her palms open. "What?"

"I don't know. I haven't figured it out yet. You've got my nose twitching and that usually spells trouble."

Bax began to laugh as Tawn looked down at a robotic dog that was attempting to latch onto her leg.

Tawn glared at Farker. "I thought we had an agreement!"

Harris said, "Come on. Let's get this done so we can get on with our lives."

The pickup, delivery and payoff went as scheduled and predicted. The *Bangor* shot up through the Bella III atmosphere and out into space. A wormhole was opened to near Domicile and the boxy craft slipped through.

Harris propped his feet up on the console for the two hour ride to Chicago Port Station. "I'm at just over eight million credits. What's yours say?"

Tawn returned an irritated look. "Same as yours. We got paid the same for all those runs. Why you asking stupid questions?"

"I don't know." Harris laughed. "Because I'm stupid rich? Because I can afford to be stupid? All I know is you and I are each looking at a plush retirement. Where was that colony of slugs and stumps you mentioned?"

Tawn sighed. "The Rabid system. Not even sure it exists. Could have just been wishful thinking by those slugs."

Harris put his feet on the deck. "Well here's what I'm thinking I'm gonna do... when we get into port, I'm going straight to those loansharks to pay off the *Bangor*. They're gonna flip. Then I'm heading to my apartment to collect my stuff. And then I'm gonna go looking for the Rabid system. With the credits I have, I could build a palace and have a party every night with my own kind."

"That's your retirement?"

Harris spun around in his pilot's chair with his feet again raised off the floor. "If it doesn't work out, or if I get bored, I still have the credits to come back and live among the regulars, like a king. It's a win – win. What about you?"

Tawn scratched her head. "Not sure. If nothing comes up maybe I'll just tag along. But I *will* be getting my own ship. Nothing against the *Bangor*, but she's not mine."

Harris posed a question. "Ever thought you'd be owning your own ship?"

"When I was younger, maybe. Not in the last ten years. You know, there was a time when I thought I wanted to be a farmer. Just get away from the war and do nothing but grow vegetables all day. Sounded like bliss at the time. Now I can't think of anything less interesting. Maybe I'll buy a fancy ship and become an explorer. Gotta be worlds out there that need exploring.

"I had this friend once, a squad member, and a slug, she always wanted to try to find Earth. If it even exists. She claimed her commander from when she first started to fight had knowledge of a site on one of these outer planets. Said it was used to help create the first wormhole that brought the colonists through from Earth."

"And where would this site be?" Harris asked.

Tawn looked up at the ceiling in thought as she replied, "Don't know. She died about half hour later during an assault. I think the story just stuck with me because it was the last memory I have of her. She was a good egg. Took a sniper round to the center of her chest. Blew her spine out the back. Didn't deserve to go out that way."

The *Bangor* landed in her rented slip at Chicago Port Station. The next week was spent in luxury hotels, stuffing their gullets at five star restaurants and then drinking at the bars. After a particularly long late-night binge, Tawn awakened in the morning, showered, dressed, and made her way to Harris' room.

A series of loud knocks brought him to the door, rubbing his eyes. "What?"

Tawn pushed the door open. "I took the initiative. There *is* a Rabid system. And there's a single colony registered as being there. I thought we might go out and take a look."

Harris pulled his eyes open with his fingers. "So go."

"I don't want to go by myself. Come on. We need an adventure. Otherwise you're gonna become that five-hundred-kilo walrus you talked about. We can't eat and drink like this every night."

Harris chuckled. "I can. I feel like I'm living a dream right now. People *like* me. They cater to me. I eat what I want, drink what I want and do what I want... when I want. I'm kind of in a happy place right now. Don't spoil it."

Tawn followed Harris into his bedroom and to the door of his bathroom.

"You think I could get some privacy?"

"I'm serious about this," Tawn replied. "And do what you gotta do. I've seen it all before. We need to be out there living, not stuck here sending ourselves to an early grave."

Harris dropped his shorts and sat on the toilet.

Tawn raised her hand as she turned back toward the living area of the luxury suite. "OK, guess I didn't need to see that. What I'm saying is that we're wasting our time here. It's a big galaxy and we have short lives. I just think we should be doing something with them."

Several minutes later, Harris came out of his bedroom, scratching his bum through his shorts.

"I'll be back in an hour to talk about this. Get a shower... you're starting to smell."

***

Harris walked into the living area rubbing his belly. "I could use some breakfast."

Tawn winced. "You just had two large steaks about nine hours ago. Those are still digesting."

Harris picked at his teeth with a fingernail. "Think I got some gristle stuck in there."

Tawn chuckled. "You're gonna make a fine catch for some woman someday. You want breakfast? Come on. My treat. I'll take you to what used to be my favorite."

A short walk out to the promenade had the pair on a moving sidewalk. Fifteen minutes later they hopped off in one of the poorer sections of Chicago Port Station.

Harris looked around with an unhappy face as they walked. "You know we have enough credits where we don't have to see this squalor anymore. At least I don't have to, anyway."

"Come on. It's just over here. This lady used to feed me breakfast even though I couldn't pay her. I want to buy breakfast and I want her to know just how much I appreciated her generosity."

Harris asked, "Is this at least a good breakfast?"

"It's OK. That's not why we're here, though. We can talk about Rabid while we eat."

The old woman greeted Tawn at the door, taking her to the best booth in her small establishment. "I'm so happy you're doing OK. You just disappeared like so may others here do. I thought you might have gone back down to the surface."

"Nope." Tawn smiled. "I got a business partner and we've done pretty well for ourselves. I thought I'd bring him over for a meal."

Harris thumbed through the menu. "How about... one of everything."

The old woman raised her eyebrows at the thought of what she would need to prepare.

Tawn said, "He'll have two of the special and I'll have one. And as I said, we've been doing well with our business, so I'll be paying this time."

The old woman smiled as she turned back toward her kitchen.

Harris held a hand above the table, palm flat, "Shouldn't have mentioned that. Probably made her feel about this tall."

"Why would you say that?"

"She gave from her heart. You appear to be giving from your credit store. Not quite the same thing. What you could have done was to show up here and to volunteer for a week and at the end leave an anonymous gift in her business account. Now you just made the relationship awkward."

Tawn looked on in fascination. "When did you become a relationship expert?"

Harris laughed. "Always have been, just not when it's my own. Now tell me about what you found on Rabid."

"It's a small world, different grav. Mostly rocky with a few patches of fertile land that are tucked down in deep valleys that keep the more violent weather away. Oxygen is low as well, so no regulars there.

"Was founded by a stump colonel and has anywhere from two to fifteen hundred inhabitants. One town in the valley where 95 percent of them live. At least that's what I could dig up from rumors and the media. Most of it from a single source."

Harris stared at his partner. "And you think that sounds like paradise as compared to having everything here?"

Tawn propped her elbows on the table. "Come on. Even you have to admit this non-stop festival of gluttony is getting boring. We have both accomplished exactly zero over the last week."

"Well I for one am not bored yet. But for the sake of your sanity, I'll ride out to Rabid with you. Can't hurt to just take a look."

Tawn leaned back on the booth bench she occupied. "I found out something else with my poking around. Our wormhole drives don't work past the far colonies. There's some kind of field that permeates this area of space that allows the drive to function. Just past the outer colonies and the field falls off. You want to travel anywhere else it's using normal engines, which are about one-sixteenth light-speed.

Harris replied, "Didn't know about the field, but I did know the far colonies were it, at least for jumps, anyway."

The old woman brought out the breakfasts. Harris tore into his like a pig in a trough. Tawn attempted to hold back the urge but was soon overtaken by habit. As a Biomarine she had been taught to consume her meal quickly, as you never knew when it might be interrupted. The feeding frenzy was over in five minutes.

Tawn attempted to pay for the meal but the old woman refused. After several minutes of friendly argument, a tip was accepted. The old woman scowled as Tawn passed two thousand credits into her account store.

As they walked back out into the promenade, Harris said, "This tall."

"She'll appreciate it later. She deserves it. And maybe she can help some other poor sap that's down on their luck."

A walk was made to the docking bays where an order was placed with a food supplier. Six crates of food and other supplies were to be delivered to the slip where the *Bangor* was being moored. Once aboard, a trip to the Rabid system would begin.

Chapter 11

The wealthy slug and stump were soon jumping to the supposed colony of Biomarines.

As the planet in question came into view, Harris commented. "Not impressed. Looks about a third smaller than Domicile. What'd you say the gravity was?"

Tawn shook her head. "I didn't. The info I had only said it was different."

"Hope it isn't too low. I get annoyed with every step being a hop. And after a while you start to lose your muscle mass."

Tawn looked over. "After the past week you could lose a few kilos."

"Don't want that to be muscle, though. I have a beacon signal for their spaceport. I'm taking us almost straight in this time."

"No practice flying?"

Harris shook his head. "I'm confident with what I can do now."

As the ship dropped through the atmosphere, the target valley came into view.

"That's it?" Harris said. "You want to move here? What is that... a kilometer wide by twenty long?"

"Let's not judge it until we're on the ground."

The spaceport came up quickly, with the retrojets only being fired at the last possible moment. The *Bangor* slowed to a stop just short of a grassy field where a small building held the beacon.

Harris laughed. "Welcome to beautiful downtown Rabid. I see they sent out the welcome committee for you."

Two dog-size animals scampered across the field toward a clump of trees.

Tawn said, "I'm sure we can get all the info we want on this place at that round building over there. Looks like some kind of office."

The grav system of the *Bangor* shut down. Both Tawn and Harris could feel the immediate pull of a stronger gravity field.

Harris looked over the sensors on his console. "Grav is at 112 percent standard. Haven't been on a planet like this in a while. Sensors show a large molten palladium core. That density would account for the gravity difference. Not sure I remember ever hearing about that inside a planet."

Tawn stepped out. "I kind of like it. I could see myself getting back into fighting shape here."

"I can see this being a drag after a couple hours. Let's go check out your building. I don't think I want to stay here any longer than I have to."

Tawn laughed as she began to walk. "Sounds like the king is getting lazy."

Harris said, "Hang on, speedy. I'll be right out."

Two minutes passed before the overweight, stump Biomarine emerged on a scooter, rolling it down onto the grass and riding it over to his partner.

Tawn gave a half scowl. "What is that?"

Harris stepped off, handing the unit over to Tawn. "It's transportation. We keep landing on these colonies where the spaceport's a kilometer from the nearest building. Get on. This will speed up our treks around town."

Tawn winced. "It's like half the size it should be. Will it even carry us?"

Harris walked back aboard the *Bangor*, popping through the hatch seconds later on a second scooter. "It was a last-minute purchase. I guess I could have done a better job of specifying our needs. Had them picked up with those supplies. Now get on and let's go."

Tawn glanced back at the ship. "We gonna take Farker with us?"

Harris whistled into his bracelet. An eager Farker came to the door, hopping down onto the grass. The two scooters began the run across the field toward the round building, their wheels sinking into the soft earth the grass grew from. It was quickly evident that progress would be slower than walking as the scooters struggled with the oversize occupants and less than ideal terrain.

Thirty seconds into the effort, Tawn stepped off her scooter, pushing it over on its side. "That was just humiliating. I hope no one was watching."

Harris continued in an effort to justify his purchase. Another thirty seconds passed before he tossed his scooter aside as well.

Tawn laughed. "Nothing like a little reality to bring you back to what the physical world allows."

Harris glanced back with a scowl as they walked. "Really thought those were gonna be a welcome surprise. Maybe for paved roads. We'll collect them when we get back."

A short walk had the duo entering the round building they had first spotted from the air. A lone slug sat at a desk in the center of the room, her head slumped over as she slept.

Tawn approached. "Excuse me. Excuse me!"

The woman came to life. "Oh. Sorry. Don't get much activity around here. How can I help you?"

Tawn asked. "We heard this was a community for slugs and stumps so we thought we'd come check it out."

The woman nodded as she stood. "Dawn Eureka."

Harris asked, "What?"

Tawn glanced his way. "It's her name, Igmo. I'm Tawnish Freely and this is Harris Gruberg. What can you tell us about this place?"

A stretching Dawn stood before them. Despite her sleeping on the job, she was leaner and more muscular than the two Biomarines now in front of her.

"We call it the Retreat. Was started by Colonel Robert Thomas, a fellow stump. The valley is divided into ten acre homesites where you can build what you want and do what you want, so long as it doesn't disturb your neighbors. The properties are all leased from the colonel, who claimed this valley after discovering it. Regulars can come to visit but are not allowed to live here. This is just for us."

Harris asked, "How many of us are there here?"

Dawn replied, "Fifty-two and counting. We get about one new occupant a month and one that leaves every other month. Most don't care for the heavy gravity. Others aren't into the solitude. After spending time out and among the regulars, some find it a pleasant change to live among others like themselves. There's a lot of bias out there against us. We're living in peacetime and people don't want warriors as neighbors. Even if we are ourselves peaceful."

Harris patted Tawn on the shoulder. "You're welcome to stay if you want, but I think I've seen and heard enough."

Tawn asked, "The property leases, how much are they?"

Dawn replied, "Cheap. Two credits a month. Buy five years worth and you get a 20 percent discount. And it's on a first-come, first-served basis. You want the prime pieces of land, you'll want to get in early. That's the plot map over on the wall."

Tawn walked over to examine the valley layout.

Harris crossed his arms as he looked around the sparse office.

Dawn gestured toward his weapon. "I like your Fox."

Harris smiled, "Oh. Thanks."

"Where'd you get it?"

Harris replied, "Well, we actually used to sell them. We were suppliers."

Dawn reached out her hand. "Can I see it?"

A suspicious Harris pulled it from its clip, turning it over to the slug.

"Mmm. I've missed my Fox. Kept the same one with me for twelve years. When they rolled us out I was kind of despondent about having to give her up. Would love to have another one."

Harris asked, "Nobody out here to sell you one?"

Dawn sighed. "Nobody out here has one. The colonel is the only resident with a weapon. Not that there's a ban or anything, just most couldn't afford one before coming out. Since we discovered a gold vein about three miles from here, everyone has been clamoring for a trader to come out here to take orders.

"We still only have a modest amount of wealth, but no traders are willing to come this far to supply fifty people. We have one government ship that comes out once a year, but they only deliver the basics. And weapons are not considered a basic."

Harris nodded. "I could probably get you a few weapons. Make up a list of what you'd want and I'll see what I can do."

Dawn returned a grin as she handed back the pistol. "You do that, and you'll make a lot of friends out here."

"For my people... I might even be willing to do it at wholesale."

Dawn reached down to pet the robotic dog on the head as it eyed her leg. "He's friendly."

The mechanical pest hopped up, grabbing around her kneecap as it began its routine.

Harris chuckled. "Well, look at that. He just seems to be fond of slugs."

Tawn walked back to the woman at the desk with a scowl. "You'll have to push him away or he won't respect you. And I'd like to lease plots G16 to G31 please."

Dawn pulled her head back slightly in amazement. "Sixteen plots? Did I hear you right?"

Farker released her leg, taking a seat on the floor beside his new friend as he looked up with admiration.

Tawn nodded in disgust as she glanced down at the mechanical pet. "At two credits apiece, it sounds like a bargain."

Harris asked, "And what are you gonna do with a hundred sixty acres?"

Tawn smiled, "You heard her... whatever I want. And I want fifty-year leases on those."

Harris said, "Sounds permanent."

Dawn tapped away on a tablet at her desk. "That's fifteen thousand three hundred sixty credits. You sure you want to do that?"

Tawn glanced back at the plot-map. "You know what? Add from H16 to H31 on to that. And stretch it out to seventy standard years. That'll take me past a hundred years of age."

Harris laughed. "You think we'll make it to a hundred?"

"Who knows?" Tawn shrugged. "We were the first to be genetically engineered this way. We might live to be two hundred."

"Or we might live to be fifty."

The woman totaled up the lease fee. Tawn gave her approval stamp and transferred the credits.

"Miss Freely, you are now the proud leaseholder of three hundred twenty acres of prime Retreat real-estate. Welcome to the community!"

Tawn turned to face Harris. "You might want to get in on this while it's cheap."

Harris laughed. "If I want in at some point I'll just come and camp on your massive estate in the middle of the valley."

"No you won't. Now go lease something. If anything you can sublease it to needy stumps or slugs in the future."

Harris looked at Dawn. "Is subleasing allowed?"

Dawn nodded. "It's yours to do with as you will, so long as you follow the rules, respect your neighbors and be a stump or a slug."

Harris walked over to the plot map. "I and J, same plots right next to hers. If I don't make use of them, at least I can sublease to someone that will be a nuisance to her, within the rules of course."

Dawn pulled together the lease and Harris gave his stamp. A transfer of credits sealed the deal.

Tawn smiled. "Howdy, neighbor."

"Not happening anytime soon. Miss Eureka? Is there anything else to see here in the valley?"

Dawn glanced at the plot map. "The colonel occupies the north end of the valley. You'll find the occasional home on the leased plots. This building and that spaceport are the only official buildings. So one quick flyover and you've seen it."

"And what about the lands outside the valley?"

Dawn replied, "Those belong to Domicile. You'll have to register as a pioneer to make a claim. Have to show a valid use at that time. And pay a registration fee. If approved, it becomes yours. Just keep in mind, you have to take up permanent residence for the claim to stick."

Harris turned toward the door.

Tawn asked. "Where you going?"

"I'm gonna take one quick flyover and then head back to civilization for some lunch. You coming or you want to start work on your homestead?"

Tawn followed, "Well I would like to at least set foot on my property. Can we do that as a minimum?"

"Fine. But we're flying there and not walking. I can feel the gravity pull on my legs already."

As they walked out of the round building, Farker was torn between the two genetically altered, female Biomarines that he so admired. A whistle into Harris' bracelet saw the robotic dog scampering for the door. The scooters were collected as they approached the ship.

The *Bangor* lifted off with Harris at the controls. "Were those on the left or right side of the valley?"

"Eastern... right side. From there we'll get to see the Rabid sun setting."

Harris laughed. "You mean *you'll* get to see the Rabid sun setting. Unless I can see it from my hotel room back on Chicago Port, I won't be watching."

"You trying to be a buzz-kill? I'm actually excited at the prospect. First time I've ever owned land."

"You don't own land. You're leasing it. And you suckered me into leasing some as well. I guarantee that if you move out here, you'll be moving back after the first month."

"How about this... if I do move out here, I'll wager five thousand credits that I would stay at least six months."

"Six months and you can't leave the planet for any reason. You throw that in and I'll take that bet."

"Agreed," Tawn said. "I can do six months standing on my head."

Harris smirked. "You couldn't do a week in a luxury hotel. You spending six months out here was a sucker's bet. And you fell for it. This should be yours coming up on the right."

Tawn looked out the viewport. "That's perfect! Set us down!"

The hatch opened. Tawn Freely stepped out onto her property with a huge smile on her face. She reached down, taking a clump of the bright green grass in her hand, picking it up and smelling it with her wide nostrils. A glance upward at the ultra-blue sky brought a tear as she shielded her eyes from the bright sun.

Harris stood behind her in the doorway. "Gonna ruin your sight."

Tawn took three steps, climbing up onto a piece of granite that sprung from her property. "This is awesome. I might have to move out here sooner than I thought."

Harris looked around. "Granted, it isn't a bad piece of land. I'd be wanting a few more of the conveniences a city has to offer though."

As Tawn turned back to face the ship, two of the muscular dog-like animals emerged from some nearby brush. Both offered intimidating growls along with sharply fanged teeth. Tawn casually pulled her Fox-40, firing off a round into the ground in front of the wild animals. A lump of dirt and grass flew into the air with a zap as the native dogs retreated to the brush from where they had come.

Harris laughed. "Looks like the local wildlife is friendly."

"They just need training."

The ship was boarded and the run up to free space made. After a jump and a short ride, the *Bangor* was back in its slip at Chicago Port Station. A quick visit to see Baxter Rumford had a new cache of weapons delivered, but only after the promise was made for another large run to Bella III.

Once the rental ship was dropped off and the insane transfer of credits again made, the *Bangor* and her crew made another run out to the Rabid system and down to the colony of Retreat. Feeling generous upon their arrival, they donated enough weapons to form an armory the locals could draw from as needed. As a like-kind measure, Robert Thomas reassigned full ownership of their properties to Tawn Freely and Harris Gruberg.

An order for supplies was taken, and the small transport returned to the civilized world to fulfill it. A new business opportunity had fallen into the Biomarines' hands. Harris was all too happy to take it on. As Tawn had predicted, the luxury hotel life of constant eat and drink was beginning to get old.

Chapter 12

The *Bangor* was moored in her slip on Chicago Port Station. Tawn was out looking over materials that could be used to build a home at Retreat. A local architect had been hired to design the home of her dreams. Dreams she had never before had or contemplated. Everything was new, and every design suggestion exciting and fresh.

Harris sat on his ship with Farker at his feet, waiting for a delivery from a local supplier. He had promised an immediate return of the materials to Colonel Thomas. The colonel, as it turned out, had trained him in combat maneuvers in his early years as a cadet. Hours of stories had been exchanged during each of the prior visits. Harris had found the talks to be cathartic.

Farker nudged Harris for a rub as he watched a local news channel. An anchorwoman gave a special report. "The unrest on the colony of Eden continues to grow. The protest marches and riots from last month have been replaced by violence. Last week, two of the colony councilmen were found dead of plasma wounds. This week, a new colonist, who had previously been seen in protest opposition, was found dead of a knife wound in an apparent tit-for-tat execution. No suspects are in custody at this time."

A second anchor commented, "I thought Eden was a pacifist colony, Kim. They've always claimed to abhor violence of any kind."

"Maybe we're seeing a new Eden, John. As more colonists move out there, and with their lack of any official police force, you are bound to eventually have people with differing opinions come to blows. Anyway, the colony board is sending out a team of investigators."

John winced at his co-anchor. "We've been hearing about more violence in the outer colonies of late. Given the recent spate of shootings on Bella III and now this. Just this morning there was a report of the chief customs agent on Bella taking his own life. An illegal repeating plasma rifle was found by his side. Are we seeing the beginnings of an epidemic of arms from the war making it to the common citizen?"

Kim shrugged. "Hard to say. Kind of makes you appreciate our safe, secure environment here at home, doesn't it?"

"Indeed it does."

Tawn stepped up into the ship. "Got some great ideas today. The goods come yet?"

Harris shook his head. "No. News was just talking about Eden and Bella. You think any of the talk about titanium is real? They seem to have had an influx of colonists lately that don't share their pacifist beliefs. Three are dead in the last weak. And on Bella they found Mr. Vontmier dead this morning. They're saying it's suicide by a plasma weapon. We gave him that rifle."

Tawn frowned. "He was nice guy. Must have had problems."

"They also said the colony board is sending a team out to investigate. If they look into that they're gonna see our visits in the logs."

Baxter Rumford stepped into the cabin. "No they won't. Those records have been scrubbed. It seems Mr. Vontmier was on the take for more than one set of deliveries. And with that data gone and now him gone, we have nothing to worry about."

Tawn winced. "You did this?"

"Pfft. No. Look, we aren't violent people. That was much more likely to have been drug related. I've heard Bella is a partying place."

Harris asked, "How'd you get in here?"

Tawn replied, "That would be me. I left the hatch open for the delivery."

Bax said, "Speaking of that. Would you be interested in making a run out to Geldon? I have a buyer in wait out there."

Harris shook his head. "No thanks. We're out of that business. Have a lawful, regulated supply business going now. We don't need anymore credits."

Bax crossed her arms. "Too bad. Pays the same as the last two. Just a simple drop and run."

Tawn said, "You know, we could actually spend those credits at the Retreat, for the other residents."

"I'm really not interested in doing that anymore," Harris replied. "You're welcome to make that run yourself, but I don't want any part of it."

Tawn rubbed her chin. "Would you just meet me out there for a pickup?"

Harris sighed. "You're gonna have to start closing the hatch. Too many flies getting in."

"So is that a yes or no?"

Harris gave a half smile, half frown. "If you're set on doing this, I guess I could swing out there after I drop off the colonel's stuff."

Tawn turned to Bax. "Sign me up. When do we leave?"

Bax grinned. "We're ready to go now. I can take you out."

Tawn placed her hand on Harris' shoulder. "I'll be waiting at the spaceport on Geldon."

As the Biomarine followed Baxter Rumford out through the hatch, Harris looked down at his dog. "I don't trust her. None of these deals are right. Are we burying ourselves here? Can we expect Colony Board agents to be knocking on our door?"

Farker farked three times.

Harris laughed. "I'll take that as a yes. And I'll see to it that this is the last run with Rumford."

***

The drop at the Retreat and then the pick up from Geldon was made. A return to the Retreat saw the establishment of a fund, seeded with ten million credits, that would be used to bring slugs and stumps to the Rabid system. Free leases, starter homes, and food for a year would be provided, giving any who chose to come a chance to get established.

After an ad was taken out on Domicile, three hundred thirty-two applicants were flown out to their new homes. All were grateful, and all promised to do their best to not only contribute, but to also welcome any others that would come. In the month that followed, the population of the Retreat swelled to more than twenty-two hundred... all slugs and stumps who had chosen to try life among their own.

The *Bangor* docked at Chicago Port Station.

Baxter Rumford was waiting outside as the hatch opened. "I have another job for you."

Tawn shook her head. "Sorry. We're finished. I appreciate the offer, but we have our own thriving, legit business going making supply runs to outer colony customers. Certainly not as profitable as what you offer, but we're not under any legal threat."

Baxter winced. "Hmm. Not what I was hoping to hear. Too bad though. My suppliers need this last run done immediately. The pay is double the last one, same type of drop.

Tawn replied, "Not interested."

Baxter sighed. "OK, but just so you know, my suppliers are the ones who made those records on Bella disappear. I suppose they could make them reappear as well. Would be a shame if that were to happen."

Harris stepped forward. "So it's come to blackmail? That fast? You know if we go down, you're going down with us. We have all the logs of our interactions recorded right here on the *Bangor*."

Baxter laughed. "Well that just makes you an idiot, doesn't it? An investigation is getting underway and you're keeping records of your criminal activity? I would have thought you two would know better than that."

Tawn scowled. "Where would this delivery be heading?"

114

"To Bella. There's a new customs agent there who's in need of paying off a few debts. And I promise you, this is the last delivery. After this, you won't see me or the *Fargo* again. This is my ticket out of the arms trade too. And just so you know this isn't a setup, I've been asked to ride out with you. I will require a ride back though."

Tawn scratched her chin. "Pays double, you say?"

Harris shook his head. "You aren't seriously considering this are you?"

"And you're certain this is the last haul?"

Bax nodded. "It's the last of the supply they have available, so I'm certain. Look, I want out of this business, too. I've made my share of profits. Time for Baxter Rumford to go out and enjoy the spoils of wealth."

Harris said, "I still don't get why you can't make this run yourself."

"As I said before, you two are registered as licensed traders on Bella III. Just as before, the records will state it was a delivery of household goods. There will be an equivalent record on Domicile showing the same. Unless they catch us with the cargo, there's no tie back to us.

"Oh, and did I mention Bonn Herrick is no longer around? And before you get upset, his flyerlight went down in a windstorm. We had nothing to do with it."

Tawn replied, "There's still the several hundred buyers who attended the first auction. They all got a good look at us. You aren't likely to forget a stump and a slug."

"I can't help you with that one. I can't fix stupid. Anyway, this run and we're done." Baxter Rumford clasped her hands together. "So who's ready for one last payoff?"

Tawn looked at Harris. "Not like we have a choice. Let's just do this. And Bax... if you or anyone else related to these transactions comes looking for us afterward... I'll be coming back to snap your skinny neck personally."

Bax smiled. "Fair enough. Are we ready to go?"

114

The *Bangor* lifted out of the port. After a jump to a remote location, the cargo hauler was picked up and a jump to Bella III was made.

As the ships dropped through the atmosphere, Harris opened a comm to Tawn. "That ship is five times larger than any of the others. You didn't happen to look in the cargo bay did you?"

Tawn shook her head. "Nope. Don't want to know. Just want this to be over with. I'll be donating my half to the Retreat fund."

Harris winced. "Your half? This is all yours. I don't want this transaction showing on my account. I have more than enough already."

Tawn crossed her arms. "Well then, I guess the Retreat is coming into a windfall. They can use the credits anyway. More of us are moving out there. And they'll need food and shelter and normal supplies. Almost like we're building our own market out there."

As the comm closed, Harris looked down at his robotic friend. "We doing the right thing here, Farker?"

The dog returned a single fark.

***

The ship was delivered without incident. The new customs agent signed the delivery log and the transfer of credits to Tawn Freely was conducted.

Baxter Rumford smiled as the agent for Bella III walked back to his tracked vehicle. "I'd say that went well. Now, if you'd be so kind as to return me to Chicago Port I'll be out of your lives for good."

The *Bangor* shot up through the Bella III sky, quickly slipping out into open space. A jump was made back to the station and Baxter Rumford sent on her way.

Tawn stood in the hatch of the ship as the red-haired nemesis walked away. "If I never see her again I'll be happy."

Harris frowned. "Not that I approve of her in any way, but she did make us rich."

Tawn scowled. "You're acting like you like her or something? She's a snake. And I guarantee she has no fond feelings for you or me. I still think we're nothing more than a couple rubes in this whole thing."

Harris smacked her on the shoulder. "Well, at least we're rich rubes. And you know what we should do? We should go buy you a ship. And I need to go pay off this one. You can check with your material suppliers down on planet while we're there."

"Why would we go down there?"

Harris shook his head. "Have you looked into buying a ship up here? Few deals to be had and the selection is abysmal."

"You bought the *Bangor* here."

"I did, but it's not like I had a choice. The sharks planetside wouldn't take me on as a credit risk. Anyway, think about what ship you might want while Farker and I go to pay mine off."

Harris looked down. "You ready to see the thugs, boy?"

The dog returned three farks.

✳✳✳

Harris walked into the Moonlight Lounge. Clovis Bagman was seated in his usual booth. Farker trotted alongside his master.

"Mr. Bagman."

Clovis looked up. "Gruberg... you here to make a payment?"

Harris sat across from the loanshark. "Better. I'm here to pay you off."

Clovis tilted his head to one side. "You rob a cruise ship or something?"

Harris smirked. "Or something. Anyway, I'd love to make chat, but I'm a busy person of late. So I'd like to pay off the *Bangor* in full."

Clovis slowly nodded. "I see. You do realize there is no out-clause in your contract, right? You want out you pay the interest in full... twenty years worth."

Harris nodded. "Just give me the number, Bagman. As I said, I don't have all day."

Clovis typed away on a tablet. "Very well. That will be three hundred seventy-three thousand one hundred eighty-six credits. And I'll round down the partial portion just to keep it easy."

Harris sat forward. "Wait. I thought the ship was two hundred fifty thousand, minus what I already paid. What's the excess?"

Clovis smiled as he turned the tablet to face Harris. "The contract specifically states that if there is no out-clause, a fee of 50 percent of the amount still owed can be applied. You see, Mr. Gruberg, the interest rate you are paying has tremendous value as an investment. That type of return is difficult to come by in my line of work, without placing my investment at tremendous risk."

Harris pointed, "But I'm paying off the full amount already, including the interest."

Clovis nodded. "True, but I will now have to go out and place those credits at risk again."

Harris sat with a dropped jaw. "Yeah, so, you already made twenty years worth of interest off those credits. What you're saying doesn't make any sense. I'm paying you a fee so you can loan your credits out to someone else?"

"Would you like to fully purchase the ship or not?"

Harris held out his credit store. "I won't forget this move, Bagman. One day you're gonna be looking for help from someone you fleeced and they're gonna turn and walk. I'd like to be there when that day comes."

Farker gave out a displeased fark before hiking up his rear leg to simulate peeing on the offender of his master. The credits moved to the account of a smiling Clovis Bagman. Harris returned to the docking slip.

Tawn was standing in the hatch. "You got it?"

Harris scowled. "I got it, all right. They pulled a fast one on me with an added 50 percent fee."

"Well, at least she's yours now. Better than what I have."

Harris sighed. "Doesn't feel better at the moment. Kind of took the party out of becoming a full owner. Oh well, guess I should be happy it's mine. Let's go see if we can find one for you."

Chapter 13

The planetary port of Tammingdale claimed to have the largest supply of personal spacecraft. Newer models ran from just under a cool million credits up to several million, with elite personal cruisers that topped out at close to ten million.

The salesmen in the showroom of the vast ship lot ignored the slug and stump as they came through the door. A rookie salesman was instead sent their way as the veterans smirked and joked over the prospects of selling the two a third world garbage scow.

The rookie timidly approached. "Can I help you?"

Tawn said, "I'm looking to buy a ship. Not yet sure what I want. Could be a shuttle. Could be a cargo hauler. Show me what you've got."

The salesman held out his hand. "Gandy Boleman. Are you thinking used or new?"

Tawn's huge hand dwarfed Gandy's skinny fingers as she confidently replied, "I'm open to either. If a shuttle, maybe something in the twenty-four passenger range. For cargo... I don't know, ten tons maybe?"

Gandy withdrew his hand in awe. "Uh, I'm sorry, but I have to ask new customers to show a credit account or score before I'm allowed to show any ships. It's policy."

Tawn held out her store. "That good enough? I'll probably be paying in full."

Gandy's eyes grew large. "I don't think I've seen an account with that much before."

The rookie looked toward the snickering pros before returning his gaze with a wide grin. "Please, follow me to the virtual room. We'll have a look over the new stock as well as what can be ordered. If we don't see anything to your liking, we can browse through our inventory of gently used craft. Once we designate any you have interest in, I can take us out to see them in a flyer."

Four ships were shown before Tawn took interest.

"This one offers comfortable seating for thirty-two. Called the Dreambus. It has a crew cabin that accommodates three, with bunks, a restroom and a shower. And two restrooms for your passengers. She comes with a standard Horton drive and Righolm retros for your normal travels. And a Wheeler wormhole generator that offers a twelve second spin-up. The fastest in the industry, outside the military of course."

Tawn nodded. "And what's she cost?"

Gandy looked around to make sure none of the other salesman were eavesdropping. "List is seven million, but I know for a fact we sold one for six last month. You a good negotiator?"

Harris replied, "She is now."

Tawn asked, "That's close to 15 percent. Gonna cut deep into any commission you get."

Gandy scowled. "I don't get commission. I'm on sixty days probation where I'm only paid by the hour. Kind of a ripoff because I would have already made triple that with the minimum commissions. Anyway, if this is what you want, fight with them over the price. They will go lower."

Tawn looked at Harris. "You know what I'm thinking?"

"How could I possibly know that?"

Tawn sighed. "I was inferring... oh never mind. I'm thinking I buy this with the funds for the Retreat. They could use a shuttle for bringing new people out. That price would leave plenty for a crew and fuel."

Harris chuckled. "You planning on moving every slug and stump in existence out there?"

Tawn shrugged. "Sure. Why not? This would even give them transport for coming back here for business and such."

Harris looked over the shiny hologram that floated in front of them. "You sure you need to spend that much on a new ship?

Could get a good used one for a quarter the price that would do everything you need, minus some of the comfort maybe."

Tawn nodded. "What's the maintenance like on this one?"

Gandy replied, "The base model of this has been out for six years now. Maintenance has been excellent. And this one comes with a five year stem-to-stern agreement where full labor and parts are covered here, and 66 percent if off- world, when approved. The insurer negotiates the repair cost for you, getting you the best price."

Tawn smiled. "I like it. Put it on our list to check out. And now on to something for me."

Gandy grinned. "You're really buying two ships?"

Tawn replied, "That's the current plan. My friend here has an old military surplus. You have anything like that used?"

"Can I ask what he has? And are you wanting something similar?"

Harris said, "It's called a Zwicker. Kind of a cross between a small shuttle and a cargo hauler. Came with a thick, heavy armor on it. Actually had rail guns in it at one time, they aren't functional now though."

Gandy flipped through images in the ship database. "Here we are. The Zwicker Stingbat. That the one."

Tawn laughed. "The Stingbat? Hahaha! That's it exactly!"

Gandy read the base specs. "Commissioned three hundred eighty-two years ago. Decommissioned eighty-nine years later. Only shows that five are still flying. Two have functional wormhole generators. Yours still work?"

Harris replied, "She works."

"You have the *Bangor* or the *Kingfisher*?"

"The *Bangor*."

Gandy held up a hand. "Hold on... wanna see what she did when in service? Those files were all declassified a couple centuries ago."

Tawn cut in. "While interesting, can we stick to finding me a ship?"

122

Harris replied, "Now hold on. This is good stuff. Any way to transfer it to me?"

Gandy nodded. "This is the global database, so you can fish through it yourself. I'll send a link if you have a comm account."

The exchange was made.

Gandy added, "You mentioned rail guns not working. I bet you could find one in a boneyard that has parts. The Magnessen yard has ships that are centuries old out there. Might be worth a look. Lots of parts would have been picked over by now, but not those."

Tawn said, "You know having a railgun on a personal craft is illegal, right?"

Gandy shrugged. "Yeah, but it would be cool to have, wouldn't it?"

"Yes it would." Harris nodded. "Thanks for the tip. I'll have to check it out."

Gandy grinned, "Man, would I love to see one of those fire. I love all the old war movies where they used them. You had to get in close to shoot at each other. I'm talking a few kilometers. Now they just sit back from a thousand times that distance. Where's the fun in that?"

Tawn replied, "Not all fun and games out there, you know. People die."

Gandy lowered his eyes. "Sorry. I get carried away sometimes. You two have experienced it all. Didn't mean to be disrespectful. I'm actually grateful for all you did for us."

Tawn slowly closed and reopened her eyes in frustration. "Ships for sale?"

Gandy nodded. "OK. Let's see what we have along those lines. I have a Lambaster. Was basically a gunship. This one of course had all the guns stripped out. Was converted for cargo."

"What kind of armor on her?" Tawn asked.

"She has... level II titanium with an enhanced plasma shield. Kind of meaningless now with the power of those new cannons."

Tawn frowned. "Anything older? Something with armor like the Zwicker?"

Gandy browsed through several pages of ships after a search. "Nope. You have a classic. Doesn't show any specs for what her armor will take."

Harris smiled. "Will take a lot."

Tawn sighed. "How about anything with a near real-time wormhole generator?"

Gandy looked. "Mmm. Nope. Best we have is that Dreambus you were already looking at. You have to go military if you want to beat that. All the surplus ones have been de-tuned to standard. And without those specific generator parts, there's no going back."

Harris said, "You seem to know an awful lot about these old ships."

Gandy nodded. "I studied to be a ship mechanic since I was a kid. Had posters of drives and systems on the walls of my bedroom. That dream died when the truce was signed. No offense, but all the vets came home and sucked up all those jobs. Was surprised to get this sales gig."

Harris asked, "The *Kingfisher*... that database show who the owner is?"

Gandy pulled the information up on the display. "It's registered to a company called... Shipmasters of Chicago Port. And it shows as for sale."

Tawn's eyes lit up. "The other Zwicker is for sale?"

Gandy nodded. "That's what it shows. Our buyers could get it for you, but you'd just be paying them a premium for that service. If you can get to the station you can talk with the owner directly."

Harris scowled. "Don't bother."

Tawn placed her hands on her hips. "Why? You scared I'll have a ship just like yours?"

Harris slowly shook his head. "No. I say that because I know who Shipmasters is. It's Clovis Bagman. You want to pay through the nose for it, go ahead."

124

Gandy walked to a desk, picking up a comm device.

Harris crossed his arms. "If Clovis has that ship, he's gonna want a mint for it."

Tawn shrugged. "I have the credits. And I do like that ship."

Gandy closed the comm and returned. "He said it's for sale. And he said it's the better of the two he had, the other he just sold."

Tawn asked, "He say what he wanted for it?"

Gandy nodded. "Ninety-eight thousand. I'm sure I could talk him down, though. Not worth much if the wormhole generator goes out."

Tawn grinned. "Any interest in being my broker?"

Gandy looked back out onto the showroom floor. "I can't do it from here. But my shift ends in an hour. The registration and payment for that Dreambus will take at least that long. If you want, I'll do this after that sale."

Tawn returned a wide grin. "I want. You ever have any desire to be a first mate?"

Gandy pulled his fist to his chest. "Are you serious? On a Zwicker? That would be awesome!"

Tawn gestured toward the door. "Tell you what. I don't even need to see the Dreambus. Let's just go buy it. And if you can get me the *Kingfisher*, I'll be in need of a first mate. Pays three hundred credits a week, plus a food allowance when we're in port."

Gandy stuck out his hand for a shake. "You, ma'am, have a deal."

As they walked toward the sales office, Tawn was all smiles. "This kid is a gold mine."

Harris half smiled. "Yeah, whatever."

Tawn laughed. "Hey, you got a raw deal, I know. But you didn't have a choice. You needed a ship. And none of this would have happened without the *Bangor*. So I'm grateful. And just think, we will have the only two working Zwickers there are. No

124

other ship can take a full plasma round like her. I for one am excited."

Harris took a deep breath. "I don't know if I'm more upset about you getting a deal or you snaking the kid for first mate. That thought didn't even cross my mind. And with you leaving, I'll be needing a new first mate."

Tawn patted Harris on the shoulder. "OK, first of all, I wasn't your first mate. We were partners. Secondly, we're still partners. You need the kid, I'll be happy to let you borrow him. Hey, maybe he's got a friend who's looking for a job too? Gandy? Anyone else you know need work on a Zwicker?"

Gandy stopped. "For Mr. Gruberg?"

Tawn nodded. "He's in need of one too."

Gandy half winced. "The only one I know of is my twin sister. Trish. She took an apprentice mechanic job before she graduated. We studied the same stuff. Anyway, she's been stuck at the apprentice level to two years now. And they work her like a rented flyer. I could see if she's interested, but—"

Harris asked, "But what?"

Gandy continued to walk. "She's my sister, and I love her and all, but we fight like cats and dogs. Only over mechanical things though. Otherwise she's cool."

Harris smirked. "If she fights with you that will make her loyal to me. Will still want to interview her first though."

Gandy smiled. "I'll arrange it."

The Dreambus negotiations lasted the full remaining hour of Gandy's shift. The finance manager handling the transaction was itching to get home. Tawn pushed for the deal of deals, striking an agreement at a hundred fifty thousand credits below Gandy's recommendation. The Retreat would be getting a Dreambus to ferry prospective residents, in comfort, to the exclusive slug and stump colony in the Rabid system.

When the deal was stamped and the credits transferred, Gandy turned in his resignation, shaking his fist at the other sales veterans who had missed out on a healthy commission. The threesome caught a flyer back to the spaceport.

Gandy said, "You know, the boneyard is open around the clock. We could go looking for parts if you wanted. The *Kingfisher* won't be available until the morning anyway."

Harris replied, "Would your sister be interested in meeting us there?"

Gandy shrugged, "I could try her."

A comm call was placed. After a short discussion, Trish Boleman was on her way.

"You'll like her, Mr. Gruberg. She knows her stuff. Not so much on the small ships, but the big cruiseliners and megahaulers. She likes the big power systems of the new boats."

"So now you're saying I shouldn't hire her?"

Gandy shook his head. "Not at all. She's a great mechanic and should make a good first mate. I was just referring to her interests."

Harris rubbed his belly as he looked over at Tawn. "You getting hungry?"

Tawn chuckled. "Not really. Since the girl is on the way to meet us, how about we wait until after checking the boneyard to get food. Gandy? You gonna be hungry?"

Gandy nodded. "I am now, but I can wait. I love going to the boneyard to just walk around. They have one section where the ships are all over five hundred standard years old. They're mostly junk, but it's cool to see stuff that old. I think they just keep them around for marketing. Doubt any parts have been taken off them for centuries."

Another taxi-flyer was called and a short trip made out to the vast Magnessen ship graveyard. The sign on the front of the building beside the landing port reported more than forty square kilometers of 'Retired Transportation'. Trish Boleman was standing near the building in wait.

"You Mr. Goober?"

Tawn laughed.

"That's Gruberg."

Trish's expression changed as the two hulking Biomarines stopped in front of her. "Gandy, can I speak with you over here for a minute?"

Gandy replied, "Yes, they're a slug and a stump. But they're also nice people. Nothing like what you see on the news where they're getting in trouble. These two are business people. And they have money. And they have ships. You wanted experience on a real ship... these two have them."

Tawn said, "Hey. You can relax. We aren't gonna eat your face or anything."

Trish folder her arms. "Didn't say that. Just wasn't expecting you, that's all."

Harris said, "Well, just so you know, she can be a little difficult to get along with, but my dog likes her."

"What kind of dog do you have?"

Harris grinned. "A robotic one. His name's Farker."

Trish scowled. "A robot dog? Why not a real one?"

Harris leaned in. "I had a real one once... ate his face off."

Trish stared for several seconds. "Hmm. Didn't think you people had a sense of humor."

Gandy raised his hand. "Hello... boneyard... can we go look around?"

Tawn nodded. "Yeah. The humor out here is kind of stale. What are we looking for exactly?"

"We're looking for Zwickers, or any other ships from that time period we can strip parts from. If I'm going to be maintaining one of those, I want to know where I can get replacement parts from. There's two other boneyards this size on this planet. This one's the closest, and we're here, so let's get going."

Chapter 14

Tawn asked, "We're walking. Would this be better done from a flyer?"

"Yep." Gandy replied, "Got one coming. Just thought it would be cool to walk for a few minutes."

They came to a stop in front of a strange looking ship.

Harris asked, "What the heck is that?"

Gandy replied, "That one was called a Beeman. It's an asteroid miner. All of those bubble-looking extensions are drill and scraper heads. The ship latches itself onto the asteroid. Those arms wrap around and start consuming it. Can chew up an asteroid the size of that hopper in about an hour."

Harris half scowled at the hideous looking ship. "Was there that much to be made in asteroid mining?"

"At first." Gandy nodded. "They had a big fleet going at one time. Nickel was at a premium for the war effort back then and everyone wanted a piece of the bonanza. Once they had mined out the easy stuff, the deep nickel mines up at Hollinger were discovered. The fleet collapsed almost overnight. Cool ships though."

The yard flyer landed next to the group.

The pilot asked, "What you hunting for?"

Gandy leaned forward, placing his hand on the back of the pilot's seat. "Specifically Zwickers. That or anything in the two-to-three-hundred-year-old range."

The pilot nodded. "That would be Lot F. How long you gonna be there?"

Gandy shrugged. "Couple hours?"

After a quick ride the pilot set the flyer down at the desired location. "I'll be back in two to pick you up. If you change your plans just call in."

The flyer lifted, blowing air from its retrojets before zipping away.

Trish waved the dust from in front of her face. "He could have waited for us to get clear."

Harris asked, "How big is Lot F?"

Gandy pointed. "See that hilltop over there and that stand of trees this way?"

Harris nodded.

"That's just the start of it. I figured if we could make it to the hilltop we should be able to see most of what's in this section of the yard."

Tawn looked around with her hands on her hips. "They don't have an inventory of their ships? I would think we could have been taken right to any Zwickers."

Gandy half smiled. "I guess we could do that, too. Was hoping to get an idea of what-all was out here. You don't have to get Zwicker parts specifically if you're doing something like re-plumbing a shower or installing a new air filtration system."

"Where are the Zwickers?" Tawn asked.

"Just over the hill."

Fifteen minutes of walking had the foursome standing on the hilltop. "Zwickers are down there. Looks like four of them. Oh wow... they have a Banshee. I didn't notice that last time I was here. Trish, can you take them down to the Zwickers while I go check that out?"

"Sure." Trish sighed. "Dump them on me and run. He gets all excited over the old fighters."

Gandy began to run down the hill as Trish yelled out. "There's a reason they don't make those anymore, you know! It's called a plasma cannon!"

The twenty-one-year-old fledgling mechanic gestured to the others. "Come on. Let's have a look at these. I'd say the one on the left had a hard crash. It's warped going from front to back. Hulls look intact on all four of them, though. That could be a good sign."

Harris asked, "The fighter he's going to look at, why'd they quit making those?"

Trish laughed. "Seriously? One shot from a plasma cannon and you were vapor. In a bigger ship you at least have bulkheads to limit damage to a section. With the fighter it was one hit and you're out."

"Wouldn't they be harder to hit?"

"At first they were, but then the engineers figured out how to widen the plasma round's effective area. Didn't take the power of a full round to knock out all your systems. So the big ships would blast these fat pulses all over the place and then come back through with the powershot for the kill once they were disabled.

"Fighter Corps used to be where it was at in the fleet. Six months after the wide-shot came out they parked the last of 'em. Couldn't get pilots crazy enough to throw away their lives. The Banshee was one of the last fighter models to be deployed. It's Gandy's favorite ship of all time."

Trish pushed a dead shrub to the side to get to the hatch of the first Zwicker. "One of you want to give me a hand? Doubt this thing will even open. Although, I don't see any corrosion."

Tawn stepped up. "Here... this one pushes in and slides. The manual interlock is down here."

Tawn pushed on a small disk before twisting it clockwise. The hatch of the Zwicker puffed as it sucked in, dumping a centuries worth of dust on the unsuspecting openers. Harris laughed at the gray covered duo.

Tawn turned. "Zip it or I'll come over there and punch your block head."

Harris held up a hand. "OK. You'd have laughed at me, too. Can we get in?"

Tawn turned. Pushing in and to the right, she slid the ancient door of the Zwicker transport to the open position.

Trish looked in over her shoulder. "Wow. Looks like no one has been in it since it was put here. I've been in others and there's at least some dust on the floor. This looks pristine."

Tawn laughed. "Smells pristine. Harris, get over here. Tell me that doesn't smell just like yours."

Harris stepped up to the hatch. "Hmm. It's familiar."

"Smells like there's a dead stump in here or something."

"Hey now. Let's not be rude."

Trish stepped up into the craft. "I bet we could pick just about anything we wanted out of here. Gaskets and seals will be worthless, as would any plastics. Metal flanges, piping, ducts, even the seats look decent."

The young mechanic sat on a bench. "Wow. Those are horrible."

"Yep. Same as his." Tawn laughed as she walked into the cockpit. "Console looks like it's in better shape than ours. Harris? Aren't we missing this gauge? Power of something?"

Harris glanced over her shoulder. "Huh. Wondered what that was supposed to be. Miss Boleman, you bring your tools?"

Trish patted a pouch on her hip. "The basics."

"You pull that gauge and hook it up in the *Bangor* and you've got yourself a job as a first mate."

Trish frowned. "I have to be honest. I only came out here to humor my brother. I kind of like where I'm at. And if I leave I know there's no going back. It's still just an apprenticeship, but if I stick it out, the full mechanic position pays well."

Harris asked. "How much you make there in a week?"

"With O.T.?"

Harris nodded. "Sure, with O.T."

Trish sighed. "Three fifty a week, but I could easily make five hundred if I get a mechanic slot."

"My first mate position pays five hundred credits a week. You're always on call, and you pay for your own meals, room and board when off the ship. A uniform is optional."

Tawn chuckled.

Harris shook his head. "Not *optional* optional, just 'you don't have to wear one' optional."

Trish leaned her head to one side as she looked over the gauge and pondered the offer. "That sounds generous."

Harris grinned. "It's more than Tawn offered your brother."

Tawn scowled. "Really? You're going there?"

Trish nodded. "If that's true then I'll take it. He's been lauding that sales job over me for a month."

"He wasn't commissioned yet, so whatever he told you was fabricated. He was earning the minimum hourly rate."

Trish placed her hands on her hips. "That little weasel. He told me he got 3 percent of sales on top of a base salary."

"That would be what a veteran salesman draws. He was far from that. Anyway, what I offered him was more than fair."

Trish turned to face Harris. "So what would my duties be? What are you expecting?"

Harris crossed his arms. "I want her washed and waxed at least once per month."

"Be serious." Trish scowled. "Other than replacing this gauge, what would I be doing?"

Harris thought for a moment. "OK, I'd say keeping on top of all mechanical work. Possibly advising on upgrades should we run across any we feel we need. Inventory control. All inside cleaning, aside from the maintenance. And basically be a backup for anything I do as captain. Buy fuel, see to it that our port fees are paid... just about everything, I guess."

Tawn laughed. "Sounds like he's looking for a pack mule he can throw all his weight on."

Trish held up her hand. "Hold on. I don't have issue with taking on those duties if that's what's expected. Just don't expect me to be your slave. Treat me with some respect and I'll be the best first mate you ever had."

"You'll be the only first mate he ever had."

Harris said, "Look kid, I'm new to being a captain. You do what I ask, within reason, keep the *Bangor* flying, and crack a joke or two about Miss Freely on occasion, and we'll get along great."

Trish took a deep breath as she held out her hand. "Mr. Gruberg, I think you just landed a first mate."

Harris chuckled as he shook his head. "Not if you can't get that gauge working."

Trish pulled a tool from her pouch. Four quick-releases were twisted and a panel removed. A connector was detached and the gauge twisted out of its holder.

"You mean this gauge?"

"I'd say you're halfway home."

Trish's brother stepped up into the ship. "That was awesome. That fighter saw action. Hull is covered with pockmarks and blast scars. Cockpit was about the only thing left intact. Looked like all the nav gear was pulled from it though."

Gandy looked around. "This all looks perfect. It's like a time capsule."

The new first mate pulled a database of the Zwicker up on a tablet. "Wormhole generator died about two hundred forty years ago. And two of the retros went bad, so it was scrapped. Says this one was used to carry diplomats and officers while in service. Never made it to the front. Everything else shows as functional. Was privately owned until dumped here."

Trish said, "You have anything else you need out of here while we're at it?"

Harris shook his head. "Nothing I know of."

Tawn stepped over to the hatch. "How about we go see about getting me a ship?"

"You in a hurry? Thought we were gonna eat next?"

"I just don't want to have my ship get sold to someone else."

Gandy said, "Take me to a comm and we can put down a deposit. If he thinks it's from a legit broker he won't try to back out. Legal fees would kill a small seller in that scenario. The Vets taught me that during my first week. Were bragging about how the laws were skewed in the favor of the brokers."

Tawn nodded. "I like that option. Let's you and I go make that happen. And you might want to call that flyer back out to pick us up."

Gandy looked at the time on his wristband. "If we hustle he should be waiting when we get there."

A fast walk had the four picked up in the flyer. A comm was placed to the Shipmasters of Chicago Port and a deposit for the *Kingfisher* placed it on hold. Another flyer took the group to a local restaurant with an all-you-can-eat buffet.

Trish and Gandy sat in awe and disgust as Tawn and Harris shredded the plates of food that were stacked before them.

Gandy shook his head. "It's not humanly possible for someone to eat that much that fast. You two must be hollow."

Trish set down a half eaten barbecue bogler rib. "I was hungry when I got here. Think I might be sick."

Harris looked up from his plate, barbecue sauce lined the rim of his mouth. "We're paying for this. Eat up."

Trish began to giggle as the couple at the next table moved to the other end of the restaurant. "There goes another one. Now I see why you people aren't so popular. You're pigs."

Tawn stood as she looked at a new attendant at the buffet. "Oh... that's right. They were bringing out more pork chops. I'll be right back."

Harris pointed at the half-eaten bogler rib. "Couple months ago we were on Farmingdale for the annual bogler migration. There must have been a billion of them came down out of the mountain pastures into the plains. Took our ship, nearly thirty tons, and rolled it about a kilometer. We rode it out in this set of concrete buildings for about ten days with a bunch of mountain men. Was interesting."

Gandy asked, "If boglers are native to here, what are they doing out there?"

Harris set his meat on his plate. "The colonists said early settlers brought out a herd and it got loose. No predators and almost unlimited food on those plains for centuries. Herd just continues to grow every year. There are so many animals in that herd, if all were brought to slaughter at once, they could feed every Human for a year. All of us."

Trish shook her head. "You look like you just finished them all off."

Harris grinned. "I'm not done yet."

Three hours at the buffet had the regular Humans begging to leave.

Tawn pushed her plate away. "Boy that was good. I take back what I said about parking in a luxury hotel and eating ourselves to death. I could so do that right now."

Trish frowned. "I think I just puked up a little of that rib."

Tawn took a handful of towelettes and carefully wiped her face and hands. Harris followed with a trip to the restroom, emerging with a clean face.

Gandy sat with his arms crossed. "This mean we can go? I'm starting to rethink my resignation at the ship store."

Tawn gestured toward the door. "Let's go buy a ship."

***

It was morning. The *Bangor* settled into her rented slip on Chicago Port Station. A ten minute walk had the group standing on the promenade outside the Moonlight Lounge.

Gandy held up a hand. "Let Trish and me go in and do the talking. I'll see if I can talk him down. He sees either of you and he's gonna try to take advantage. Everybody knows slugs and stumps are—"

Gandy held his tongue.

Tawn laughed. "Go ahead. You can say it. Slow. Everybody thinks we're slow. And it's a misnomer. What we are is inexperienced with normal human interaction. IQs are about average. Dealing with people is where we have a hard time."

Trish replied, "Like that display back there at the buffet."

"That would probably qualify."

Gandy said, "Just wait here. We'll be back with the deal."

Tawn grabbed his shoulder as he began to turn. "Hold on there, Hoss. You forgetting something?"

Gandy returned a confused look.

"Here, let's load up your credit store. If you want to act like a buyer, you have to have the credits to back yourself up."

Tawn transferred a hundred thousand credits into Gandy's account. The soon-to-be first mate stood in silence as he looked at the total on his device.

Tawn said, "And I tell you what. As my broker, I'm willing to pay you 10 percent of all the credits you save me under his asking price. What was it? Ninety-eight thousand?"

Gandy nodded as he turned toward the lounge with a grin on his face.

Trish looked at Harris.

Harris replied, "What? I'm not buying anything here."

Tawn said, "You can go with him. If the two of you can get that price down by at least twenty-five thousand, I'll cut you in for 5 percent of the savings as well."

Trish grinned. "Consider it done."

The young mechanic trotted off after her twin brother.

Harris smiled. "Now that was downright nice of you. Dumb, but nice."

Tawn looked toward the door of the lounge. "I figure we're buying their loyalty right now. We give them something in their pockets and a shot at a future and they're gonna work their butts off for us."

"Look who's picking up the people skills."

Twenty minutes of waiting turned into an hour and then three.

A nervous Tawn took a step toward the lounge.

Harris asked, "Where you going?"

"I'm going to see if my hundred thousand credits are still in there."

A red faced slug walked out two minutes later. "Bartender said they left out the back an hour ago. His boss gave no indication he was coming back. And he said he left with a smile on his face. You think I just got robbed?"

Harris laughed. "Maybe Gandy's smarter than I thought. Looks like he took you for a ride. Clovis probably talked him into splitting the money and just disappearing. Twenty-five thousands credits each... that's a huge payout for two kids that young."

Tawn pounded her fist in her other palm. "If that's the case, I'll be crushing some skull."

Chapter 15

Harris said, "Here they come down the promenade."

Tawn let out a deep sigh.

Gandy was grinning. "Miss Freely, Captain, first let me say thank you for this opportunity. Second, you want to go see the *Kingfisher*? She looks to be in good shape."

Tawn replied, "Would you care to tell me what happened first? Where'd you go?"

Gandy pointed. "As we walk?"

Trish said, "Bagman tried to intimidate us because of our age. I told him 'Look, we have a buyer who is interested. Cut the crap and let's get down to business. We have other clients who have interests and if you want to be on a list of reputable sellers, you'll stick to reputable practices'. I think it caught him off guard."

"She was vicious." Gandy nodded. "After that we got down to numbers. I kept low-balling and then dangling the fruit of future sales out in front of him. I might have even talked about possible forced buys at his asking prices. He seemed to jump at that. I had him down to sixty-eight thousand credits before Trish took back over."

"I managed to knock him down another four. And he topped of the fuel tanks, including the jump fuel. Of course, I might have promised him a few clients that were in desperate straights, needing to sell their ships for hard credits."

Harris winced. "You do know the guy you were dealing with is a loanshark, right? He's the kind that, if he feels crossed, you wind up dead in a trash bin. You might be proud of your cons, but if he figures them out, he will be relentless at wanting revenge. In the business he conducts there's a certain reputation he has to uphold."

Gandy shrugged. "He's an old man. You're a slug and a stump. You were built for war. He's not gonna bother you."

Tawn frowned. "Let's just get to the ship and take her out. If he sees us with the stump he's gonna connect the dots."

Gandy held up his store. "I have your credits. I kept my thirty-four hundred and transferred seventeen hundred to Trish. If it was OK to do it that way."

Tawn nodded as she recovered the remaining monies. "You both did good. Real good. Just keep in mind what Mr. Gruberg said, that guy and guys like him are bad news. Don't mess around with them our you'll wind up as cat food coming out of some low-end meatgrinder."

Harris said, "I'll meet you there in a minute. I need to stop by the *Bangor*."

They stepped aboard the *Kingfisher*.

Tawn's expression was one of joy. "Oh this is nicely done. Clean, elegantly decorated. And... it doesn't smell."

She walked into the cockpit. "Wait... no power gauge. We'll have to start a list."

Gandy nodded. "Got it. First on my to-do."

Harris hopped up into the cabin.

Tawn checked the bunkroom. "Harris... check this out... that look like one of our old mil mattresses?"

He walked to the bunk and slid in on top. "Oh. Yes it is. I recognize that feel. I don't suppose you'd want to sell me the one off your first mate's bunk would you?"

Tawn chuckled. "Pfft. Fat chance. You'll have to buy your spare parts somewhere else."

Harris turned to Trish. "Start a list of your own. Job one is to find me one of those mattresses."

"What about the power gauge?"

"Oh yeah. Put that in first. That makes the *Bangor* a more complete ship than this... *Kingflusher*."

Tawn shook her head. "OK then. Time to get out. I won't have you insulting her on my first day as owner."

Harris took a seat on one of the benches in the cabin. "Just fire this thing up and let's take her for a ride. You can pretend you have feelings later."

Tawn looked at Gandy. "Mr. Boleman, would you care to initiate a startup? And check with the controller about a launch?"

Gandy sat in the copilot's seat. "You sure about that? This is your first time out. I mean she's registered to me still, but we can take care of that later."

Tawn stopped before taking the pilot's chair. "Wait... what? She's registered to who?"

Gandy shrugged. "We kind of forgot about that small detail. I had to take possession of it in my own name since the credits were coming from my account. When we get back we can run down to the licensing bureau and have the title changed over to you. Costs a hundred credits for the transfer, but you can afford it."

Harris laughed. "Should have been Gandy ordering me off his ship for the insult. Looks like you're the real first mate here. How much he paying you? You know what I offered Trish, right? Tell me he at least offered you that. If not, there are plenty of other captains around here looking for first mates... Like Baxter Rumford. I think she has an opening."

Tawn sighed. "Are you done flapping your trap yet?"

Harris looked up in thought and then back. "Nope."

The station controller gave the exit codes to be entered into the computer for the automated ride out of the station bay. Forty seconds later the *Kingfisher* emerged into free space.

***

A jump was made to the Rabid system.

Tawn nodded as the wormhole closed behind them. "Smooth."

Gandy replied, "All systems are showing green. Whoever owned this ship took good care of her. I have a full diagnostic running, and so far we are clean."

Tawn asked, "You two up for seeing the Retreat? It's a colony exclusively for slugs and stumps. You can visit, you just can't stay. Harris and I both own property there."

"Not to be nosy, but where did you and Mr. Gruberg get your money? I haven't heard of any other Bios making it rich. And I know you didn't inherit."

Harris replied, "Business. We deliver goods to the outer colonies."

Gandy pressed, "What kind of goods?"

A brief silence was followed with a reply. "Well, of recent, we've been shipping building supplies out here to the Retreat. There's a foundation that's supporting the building of homes for slugs and stumps who want to move out here."

"So a whole colony of nothing but you? Will there be little slugs and stumps running around?"

Tawn shook her head. "Not happening. One of their engineering feats was to make us sterile so we weren't producing more of us. I can't mother and he can't father. When the ten thousand of us are gone... we're gone."

Harris said, "They didn't want to have too much of a good thing. So they took precautions. Anyway, this colony is in one long valley. Probably twenty-five hundred of us living there now."

Tawn corrected. "Thirty-two hundred and growing. And we have room for everyone."

Farker nudged Trish. "What the—"

Harris laughed. "Meet Farker. My robotic dog. And my second mate."

The dog looked up with his usual creepy grin.

Trish reached down to pet his head. "He's adorable! Where'd you get him? I've never seen anything like him."

"Tawn gave him to me. She didn't want the poor thing. Kind of heartless, that one."

Tawn rolled her eyes. "It wasn't mine to give. It ran onto a ship I was on just before the ship we were docked with was destroyed. The owner was killed."

Gandy asked, "How was a ship destroyed?"

Tawn looked at her new first mate. "Boom. It blew up. Can we leave it at that?"

Gandy crossed his arms. "Blew up? From what? Drive failure? A bomb? What?"

Harris said, "We might as well tell them."

Tawn turned. "What? I think that's a bad idea."

Harris sighed. "It's gonna come out sooner or later. She undocked just as another ship approached. They blasted the other guy. Her ship slipped away."

Gandy frowned. "Who would do that?"

Harris replied, "We think it was alien space pirates."

Trish laughed. "Good one."

Gandy shook his head. "You don't want to tell me, then fine."

Trish sat forward. "Hey. There's a panel here on your pet. How do you open it?"

Harris looked down. "Don't know. Never tried. Farker? Can you open the panel for her?"

A small access door slid back, exposing the electronics just behind the dog's shoulder.

"Whoa." Trish moved closer for a better look. "I don't recognize any of this."

Harris grinned. "We were told he was one of a kind."

"Can I see?" Gandy asked.

Tawn gestured toward the cabin. "Have at it. We won't be on the ground for another three or four minutes."

Gandy forced his way in between Harris and his sister. "Oh, cool. I can see his shoulder joint. Interesting. And nicely made. That has to be a titanium alloy. How much does he weigh?"

Harris shrugged. "Twenty-five kilos maybe? Tawn? You've held him up on you leg a number of times... what would you say?"

Tawn scowled. "Aren't you funny. Yeah, I'd say about twenty-five."

Gandy said, "It's probably loaded with more sensors than this ship. The programming running this thing must be impressive. Does he do any tricks?"

Harris chuckled. "Other than humping your boss's leg? None that I've seen. Although I think he understands most of what we say. He's barked a few replies that... I should say farked replies because he doesn't bark. Anyway, he responds at times as if he understands."

Trish frowned. "I don't see anything in here that points to a manufacturer. Normally that stuff would be plastered all over the chassis. Farker? Do you have any other access doors?"

Three farks were returned.

"Can you open them for us?"

A multitude of panels popped open or slid back, exposing the innards of the mechanical pet going from the top of its head to its still-wagging nub of a tail.

Gandy gazed in awe. "Wow. This is so cool. A working spine. And look at those hip joints."

Trish nodded. "And the controller running it all. It's only half the size of my fist. You said this was one of a kind... where'd it come from?"

Harris replied, "The prior owner was said to have found it on one of the uninhabited worlds. It was just roaming around by itself."

Tawn turned to face the cabin. "Wait... doesn't that thing require charging? It couldn't have been roaming around without having a charger to periodically connect to."

Trish looked around in the chassis. "I don't see a battery. Here's the power unit. There's no battery there. At least not a traditional one. You sure it uses a charger?"

Harris pointed. "It's right up here. I plug it into this socket."

"Hmm, that line just goes to the brain controller. Hang on... that's not for power. That's an interface."

Gandy said, "You have a tablet?"

Harris reached under the console beside Tawn. "No tablet, but we can hook into the console display right here."

Trish took the cable that had previously been plugged into the dog. Connecting it from the console to the pet, a program window opened on the console.

"Whoa."

Harris asked, "What?"

Trish gestured at the display. "I didn't do that. The dog is doing that."

Several windows of code whizzed by before the background image of the display turned into a view from the dog's eyes. A word popped up on the screen.

Hello.

Trish replied, "Uh, hi?"

Welcome to my world.

"Who are you? Or what?"

First I must apologize for the ruse. This program is not an artificial intelligence. It's merely a series of recordings. The program will attempt a best match to a question, responding with the recording believed to most likely provide an answer.

My name was Alexander Gaerten. I say was because my physical body passed away long ago. My companion, Archibald, with whom you are interacting, is a remnant of my experimentation into artificial intelligence. It was a wholly incomplete venture, but my best attempt. This program is but a shell of that attempt.

Gandy asked, "So you're dead?"

My existence in the physical world came to an end eighteen hundred years ago."

"Where are you from?"

I traveled from Earth with the colonists who took refuge on Domicile. A name which I abhorred, by the way. My team and I discovered the boson field, the primary element of force that permeates all matter. With this discovery came the knowledge of how to manipulate this field.

Through experimentation, we acquired the ability to open a wormhole. It was a single event with the field continuously running for a period of more than seventeen years. Which was fortuitous for man, as our own world, Earth, was under grave threat. A rather large gamma-ray burst was heading our way, and we had no means of stopping its progression. So we fled here.

The wormhole experiment opened the reality of travel to this region of space. Several probes were sent ahead, and the habitable worlds of New Earth and Domicile were discovered. I won't go into our wormhole discovery other than to say we had little control over where the destination end opened. And the newly discovered threat from the asteroid saw to it that our options were limited.

Massive Earth ships were constructed by two competing world teams and launched within months of each other. Each ship housed nearly five million residents. Those residents are your ancestors of both Domicile and New Earth. Each reached their destination after nearly ten years in space. The ships themselves became the first colonies of the two worlds.

Harris asked, "So this wormhole from Earth, is it still out there? Could we get back if needed?"

The wormhole to Earth is lost, possibly forever. Our knowledge of control of the boson field was limited. But perhaps your scientists have made progress since our time. After years of experimentation, the best we could accomplish was to create our own field here in local space. Jump generators were added to ships, and travel within this area expanded.

We constructed two field generators within this region. One in Domicile space and one in New Earth space. A large portion of the two fields overlap. And the two fields are dependent on one another. Should one collapse or cease to exist, the other will follow. The overlap and the dependence were made to ensure cooperation between the two colonies.

Gandy said, "That's why our jump drives only go so far. And I bet we can find right where the field generators are. Archibald, where are the generators located? What planets?"

The location of the field generators is held in confidence by the science community who created these fields. Attempted facility access may result in the collapse of the fields for both worlds. Maintenance of the field facilities is automated, and those maintenance resources should not be tampered with. In short, if you value the boson fields and the ability to travel using wormhole generators, do not tamper with the field facilities.

Gandy frowned. "That's scary. Someone could take down our travel completely. Travel out here, what is it? Eighty light-years? That would take twelve hundred eighty years on normal drives. You'd be stuck wherever you were when they went down."

Trish asked, "Why was this dog created? As a guard for one of the facilities? To give warning?"

Archibald was placed outside the facility as an interface to the security system. He is the eyes and ears of that system, having the ability to sit and listen to those who have discovered a facility. Those individuals could then be appropriately warned if a facility was approached.

Tawn piloted the *Kingfisher* to a stop in the grassy field beside the port beacon for the Retreat colony. "I'd say we need to return that dog to where Cletus found him. We lose our jump drives and the party is definitely over."

Harris said, "Where'd that taxi driver say he picked him up? Del something?"

Tawn pulled up a nav map. "A hundred twelve habitable worlds. None with names like that."

Gandy asked, "Is there a center to the field of travel? I would think it would extend out in all directions for an equal distance."

Tawn looked over the maps. "Our known space is actually a long, thin region. Same for the New Earthers. They overlap from here to here. The centers of those spaces are Domicile and New Earth."

Harris said, "Maybe the facility is back home."

Tawn shook her head. "Why would Cletus say he found him elsewhere?"

Harris asked, "Farker, do you know the location of where Cletus Dodger found you?"

Yes.

"Can you tell us?"

The location of the field generators is held in confidence by the science community who created these fields. Attempted facility access may result in the collapse of the fields for both worlds. Maintenance —

Harris held up a hand. "Save it. We know what you're gonna say."

Trish crossed her arms. "Looks like we've got a mystery on our hands."

Chapter 16

Tawn opened the hatch and flipped off the inertial dampeners. The heavy gravity of the colony planet took hold.

Gandy remarked as he stood. "Wow. I feel like I'm carrying a thirty-kilo pack. It like this all the time?"

Harris smirked. "Yeah, it's called gravity."

Gandy frowned. "And you people are OK with this?"

"It takes a bit of getting used to." Harris replied. "Couple days of dragging around and you'll start to get your legs back."

Trish stood and then sat. "Maybe for you. This is horrible. Can we turn the dampening field back on?"

Tawn flipped a switch. Gandy shook his shoulders in an attempt to relax as the dampener field again surrounded them, bringing the gravity back to standard.

Trish said, "Thank you. It was getting hard to breathe."

Harris laughed. "Hard to breathe? That was like two seconds. You two need to bulk up a bit. You're too soft."

Tawn sat back in her chair. "This the first time either of you have been off Domicile, isn't it? Aside from Chicago, you haven't been anywhere."

Trish returned a half smile. "Was hoping to at my job, but it never came up."

Gandy shrugged. "I sold ships. Didn't get to ride in them."

Harris said, "You do realize about a third of the colonies have at least a slightly higher grav, right?"

Gandy gestured by pointing his thumb over his shoulder toward the door. "Nothing like that, though. What is that? Twenty percent over?"

Harris laughed. "Twelve. Guess that means the two of you will be staying on the ships when you come out here."

Trish said, "Farker, what is the gravity level where Mr. Dodger found you?"

It is 4 percent above standard.

Trish grinned. "Now you can't tell me we can't find that. How many one-oh-fours can there be?"

Tawn looked back at the nav display. "Six. Good job."

Gandy said, "Mr. Gaerten's algorithms must not be all that good. Should have screened that question out."

Harris sat back on the bench. "Since these two have no interest in seeing the Retreat, why don't we head back and grab the *Bangor*. We can split the planet list between us and find out where our little buddy came from."

Harris looked down at his dog with its wide open chassis. "Farker, close yourself up."

The panels and doors flipped and slid shut, returning the pet's exterior to one of a friendly and familiar dog. The unnatural grin returned to his face.

A jump was made back to Chicago Port Station where Harris and Trish walked aboard the *Bangor*. A comm was opened.

"Give us three coordinates." Harris said as the retros for the ship were initiated and control was turned over to the automated exit system.

Tawn pushed over the coordinates. "I'm sending you Imedia, Grytus and Wet Blanket."

Harris laughed. "Wet Blanket? I don't remember ever hearing about that one."

"It's out on the edge like the Rabid system, only on the other end. The other two are on your way out to it."

***

The *Bangor* was soon out into free space.

Harris said, "OK, *Kingflusher*, we'll meet you back here when we have the data."

Tawn scowled. "It's *Fisher*. Now cut it out or I'll start calling yours the *Bummer*."

"Roger that, *Flasher*. We'll see you shortly."

The comm was closed.

Harris said, "Miss Boleman, would you like to do the honors?"

Trish nodded. "I would. You think we'll find anything?"

"Couldn't say. Who knew a blossom field or whatever it's called even existed?"

"Boson field. And yeah, they kind of left that important fact out of our schooling. Weird that we have a confined space we can travel in because of it. I always wondered why, but nobody had a good answer. You have to wonder how something so crucial to our existence remains an unknown to the populace. Someone has to be studying that stuff."

Harris propped his feet up on the console. Trish returned an angry stare.

Harris chuckled. "What? It's my ship. If the captain wants to prop his feet up, he can."

"And if the first mate wants to maintain a properly functioning vessel, she'll complain. You scrape over those buttons and dials with that fat boot and we won't be able to read them."

Harris sighed as he pulled his feet down. "Fine. Once we jump we'll have an hour to reach... Imedia. You can take the time to install our new gauge."

Trish smiled. "I could do that."

***

"I don't get it. Four. That's exactly what it said before I hooked it up. What's it even mean? Could be that it's broken, but we don't know because we don't know what it is."

Harris replied, "I'd say you have a research project waiting when we get back to port. It had to do something or they wouldn't have put it in here."

Trish scowled. "I don't like it. Think I'd rather just look at the hole."

Harris leaned forward. "Sorry, but it stays. I made a big deal about it to Tawn and I'd like her to think she's missing out on something."

Trish replied, "What's with you two, anyway? You fight like you're a couple."

Harris grimaced. "That's just disgusting."

"Why? She seems like a reasonable person."

Harris chuckled. "Yeah, she's tolerable. It's slugs and stumps. We all came from the same base DNA. It would be like getting together with my sister. Kind of like you and Gandy."

Trish frowned. "Eww. I see what you mean."

"Yeah. The designers did all they could to design out fraternization among us. Sterile and the same base DNA. Not that we don't have urges or anything, but—"

Trish held up her hand with a scowl. "OK, not really a conversation I was looking to have with my new boss."

Harris laughed. "I take it there's no boy back home?"

"I just said I'm not comfortable with this."

Harris shook his head. "One thing you'll have to learn about Miss Freely and me, we've been through massive amounts of psychological training. You're gonna have a tough time hurting our feelings or shocking us. Thick skin, you might say.

"As a consequence, though, we can be a bit blunt. One of the reasons some regulars don't care to have us around. I mean, we desperately want to be liked, but... hahaha! I can't even say that with a straight face."

Trish half smiled. "I think there's feeling buried in there somewhere. Even with your alterations, you're still Human."

Harris smirked. "Stop it. Before you make me tear up."

The *Bangor* dropped into the atmosphere of Imedia. The retrojets were flipped on, slowing the ship as she fell.

Harris said, "Want to have some fun?"

"Depends."

"Flip off the auto-descent switch. Let's see if you can pilot this pup manually."

Trish sat forward. "I take that as a challenge. Can't be that tough. I've done it in a simulator a hundred times."

Harris grinned. "Not in this ship you haven't. And you might want to cinch up that lap belt."

Trish returned an arrogant smile. "I'm fine."

The button was pressed and unlocked. Immediately the ship began to buck and rock before rolling into a spin. Trish jerked the controls one way and then the other in an attempt to correct the unruly flight of the craft.

"Grrr! Why is this so hard? What's wrong with this thing?" she exclaimed.

Harris reached over, re-engaging the auto-descent control system. "Not the picnic you thought it would be, huh? Ever tried to pilot an oversize refrigerator as it plummeted toward a planet? Didn't think so."

Harris took the controls, again flipping the button to off. Repeated jerks of his hand kept the decent smooth and easy.

"How are you doing that?"

"Practice. I'll take us in. Once we've leveled-off you can take over and learn how to drive this box."

Trish shook her head as she watched the constant maneuvering of the controls. "How's that possible?"

Harris grinned. "Skill. Actually, it's just practice. Took me a half dozen tries to get the hang of it. You get forced feedback through the stick. You just have to learn how to react to it. Not so bad once you figure it out."

"Why are we doing this in the first place?"

Harris held up a finger on his free hand. "The million-credit question. Now let's suppose an enemy ship has decided to chase you. Are you going to do whatever it takes to get away? Or are you planning to just set the autopilot and let the ship's computer fly you to safety?"

Trish shrugged. "I kind of like the second one."

Harris shook his head. "That leaves you dead. Let's reverse the roles. If you were chasing someone, would you rather they were flying straight and level for you to follow? Or would you want them dipping and swerving and making every turn or change in speed they could to get away?"

Trish slowly nodded. "I see. Guess I never thought about it. Besides, we don't have an enemy."

Harris winced. "Hate to burst your bubble, but the truce didn't make us instant friends with the New Earthers. They still hate us and want control of what we have. Out here on the frontiers, where no one is watching, things can get nasty. The war may be at a stop, but it's not over."

Harris pulled the ship to level before bringing it to a stop at five kilometers from the surface. "Before we get started with your flight lessons, why don't you tell me what you know about the truce?"

Trish shrugged. "It was signed? We quit fighting and everyone came home?"

"Do you know why we quit fighting?"

Trish shook her head.

"The New Earthers were in trouble. They had exhausted their supply of titanium. For every five ships they lost in battle, they could only replace four. Their navy was getting thin and they knew it. There's sixteen star systems in the truce zone. They controlled twelve of those before the truce was signed. We gave up four of ours.

"Had we pushed ahead with the war I believe we could have defeated them once and for all. Our politicians thought it best not to risk any more lives. If you ask me, all they did was postpone the war for as long as it takes for the Earthers to gain a new titanium supply."

Trish nodded. "Well no fighting is better than fighting. I think they did the right thing by ending it. Besides, if the Earthers had any titanium available, they would have found it by now, wouldn't they?"

Harris scratched the back of his head. "That's where the problem lies. They were smart enough to negotiate putting Eden into that truce zone. Our people didn't care. To them it was just a hot, hostile desert planet. But I've heard rumors it's loaded with titanium. If the New Earth people can mine that supply, this war kicks back on."

Trish asked, "Is that the one that's been in the news lately? Some escalating violence or something?"

Harris smiled. "Wow. An informed youth. I'm impressed."

"Don't be. One of my friends is a devout pacifist. Eden is like some kind of cult shrine to her."

Harris nodded. "Dove is the main colony there. They just want to be left alone and have no interest in mining or trade. However, if the rumors about titanium are true, New Earth could be meddling in their affairs."

"Well, now you've got me all depressed."

Harris laughed. "OK then, I guess it's time we occupied your mind. Set us a nav pattern to circle this planet while I scan for structures. Will take us a couple hours, but we'll know if there's a facility down there. And in the meantime, you'll be getting practice."

Harris programmed in the waypoints for the flight. "We're flying level, which should make it a bit easier on you. Just remember what I said about the feedback through the stick. Don't fight it. Use it. You ready?"

Trish nodded as she cinched her belt. "Ready as I'll ever be."

The *Bangor* began to move forward and immediately dropped by fifty meters as the front nosed over. Several hasty stops and restarts saw a ship that was moving, but rocking and jerking as it went.

Trish frowned. "I think this is gonna make me sick."

Harris reached to the console, depressing a button. The visual display in front of them, the view in front of the ship, became steady.

Trish let out a deep breath. "That's much better."

"That mode has its own problems. Like you might be flying upside down right now. You just have to keep watch on your instruments and don't try to make adjustments by what you're seeing on the viewscreen. Such as, right now you're down a kilometer from target."

Trish reached up and flipped off the view stabilization. The image flipped upside down and began to jerk back and forth.

"I see what you mean. That can be disorienting."

Harris propped his leg up on the console. "Just give this mode a little more time. And if you feel you're losing it, reach up and press the button. You don't have to learn it all today."

The bumpy ride went on for forty-five minutes before the young first mate threw in the towel. "I'm done. I think I hurt my brain. My eyes are shaking."

Harris laughed. "As I said, you'll get used to it. It gets a lot better with time."

"We see anything down there?"

"Two small colonies and their associated buildings. All registered in the property database we brought. We have... about an hour twenty before we're done here."

Trish sat back, propping her legs up on the corner of the console.

Harris shook his head. "So, Miss Boleman, what do you think of your new job?"

"It's interesting. I've traveled to the far reaches of known space... bought a ship... flown a ship. And I got paid a fat commission before even starting. So far I like it. What do you think of your new hire?"

Harris crossed his arms. "I guess I can't complain too much so far. You seem competent and willing to learn. I'm sure given time I'll find out what your annoying habits are."

Trish smirked. "Yeah. You'll find out. When I get my mind set I can be stubborn. I don't like to give up and I don't like to lose."

Harris smiled. "I think we're gonna get along just fine."

Silence permeated the cockpit for fifteen minutes as the pair watched the terrain below going by.

Trish asked, "You said before this ship can take a plasma cannon round. If it was built and in service before those cannons came about, how do you know?"

Harris cleared his throat. "I'm probably jumping the gun on this and Tawn will be pissed, but if we're gonna be a team we have to be able to trust one another. Can I trust you, Trish Boleman?"

"You're not a pirate, are you?"

Harris laughed. "No. Not exactly. You and your brother asked before how we made our money? Well, we sort of did a bit of gun-running to the outer colonies."

"Illegal like?"

Harris tilted his hand back and forth. "Some of it at least is a gray area, but yeah, I think you'd have to say illegal. But we aren't doing it anymore. Those days are over. We're all legit now. We run supplies out to the Retreat."

Trish said, "As long as we're confessing... I have a sordid past of my own."

Harris set his feet on the deck. "Do tell."

"When I was sixteen, I might have borrowed my neighbor's flyer without permission. Went for a little joyride. And I might have managed to put a small little dent in the passenger side. And I might have let my friend Randall take the fall for it. He didn't go or anything, or know anything about it, but he did ride his heloscooter into their garage after being asked not to. I've felt bad about that for the last five years now."

"Flyer theft is a felony. I had no idea I was taking on such a hardened criminal. You have chosen to stay on a path of the straight and narrow now though, right?"

Trish half smiled. "I'll have to let you know on that one. All I can say is that so far I have."

Chapter 17

The Imedia colony offered no data leading to the possibility of an isolated facility. The Grytus and Wet Blanket colonies yielded the same. A jump was made back to Chicago Port Station where The *Kingfisher* and her crew were waiting.

Harris stepped up through the hatch. "No luck, huh?"

Tawn tilted her head back and forth. "Well... Durodurn was a bust as well as was Context. We then ran into an issue that you might find interesting. The Midelon system, which sounds surprisingly like the Midland or Del-whatever system mentioned by Cletus Dodger, doesn't allow jumps. We just happen to fall a couple years short when we entered the coordinates.

"It's on the edge of what we consider travel-able space, but you can't get there with a wormhole. And Gandy and I didn't think you wanted to wait an extra four years or so for our return. So we came back."

Harris nodded. "Now that is interesting. Kind of convenient, don't you think, that you can't quite reach it without making a big sacrifice?"

Gandy replied, "We tried every angle, too. Above, below, didn't matter. The wormhole wouldn't generate."

Harris grinned as he pointed to the hole in the pilot's console where the gauge was missing. "Might be because you don't have one of those."

Gandy asked, "You put it in?"

Trish nodded. "I did."

"And? What's it do?"

Harris cut in. "It does exactly what it's supposed to do. I guess if you had one you'd know what that was."

Trish asked. "So what do we do from here?"

Tawn replied, "I have building materials I need to get shipped out to the Retreat. I have a cargo transport and crew rented for it, but knowing the gravity, they've refused to do the unloading, so I have to round up some volunteers."

Harris frowned. "I'd love to help, but I think I'll be checking up on Trish as she swabs the deck and hoists the jib. Or whatever other maintenance is needed. You know these noobs, you have to watch them like a hawk."

Trish shook her head. "I can't even comment on any of that."

Tawn sighed. "Well go swab your jib or whatever it is you have to do. I've got work to get to. Mr. Boleman, I'm sending you a list of supplies we need for the *Kingfisher*. See to it that those are aboard before we leave at... oh-two-hundred."

Harris gestured to his first mate. "Come on kid. Let's go see what trouble we can get into. You getting hungry?"

"You going to a buffet?"

Harris chuckled. "I was thinking about it, yes."

Trish sighed. "I guess it's something I'll just have to get used to. Lead the way."

As they walked toward the Emporium, Harris said, "The *Bangor* at one time had a pair of railguns on her. Parts of them are still there, but they've been made inoperative. What would you say about having a side project of trying to bring those back to life?"

Trish thought as she walked. "Wouldn't those be illegal?"

"You the cops?"

"No."

"Then as far as you know, no. And besides, there's not an inspector out there who would go looking for a functioning railgun. They just don't exist anymore except in the old movies or games. And you have to admit, it would be kind of fun to shoot one."

Trish took a deep breath. "Am I gonna regret saying it would be?"

Harris chuckled. "I think you and I -- the crew of the DDS *Bangor*, the only, soon-to-be-fully-functioning, three-hundred-year-old defense ship -- are gonna get along great. I might even be tempted to spring for your meal this evening. Watch how I get this comped."

Trish nodded in acceptance as they walked into the Emporium. Harris flashed his fake badge, claiming to be a DDI agent. The attendant at the register requested a deposit of forty-four credits. Trish was convinced the meal would be taken care of at the end, and as such placed the deposit to be held until then.

The carnage lasted for two hours before a young manager in a clean pressed shirt came forward to check credentials for the comp. Harris stood in protest, heading for the door as Trish looked down at her depleted credit store.

The walk back to the ship saw a snickering captain and an agitated first mate.

Harris sat as he held up his credit store. "Come here. Get your credits. I was just having some fun."

Trish replied, "Not fun for me. I had to watch that. And then you made me pay for it."

The transfer of credits saw the end of the protest. Harris turned and pulled the schematics of the railgun up on his console.

"The breech for each rail is under a plate in the back of the cabin. The autoloaders are of course gone, but I'm almost certain the power circuits and capacitors are still there. We figure out how to replace those loaders and we might just be in business."

Trish looked over the diagram. "Interesting. This design looks a lot like the beverage dispensers on the big cruise-liner project I was working. It moves forty cans per minute into the pneumatic room-delivery tubes. If we could get one of those, I might be able to adapt it. Might cost you fifteen hundred credits to pick one up, though. And I'll have to track down the manufacturer."

Harris chuckled. "So we're gonna go into a fight spewing beverage cans? You think that will be effective?"

Trish giggled as she shook her head. "You have a warped sense of humor, Mr. Gruberg."

Harris nodded as he smiled. "We'd have to check, but that might actually make the weapon legal to have."

Trish looked up from the tablet display she was studying. "Don't push the comedy too far, sir. Learn to pull back from the fight when you already have a win."

"Noted."

Trish flipped through screens on her tablet. "Here... Claymonte Manufacturing. Domino Bend. Down on the surface. Retail for that unit is sixteen hundred ninety-nine credits."

"Who else would use something like that?"

Trish replied, "You ever order a beverage while in your hotel room? That tube it came through was probably fed by one of these."

"Can we go pick it up or is it an order thing?"

Trish opened a comm. After placing an order she was advised that a unit was in stock and available for immediate pickup. The *Bangor* was soon zipping down through the atmosphere.

Trish glanced up from a series of bumps and jerks. "I see what you mean about the feedback. You have to make your brain react with it and not against it. Already feels better."

Harris nodded. "Good. We'll have you trained as an expert pilot before we're done. And as a consequence of that, you'll be able to do the same with any ship with a minimum of practice. That same feedback mechanism is in most of them."

"Funny... every flight simulator I've been in, they all use the autopilot with set waypoints. Nobody pushes manual flying. I think the lack of control at first scares most everyone off from that."

The automated feeder was collected. Trish immediately got to work on its integration with the breech of the railgun. A return to Chicago Port Station saw a number of tools, including a welder, rented from a tool shop. Brackets were fastened and welded into place. The can-size holders of the feed were modified to hold the small tungsten pellet that would be fired from the gun.

Two days later, Trish stood from the floor. "You ready for a test?"

Harris laughed, "Don't you think we should take her out of the slip first?"

Trish shook her head. "No, you idio—t. Sorry. That slipped out before I could stop it."

Harris smiled. "Not my first time being called that. And I was joking about taking her out. I assume you were just referring to the feeder itself."

"I was. See that red button on the top left of the console? Push it."

Harris complied.

"Now, there are two trigger settings there. Auto and Manual. Set it to manual."

A rocker switch was flipped.

"There's an enable button beside the switch you just flipped. Press it. It should light up as yellow. From there, the red button on the control stick is your trigger. One press should advance the feed by one notch. Let's give it a shot."

Harris pressed the enable button. "And you're sure there's not a leftover round in the breech?"

Trish nodded. "I'm sure."

The trigger was pressed. A low vibration shook the ship.

Harris asked, "Were we supposed to do that?"

Trish looked over the controls. "Hmm. The rails were energized. Wasn't expecting that. Probably not a good thing to do while in port."

There was a commotion out in the docking bay with a number of individuals yelling. Harris poked his head out the hatch, talking briefly to a neighboring captain who was standing outside his ship while scratching his head. Within minutes, port officials were walking from ship to ship and checking power systems.

Harris came back in. "I think we might have a problem."

"What's happening."

Harris grimaced. "I think we're happening. Those rails going off inside this bay might not have been the best thing. EMP maybe? I think half the ships in this bay lost power."

Trish frowned. "That has to be coincidence. They're all shielded. Even if we did put out a big spike, they should be able to handle that."

Harris glanced around. "Are you certain? We are in an enclosed area and in extreme close proximity. I saw one other ship still leaving out there. We might want to slip out of here before anyone comes nosing around."

Trish looked over the console. "Here... Rail Enable. I guess we could have flipped that off first."

Harris sat in the pilot's chair. "Pull that hatch while I get us moving."

The auto-exit procedure was performed and the *Bangor* was quickly out into free space. A short ride and a jump had her parked above the colony of Grytus.

Harris pulled up an image on his console display. "This desert area... has to be a thousand kilometers in each direction. What do you say we go down there and fire this thing for real?"

Trish returned a worried look. "Shouldn't we run more tests first?"

"Did your feeder advance by one notch?"

"Yes, but that's not much of a test. We don't know if the rest of this system works or not. What if you press that trigger and it blows off the front of the ship?"

Harris laughed. "Other than your feeder, this is all military grade equipment. If it's going to work at all, it already works. Now, put us a tungsten round in there and let's see what she can do."

Trish sighed as the feeder was opened and a single tungsten pellet was placed in the hopper. "You'll have to advance it three times before it's in the breech. Your fourth press should send it on its way... if it already works."

Three flips of the trigger brought the same vibration through the cabin. Harris piloted the *Bangor* down to the surface, positioning the re-armed ship a half kilometer from a large sand dune.

"Does it look like our round went in place OK?"

Trish looked over the equipment. "It's not in the holder anymore. Don't know where else it could be."

Harris grinned as he squeezed the trigger. The vibration could be felt and was followed by a crack sound as the projectile went supersonic. The dune in front of them erupted with sand being thrown in the air, but the expected destructive power of the weapon was not perceived.

Trish said, "That was it? You can get that out of a plasma rifle. That couldn't be all there is to this. You couldn't fight a war with that."

Harris scowled. "We're missing something. Check the power to those rails."

Harris looked over the console controls while scratching the back of his neck. "There must be a setting were missing. I just don't see it."

Trish pulled a diagram of the railgun system up on her tablet. The power feeds into the rails were checked. From there, the lines going back to the capacitor and battery bank proved out as OK. She stopped as she came to a circuit on the exterior of the power bank.

"Hang on. This doesn't show on the diagram."

Harris walked back. "What is it?"

Trish looked the device over. "It appears to be a limiter."

Harris reached for it. "Well let's yank it out of there."

Trish grabbed his hand. "You might want to wait until we shut this down and bleed off any residual power. That line carries two hundred amps at fifty thousand volts. If it still has a charge you would basically explode. And I don't want to have to clean that up."

Harris lowered his arm. "I guess I'll leave the maintenance work to the mechanic, then."

Ten minutes later the device had been removed and the power lines reattached.

Trish closed up the access panel before loading in a new tungsten pellet. "We're all set."

Harris looked over the console. "Hey. Our new gauge is now reading a thousand."

Trish leaned over. "Hmm. Might be a power indicator for that weapon. If so, this round might be a bit different."

Harris smiled. "Let's find out."

The system was enabled. The feeder was advanced until a tungsten pellet entered the breech. The trigger was pressed. The vibration and crack of the pellet being expelled at a supersonic speed was followed by three quarters of the large dune lifting away from them into the air. A violent returning shockwave rocked the small ship.

Harris stood and raced to the hatch as it opened, jumping the two meters to the ground before sprinting the half mile to have a close look at the destruction. A ten-meter-deep crater, forty meters wide and running back sixty meters from the front, now sat where the large dune had once been. Fused glass shards, from the heat of the impact, lay strewn in every direction going away from him. Trish piloted the *Bangor* up to his location.

Still grinning, Harris climbed aboard. "Now that was impressive. Had I had one of these at Helm, I could have wiped out their whole army in a couple minutes, by myself."

Trish returned a half frown. "I don't know if this is a good thing to be enabling."

Harris waved the comment off. "Relax. It's not like we're going to use it. But wow, I do like having that available."

Harris pointed at the feeder. "Load us up with a dozen rounds. I want to see what the auto setting will do."

Trish counted out twelve pellets, placing them in the hopper on top. "I would use manual until the first is in the breech."

Harris sat back in the pilot's chair. "Miss Boleman, would you care to pick our next target?"

Trish sat in the copilot's seat, strapping herself in with the lap belt. "How about that one?"

"Excellent choice. You'd make a fine target selection officer."

"Really? You had those?"

Harris shook his head. "No. But if we did, you would have been right up there with the best of them."

The *Bangor* was moved back to a half-kilometer distance. Harris pressed the trigger three times with his thumb before flipping the rocker switch to auto. After a nod to his first mate, the trigger was pressed.

Twelve rapid cracks were followed by a wave of molten sand blasting the front of the *Bangor* as the selected dune disintegrated. Trish bounced up and down in her chair as Harris was thrown up to the ceiling and then slammed down to the floor, the inertial dampeners of the ship reacting slowly.

As the dust and debris began to settle, Trish unlatched her lap belt and jumped to help her captain. "Mr. Gruberg? You OK?"

Harris sat up as he winced while rubbing his shoulder. "Didn't see that coming. How'd I get down here?"

Trish chuckled in relief. "First you went up there. Then down here. Came in pretty hard from what I could see. Of course I was in the middle of getting my brains shaken out. You OK?"

Harris rotated his shoulder several times. "Yeah. Just gonna be sore for a bit."

The two stood, looking at the console displays. "Well that's not good. We crapped out our cameras."

Harris flipped a switch on the console. The blacked out images came to life in a quasi-wireframe form.

"We'll have to run with the radar system."

166

Harris walked to the hatch, sliding it open. Black shards of heat glass covered the sand just below and around the ship. Poking his head out into the still dusty air, he took a look at the destruction.

"Whoa."

Trish stuck her head out behind him. "What? Wow... we did that?"

The crater before them was fifty meters deep in the center, stretching back half a kilometer and out to a hundred meters on either side.

Trish said, "That's incredible."

Harris asked, "How many pellets does that say we can fire in auto mode?"

"Continuous. And we have another rail we haven't messed with."

Harris rubbed his shoulder. "Miss Boleman, I'd say our test was a success."

"Why did they ever get rid of these as weapons?"

"Harris moved back to his chair, taking a seat. "Proximity. You have to be within a few kilometers for it to be effective. Plasma cannons made these obsolete. Is rare that two ships come that close in battle now. Same with air-to-ground campaigns. Why get close if you don't have to?"

Trish said, "Hang on."

The *Bangor* settled on the blackened sand. Trish hopped out and walked to the front of the ship, returning a minute later.

"Sandblasted the whole front. That hull now looks like wire-brushed aluminum or something, on all the forward surfaces."

Harris said, "We can paint it when we get back."

Trish sat in the copilot's chair. "I don't know. It looks kind of cool. Like it was purposefully done."

Harris half scowled. "Well, we're gonna paint it anyway. I have no interest in drawing attention. Would rather just blend in with the rest of them."

166

The *Bangor* was soon rocketing up through the atmosphere on its way back to Chicago Port Station.

Chapter 18

Two days had been spent at the Luxus Hotel and Spa. Harris was again on his eating and drinking binge as Trish spent her days and nights on the *Bangor*. Tawn and Gandy returned from a trip to the Retreat to oversee the delivery of building supplies for the hundred fifty new homes that were under construction. The population at the Retreat had grown to thirty-six hundred.

Tawn stepped up into the cabin of the *Bangor*. "Knock knock."

Trish answered from the cockpit. "In here. Just watching the news on the console. Your trip go OK?"

Tawn nodded as she walked into the cockpit. "Where's the stump?"

Trish sighed. "Out wallowing. Been doing nothing but eating, drinking, and sleeping for two days. Thought this job was gonna be nothing but excitement. Now it's nothing but boredom. Pays good, though."

"Looks like the exterior got a paint job."

Trish nodded. "It did. But I can't talk about it. Can't talk about any of our efforts or experiences. I just spend my days in here watching the broadcast channels and talking to Mr. Farker."

Tawn half smiled. "At least he's an agreeable pet. And you don't have to walk him."

"He can be a pest when he wants. You have to scold him to get him to stop, and then he hits you with that sad face and makes you feel guilty."

Tawn scratched the dog's head. "You figure out anything more about him?"

Trish shook her head. "Not really. I quizzed his programming again but it's all the same set of recordings. His parts are mostly hand-made. Only found a half dozen chips I could identify as commercial. And those manufacturers have been gone for tens of centuries. Wish we could get out to that one planet you couldn't get to, Midelon or whatever it was."

Tawn said, "I have a few days before my next supply delivery. I suppose we could run out there and try again."

Trish frowned. "I have orders to sit and wait. Unless you can get him away from the food trough, I'm stuck here. At least the news has been interesting."

"What's happening on the news?"

"That planet Mr. Gruberg was talking about, Eden, it's had more unrest. There's a group of about fifteen hundred settlers now who aren't pacifists. They've been demanding changes from the twenty-thousand who control the government. Two more people wound up dead yesterday.

"The non-pacifists are trying to open the doors to anyone who wants to settle there, while those in charge insist on only those who pledge to uphold the non-violent principles of the colony. The nons also want the right to carry weapons, which are completely banned."

Tawn looked at the reporting on the console display. "Let's hope they don't crack open that door. New Earth wants that planet. Or at least control of it."

"That's what Mr. Gruberg was saying. If plasma rifles make it there, the pacifists will get slaughtered and pushed out of power."

Harris stepped up into the cabin of his ship. "I thought I saw a bunch of flies buzzing around outside... what's the occasion?"

Tawn said, "The occasion is that you need to give this poor girl something to do. She needs some projects."

Harris chuckled. "She's getting paid. And what do you care? Where's your lackey?"

"He's not my lackey, he's my first mate. And he's closing up the *Kingfisher*. I was giving him the afternoon off to go out and about on the station."

Harris laughed. "So you've got nothing for him to do. Sounds familiar. I gave Missy here the option of browsing the station but she declined. I may be out stuffing myself, but at least I have a goal and a purpose."

Gandy stepped up into the cabin. "All done. Hey, Mr. Gruberg."

Tawn said, "I was thinking we might try another run out to Midelon. There must be a way to get there without burning four years on regular drives."

Harris half scowled. "I guess I could go for that. The manager at the Emporium just threw me out and asked that I not come back. Seems I eat more than what I pay for."

Tawn turned. "Mr. Boleman? Would you like to prepare the *Kingfisher* for a journey?"

Harris walked over to his chair. "Don't bother. Trish. Fire this mule up and set a heading for Midelon. We'll all go together."

The automated exit procedure was implemented and the *Bangor* was on her way out of the station.

Tawn said, "You need a permanent project."

Harris laughed. "I am a permanent project."

"No. You need a goal. Something to work toward. Be productive. Do something or you're gonna drag this poor girl down with you."

"What would you suggest?"

"I don't know. Help the poor? Get an education? Add ground effects lighting to your ship? Anything is better than nothing. And you have the credits to do whatever it is you want. Just do something. Come out to the Retreat and build homes."

Harris rubbed his belly. "None of that has any appeal."

"Then make it a goal to help Trish achieve her goals."

"Not gonna do that, either. I'd just end up losing my first mate."

The wormhole generator came online. The *Bangor* cruised into the area closest to Midelon that Tawn and Gandy had reached.

"You try heading in at an angle?"

Tawn nodded. "Just about everything. We even traveled into the space the jump drive wouldn't take us to and tried from there. Wouldn't let us jump back either. It's like this barrier wall is there. When I entered the coordinates and sent them to the drive it rejected them over and over."

Trish held up her hand. "When did you get rejected? When you initiated?"

Tawn replied, "When I tried to set them. Never made it to initiation."

"Well it accepted my input."

Tawn stepped up. "Let me see... hmm. It wouldn't do that for us."

Harris joked. "Maybe that's because you're missing this gauge."

Tawn huffed. "You don't even know what that does."

"Actually, we do. We figured it out. And you're right, it has nothing to do with jumping."

Harris turned back toward Trish. "Miss Boleman. If the drive accepted those coordinates, let's go see what's there."

The *Bangor* slipped through to a location a half hour from Midelon IV.

Tawn shook her head. "Why'd it let you through and not us?"

Harris chuckled. "Because we're special. We're better. My crew is better and my ship is better."

Gandy said, "We do have one thing that's different here. Farker. If he came from here, maybe he's the key to coming back."

Harris looked down at the mechanical dog. "You the key?"

Three farks were returned.

As the *Bangor* approached orbit, Trish said, "That's a water planet. Nothing but ocean down there. At least on this side."

The ship locked into orbit and began a descent as it slowed. Trish jerked and pulled on the control stick, keeping the ship relatively stable as it dropped through the atmosphere toward a single piece of dry land. Forward progress came to a stop directly above a lone island that measured fifty kilometers square.

"I show a single building down there, Mr. Gruberg. What would you like me to do?"

Harris replied, "Take us in."

The *Bangor* settled on a grassy knoll a hundred meters from the outside of the single structure on the island. A square concrete building, it measured fifty meters to a side and eight meters tall. Grass grew on its flat top. A single door graced the north facing wall.

The hatch opened and the four visitors and their robotic dog hopped out onto the grass. Farker sprinted away, farking continuously just outside the door to the structure. It opened, allowing the dog to scurry in. The door closed immediately behind him.

Harris gestured toward the cockpit. "Miss Boleman. Could you try entering coordinates to get out of here into the generator?"

Trish replied, "We can't open one in atmosphere."

"Don't want to open one. Just want to know if we're blocked from using it."

The *Bangor*'s first mate emerged seconds later. "Blocked. It must be that dog."

Harris looked around. "Anyone happen to bring a year's worth of food with them? If not, we may be calling this place our final resting place."

The group walked down the knoll to just in front of the door.

Tawn placed her hands on her hips. "Hello? Anyone there?"

Gandy walked to the door and rapped with his knuckles. There was no indication of an answer. Options were discussed for the better part of a half hour. The *Bangor* was powered up and flown onto the roof of the structure.

Trish hopped out and walked to the roof's edge. "Nothing special up here."

Harris rubbed his forehead. "Who was it that wanted to come out here so bad?"

Tawn scowled. "You wanted to know, too. Now we know what's here. I guess we just have to wait to see if Farker comes back out."

Repeated calls were made for the dog. Harris whistled into his comm. The door to the structure remained shut.

Tawn sat down on the grass. "At least the temperature here is pleasant. And I would bet that ocean is teeming with fish. If we have to eat, we at least have that."

Harris scratched the back of his neck. "We do have one other option."

Tawn looked up.

"Trish and I... well Trish anyway, was able to get one of our railguns working. I could blow a hole in this structure that we could drive the ship through."

Gandy said, "You have a functioning railgun?"

Trish sat on the edge of the bunker's roof, looking down at the others. "Yep. And you'd love the solution we came up with."

Tawn frowned. "I don't think shooting our way in there is such a good idea. Remember what the recording said? Tamper with the facility and you risk losing the boson field. We do that and we're really stuck here. There's probably not enough years in our lives to make it back to civilization on standard drives. And not only do we not have the food, we don't have the fuel."

Harris gestured toward the door. "You have a better way in?"

Tawn laid back flat on the grass, placing the fingers of her hands under her head as she crossed her legs in a relaxing pose. "Don't see that we have any option but to wait. We probably have what... a week's worth of rations on there? And we can stretch that out if needed. You and I don't have to eat as much."

Harris chuckled. "Great. Sounds like the Emporium was my last meal. I shouldn't have let that skinny kid kick me out of there. There was nothing he could do legally."

Tawn shook her head. "Sit your stump-ass down and stop talking about food. We need to figure this thing out. Wait. I tell you what. Take Gandy with you over to the shoreline. See what our fishing prospects look like."

Harris crossed his arms. "If we're doing that, I'll just have Trish go up for a quick scan."

Tawn replied, "I say we don't use even the tiniest bit of fuel until we know our situation better. Walk your lazy feet over and look at the water. If you can't tell anything from the shore we can always take the ship up later."

Harris scowled. "Come on, Gandy. Let's check out our prospects. We might be wanting to leave the bossy women on their own side of the island anyway."

Gandy followed along. "I like the bossy women."

Trish looked down from her perch. "What are we gonna do, Miss Freely?"

Tawn smiled. "We're gonna relax and enjoy the afternoon. If they get back with reports of sea-life, we'll send them back to catch us dinner. Other than that, we wait for that stupid dog to come back. We aren't blasting this thing unless we're on the brink of death. We disrupt that boson field and we trap everybody, every Human, right where they are."

Tawn rolled onto her side, propping up her head with her hand and elbow. "Tell me about the railgun."

Trish's eyes grew big. "It's like mega-powerful. We only fired it a couple times, but wow! A twelve round burst, lasting all of about sixteen seconds, sandblasted the whole front of the ship after hitting a target a half kilometer away. That tiny stream of tungsten pellets left a crater that was five hundred meters long by a hundred wide, and fifty meters deep in the center.

And I think that's what that mystery gauge is. Something like output power from the railgun. We had to add an automatic feeder and remove a choke from the power feeds, but that was it. When we get back I can help Gandy do it to the *Kingfisher* if you want."

Tawn nodded. "I want."

Gandy stepped out onto a rock that jutted over the water at the shore's edge. "For having an ocean covering its surface, I wouldn't have expected it to be so calm."

Harris pointed up toward a cliff edge to their left. "Notice how these rocks going halfway up that cliff are wet?"

Gandy shrugged. "So?"

"That tells me a wave pushed water all the way up to there. And it happened recently, like in the last hour or so. This might not be the best place to be standing."

Gandy looked up at the cliff and then back down into the water. "There's fish in there. See the red ones."

Harris looked at the horizon. "Come on. We better get back up top. I get the feeling these waves come in from nowhere."

As the two turned and hopped from rock to rock, the ocean level began to rise. They climbed toward the cliff face they had slid down, only to be caught by the rapidly rising water. In seconds they were being lifted as the water rose and they flapped their arms and kicked their legs to stay afloat.

Moments later, the surge came to a stop and began to fall. Harris grabbed a jutting rock with one hand and a paddling Gandy with the other. As the water rushed down their legs and past their feet, eddy's and swirls developed in and around the rocks at the base. Almost as quickly as it had come, the surge was over.

Harris dropped Gandy a meter to a rock just below. "Let's get back up before another one of those comes in."

Gandy stuck his finger in his mouth. "It's freshwater. That whole ocean is fresh. That doesn't seem right. Domicile's are all salty."

The wet adventurers returned to the structure.

Tawn laughed. "Go for a swim?"

Harris replied, "Something like that. There are fish. And the water is fresh. But we'll have to watch for the surges. Water came up ten meters in a few seconds, without warning. Anything happen here?"

Tawn shook her head. "Just the sunshine and a nice breeze. I tapped on the door again and got nothing. Trish did a food inventory. We have four days normal consumption and maybe seven if we stretch it. I say we give this wait at least five days before we consider blasting our way in. And if the two of you can manage some of those fish, we could push that out for longer."

The door opened and Farker raced out, making an immediate line for Tawn, who was lying in the grass. An attempted mount was pushed away with a scowl.

"Stupid dog."

The bunker door closed behind and sealed.

Harris gestured to Trish as she sat on the roof's edge. "Bring the ship down and we'll get out of here. We have the dog, we should be able to leave."

A minute later the *Bangor* was rushing up through the blue Midelon sky. Coordinates for a jump back to Chicago Port Station were set and accepted. Once out in the blackness of space, a successful jump home was made.

Chapter 19

Harris emerged from a shower on the *Bangor* with a change of clothes. "We should carry extra foodstocks before we go out next time. A week doesn't quite seem like enough anymore. Put in an order for us when you restock."

Trish said, "You see this? Fifteen people shot with plasma weapons on Eden today."

Harris leaned in to watch the image displayed before him. "This isn't good. That last body was a victim of a military grade plasma round. I've seen enough of those to know the difference."

A comm was opened to the *Kingfisher*. "Gandy, put the boss on."

Tawn replied, "Here."

"You seeing the images from Eden?"

Tawn nodded. "I did. You thinking what I'm thinking?"

"That those were military grade rounds?"

Tawn shook her head. "No. That we need to go out there and clean up our mess. Those rounds, and probably the weapons they were fired from, probably came from what we sold. We need to go out and collect them."

Harris chuckled. "You want to plop us down in the middle of a potential civil war? One that is possibly being fueled by New Earth? I think you might need a better plan."

Tawn crossed her arms. "OK, how about this, we go in and infiltrate the resistance, take back any weapons they've acquired, and find out where they're getting them from."

Harris laughed. "Yeah, like the Earther resistance on Eden is gonna let a slug and a stump infiltrate their ranks. What fantasy world are you living in?"

Gandy said, "We could do it."

Harris returned a confused look. "Who?"

"My sister and I. We could be the infiltrators. We could feed you the information."

Harris nodded his head. "Sounds like a good way to get your throat cut. If these are New Earthers, their intent is to bring back war. They wouldn't hesitate to off a couple nosy kids who are meddling in their affairs."

Trish said, "I actually like his idea. He and I could pose as greedy Domicile business people. We'll tell them we want the titanium mines opened up because we want a cut of the business. I doubt they would be above using greedy Domicile citizens in their plot. If there is one."

Harris shook his head. "Lame. Nobody would fall for that."

Gandy said, "They have a goal. We offer a means for them to achieve that goal. They can check our past and they won't find any government connection. And no one in their right mind would do this on their own."

"Exactly," Harris replied. "I'm gonna have to say no."

Tawn said, "We should at least go there and talk to the pacifists. If this is just a minor squabble between two parties, we can walk away clean. If this is from our weapons, we can't just walk away."

Harris sighed. "I'm supposed to be retired. This being rich thing is turning out to be a lot of work."

Trish said, "You really gonna let that happen?"

After several mumbles to himself, Harris sighed. "OK. We'll go talk to the locals. Trish, update the foodstocks and then we'll see about hopping out there."

Tawn glanced at the time on her wristband. "I have a few orders to set up for supplies going out to the Retreat. Give us a comm when you're stocked up and we'll meet you there."

**

The *Bangor*, closely followed by the *Kingfisher*, dropped through the Eden atmosphere as a pair of fireballs. The twin ships pulled up short of the main port city of Dove before calling in to the port controller. Clearance was given and the two ships landed side by side on the tarmac.

Harris stepped out into the heat. "Wow. This is like a furnace."

Trish stepped out and immediately went back in. "That's too much. Didn't they say a transport was coming for us?"

Harris looked back with a laugh. You still think you and Bobo coming down here as agents was a good idea?"

"Bobo?"

Harris nodded. "You and Jim-Bob. I'm thinking a month or two down here as infiltrators would do you good. Would loosen you up. Mostly your heads from your bodies, but you'd be looser."

Trish returned a half scowl. "Aren't you Mr. Funny today."

Tawn walked up beside him. "The heat is definitely turned on here."

Harris looked around. "Where's Gandy?"

Tawn gestured toward the *Kingfisher*. "Not coming out until our ride is here."

A windowless van with enormous sand-tires pulled up beside them.

A ramp dropped down from its side. "Hurry in please."

Tawn waved at the *Kingfisher*. Gandy sprinted the thirty meters to the vehicle as the hatch closed behind him. Trish hurried just after. Harris and Tawn casually walked up the steps. The ramp flipped shut, almost throwing Tawn to the floor.

"That was rude."

The driver looked back. "You were wasting our cool. Something to know on this planet, people like their cool. If you go through a door, hurry through and shut it or the owners will shut it on you. The average person will only last about fifteen minutes out there. It's basically an oven."

Harris asked, "Why would you come out here to live?"

The driver shrugged. "Just want to be left alone. To live in peace you know. Most of us figured no one would want to bother us. Which brings me to this question. What are you here for?"

Harris replied, "You a pacifist?"

The driver nodded. "That's why I came out. You two look military."

Harris scratched the back of his neck. "We were military. She's a slug and I'm a stump."

The van screeched to a halt. "We don't want your type out here."

Tawn said, "Relax. We're here to help. We've come out to talk to your leaders. We have an idea of what might be going on with the Earthers and we think we can help."

"Dom government send you? If so, you can just turn around. The council doesn't want your help."

Tawn replied, "We aren't with any government. Just concerned citizens who want to help right what's wrong. We'd like to see Eden remain just a peaceful, quiet planet."

The driver asked, "How you planning on helping?"

Harris said, "We'll be discussing that with your council members."

The driver replied, "I'm on the council and the council is open to everyone. So whatever you hold back here I'll hear there."

Tawn leaned forward. "What's your name."

"Bizzy Mister."

Harris laughed. "Bizzy? How'd you get named that?"

The driver took some offense. "It's Biznardo. It's a family name, thank you."

Harris elbowed Tawn. "Biznardo. That's precious."

Tawn turned with a scowl. "You think you're helping?"

Harris looked at the driver. "My apologies. Was just trying to be humorous. Sometimes it works. Sometimes not."

Tawn continued, "Mr. Mister."

Harris chuckled.

"We believe the settlers who are giving you trouble are from New Earth."

Bizzy replied, "Everyone is welcome here. We just ask that you commit to being peaceful."

Tawn sighed. "Yeah, well, we don't believe their intentions are peaceful."

Bizzy cut in. "And that's why we've been having problems."

"There's likely much more to it than that. We believe they're here as agents of New Earth. And their intention is to topple your government and take control of this planet."

"That would be in violation of the treaty."

"Yes it would. Which is why they aren't official agents of New Earth. They're thugs and hired contractors sent here to take control of this colony."

Bizzy shook his head. "That doesn't make any sense. There's nothing here. Why would they want control? We came here specifically because nobody wants it."

Harris said, "Have you heard the rumor that Eden might be rich in titanium?"

Bizzy scratched his head as he turned onto a road leading into town. "I've heard that, but we don't allow mining. Residents are to live in symbiosis with their land. That's where possible, of course, more of a guide than a hard-fast rule. Businesses are precluded from mining in any form."

Harris replied, "And this is why they want control of the colony. Most people don't know this, but the Earther Emperor only signed that truce because they were running out of the titanium they needed to build more warships. They were falling behind in their replenishment production, and it was costing them planets. So they signed the truce, making certain to add Eden to the truce zone. They want your planet for its titanium."

"Well they can't have it." Bizzy replied. "We aren't giving it up."

Harris sat back in his chair. "Then you better be prepared to fight because they're here to take it. I've heard you had some citizens leave in the last few weeks. Is that true?"

Bizzy nodded. "A few hundred have chosen to go. Most were recent settlers and just didn't like the heat. We still have more than twenty thousand here. Not including the troublemakers. Who have been asked repeatedly to leave."

Tawn said, "They aren't leaving. Right now they are just trying to scare you off. Easiest way to reduce your numbers. I bet they've had more settlers showing up every week while you're losing some. Am I right?"

"That's recent, and can't be construed as a trend. And I'll admit that I'm fearful, too. But we aren't giving up. The council is already meeting to figure out ways we can reduce any confrontations.

"Just this week we started a new 'don't reply' initiative. If they call you out in town or wherever, just don't reply. That gives them nothing to escalate the situation with."

Tawn let out a deep breath. "Oh boy. This is going to be tough. Convincing pacifists to fight for their freedom. This may be unwinnable."

Bizzy smiled. "There is no winner or loser if there's no fight."

Harris said, "This planet has a large supply of titanium ore. New Earth is desperate for that ore because they need it to rebuild their fleet. They want the war turned on again and this planet is their way to do that. They are here. And their numbers will only grow until they take control. You'll be pushed aside or killed. They don't care which."

The van pulled into a garage and then to a stop. "Welcome to Dove. Through the doors and straight down the hall will take you to the grand room. A number of our citizens will be meeting in there. I'll be joining you shortly."

Tawn said as they walked. "So how do we convince a group of pacifists they have to fight or they'll lose everything?"

Trish replied, "Especially when they consider having to fight *losing* everything. Everything they care about, anyway."

Harris pulled open the door to the hall. "I'm surprised Domicile hasn't had reps out here to try to deal with this. They've just been hands-off. They have to know about the titanium."

Tawn shook her head. "The truce states that no official or unofficial representative of either New Earth or Domicile will set foot on this planet. They can give advice or offer supplies, but they can't come here without it being a violation. And from what we hear on the news, both sides are watching carefully for any violations."

The group walked into the grand meeting room. A raised platform stood on the middle of the room. Hundreds of lounge pillows lined the floors surrounding the platform. Several dozen Eden citizens were laid out in a relaxed fashion as they listened to a speaker.

"I returned from my trek north to find a handful of new settlers in my home. I kindly asked them to leave over the course of a week if possible. They moved on without incident. I believe we can sit with these other new settlers over a cup of tea and calmly discuss all grievances. They are human beings just like us. Thank you."

A handful of applauders praised the short speech as the citizen stepped down off the platform.

Harris said, "Is there a sign-up form or something? How do we get up there."

A woman sprawled out on a set of pillows beside them offered her counsel. "Anyone can speak. All we ask is that you be courteous and non-confrontational."

Tawn stood. "I'll give it a shot."

Harris chuckled. "Well, this should be good."

Tawn climbed the four steps to the center of the platform. Turning in both directions as she took a headcount of the small crowd. Twenty eight citizens lay about, most involved in quiet conversations with others beside them.

The Biomarine began. "Hi, uh, my name is Tawn Freely and I'm here to talk about the new settlers who are causing problems."

A single audience member clapped, balancing on their pillow as they leaned forward to have a sip of a beverage from a straw. Tawn continued for several minutes before it became apparent that most if not all of the Eden citizens surrounding her were not paying attention. An agitated stare came the way of the other three.

Harris gave a quiet laugh. "She's bombing. She needs an attention-getter."

Harris stood, walking to the platform and up the steps. Once atop he raised a heavy boot and slammed it hard into the metal decking that made up the raised stage. All eyes in the room turned his way.

"Miss Freely, I believe you have the floor." Harris returned to the others.

Tawn looked out at the crowd. A handful of Dove citizens came in through a side door.

"Citizens of Eden. This is your home. Your paradise. You've come here to live in peace and tranquility. Which is both admirable and noble. But you still live in the real world. A world with other planets and peoples who are hostile. And people with bad intent. Sometimes you have no option but to defend what you have from those who would take it.

"Those people are here now. They are on your world. They want what you have."

Tawn looked around the room. The attention of most had returned to their own private conversations.

Walking down the steps, she returned to the company of the others, plopping down on one of the pillows. "Blind idiots. They don't even care."

Harris laughed. "I thought you were boring. No charisma."

Tawn challenged. "You think you can do better?"

Harris thought and then stood. "I think I can."

The thick, genetically engineered Human, stomped up the steps as he let out a roar and beat his chest. "People of Eden! A plague is descending upon your house! That plague is a conspiracy by New Earth to take your planet from you... by force! You must join now in her defense!"

With that sentence the watchers began to turn away. One by one their quiet conversations resumed. Harris looked around the room in disbelief.

A short walk back to the group had him standing over the others. "You're right. They're idiots."

Gandy asked. "So what do we do? How do we stop this?"

Harris frowned. "We have to go to the source of the problem. We go see the Earthers. Maybe letting them know that their plans have been exposed will be enough to turn them back."

Trish said, "I can't say I think poking our heads in on the business of armed conspirators sounds like a good option. You have anything else?"

Tawn stood. "I think he's right. This is a people problem. And we can work to resolve it on this end or that. And we just saw what our chances here are."

As the group stood, Bizzy walked into the meeting room.

Harris waved him over. "We tried to talk. Nobody seemed interested in listening."

Bizzy nodded. "Any talk that sounds confrontational and they will turn away. I tried to mention that to you on the way over here."

Tawn asked, "How do we get to the other colonists? The troublemakers."

Bizzy replied, "Someone has to drive you. We don't allow ships anywhere but the port itself."

Harris scratched his head. "That something you could do? Drive us?"

Bizzy shrugged. "Sure. If you want. I will have to leave you there, though. They don't care for visitors from Dove. You'll have to find your own way back to the port when you're done."

186

Harris nodded. "Fair enough. When can we leave?"

Bizzy gestured toward the garage. "Now, if you like. Sorry you didn't find our citizens welcoming. Sometimes it takes time for them to warm up to others."

The van pulled out onto the baking sand of Eden. The hundred fifty kilometer ride took nearly five hours. Bizzy pulled to a stop at the edge of a cluster of buildings.

"One of you has to go in and see if they'll accept you. I won't leave until you're all inside. To do otherwise would be sending you to your death."

Harris hopped down the ramp into the hot sand. A quick walk had him through a door to a welcoming room. After a short discussion with a local, he returned to the door, stepping outside to wave his hand. The group disappeared into the building as Bizzy Mister quickly pulled away.

Chapter 20

"**W**elcome to Boxton." The shift worker assigned to the welcome room said. "What's your business here?"

Harris replied, "We'd like to talk to your officials about doing some mining."

The man shook his head. "No mining going on here. The pacies won't allow it. We're out here trying to scratch out a living while they walk around all smug in their robes and sandals, sitting atop the only decent water source on the planet."

Tawn said, "You must have water here. With this heat you wouldn't be able to survive."

The man crossed his arms. "We recycle what we use and are forced to purchase more from them. They claim it's donations, we all know it's a shakedown.

"We have plenty of water, two kilometers below. The pacies won't allow us to drill for it. They took over a well from a former settler and have since blocked all others from tapping into it."

Harris shook his head. "Why don't you just drill it anyway?"

The man sighed. "Can't get equipment here. They control all imports through that port. We're all slowly going broke because of the water donations. They don't seem to care. What is it you're visiting us for again? Mining?"

Tawn said, "Actually we're traders. Looking to do business."

The man gestured toward a door as he stood. "Come on. Follow me. I'll take you to see the commissioner. I don't think you'll find much of a market here, but I guess you can decide that."

After a walk down a long hall they turned a corner into a room. "Daniel, we have visitors. They claim they're traders out scouting for business."

Daniel Falburn pointed at a set of chairs. "Have a seat while I call you a transport back out of here. Maybe we can catch the one that dropped you before they get too far."

Several attempts at a comm were denied. "Putz. Once they drop they don't like to come back. You say you're traders? I can't say we have much to trade for unless you have drilling equipment. We could turn this place into the Eden it's supposed to be if we had a well."

Harris asked, "What reason do they give for denying you a well?"

"They claim we'll be destroying the pristine planet. That the water belongs to them and they want it to stay where it is. What they want is for us to dry up and go away. A wellhead here would bring more homesteaders and they don't want more."

Harris leaned in. "We're more interested in mining titanium. I hear this planet is crawling with it."

Daniel leaned toward Harris. "I hear you're a moron that believes every rumor the pacies put out. There's no titanium here. They started that rumor to help justify their position back on Domicile."

Harris smiled at the directness of the Earther. "OK then, please tell me why any of you would move to this burning pit of a world?"

Daniel sighed. "We were told not to talk about it, but we had private companies offer a stipend to any settlers who would move to here or any of the other truce worlds. It's that simple. They saw influence from Domers spreading out here and wanted to counter that with our own settlers. Government is probably responsible, but can't claim it. We've sent back requests for assistance, but our government says they can't get involved."

Tawn said, "There's been a number of news reports about unrest and people being killed. What can you tell us about those?"

"Out here? The only deaths we've had are from dehydration."

Gandy asked, "No one killed by plasma rifles?"

Daniel shook his head. "Weapons aren't allowed here. A couple of the settlers did try to sneak them in, but they were all caught at the port and confiscated. Those individuals were also put back on ships heading out of here."

Trish said, "I still don't get why any of you would come here. Even with the stipend, what does this planet have to offer?"

"It has what most of us want. A quiet peaceful life where we are in control of our own destinies. Out here you work for yourself. We were also told that even though the deserts covered most of this planet, there was water to be had. Not really how it worked out."

A man came into the doorway. "Dan, the Fletchers just came in. Barely alive. Said their condenser broke a few days ago. They think it was tampered with."

The commissioner rose. "I have to see to this. I'll be back shortly."

Daniel hurried out of the room.

Tawn lifted an eyebrow as she looked at Harris. "Wasn't expecting to hear any of that. Sounds like the unrest out here is from hoarding water and not over some titanium ore deposits."

Trish said, "We should help these people."

Harris slowly shook his head. "How can we? This is still a New Earth versus Domicile issue. These Earthers are only here because of their government wanting influence out here. If we help we are also helping the New Earth.

"And I'm starting to think those news reports were planted by the DDI or something, with a purpose to influence opinion back there. Might be they're trying to stir up more pacifists to move out here. This complicates things."

"How you figure?" Tawn asked.

"I figure because we have both worlds poking their noses in, and it's the people here who are paying for it. If word spreads among our colonies that the New Earthers are trying to colonize the truce planets... support for our colonizing them first would go wild. There are no restrictions on private entities meddling."

Tawn said, "This is an impossible situation. One for which there is no action we can take to make anything different. We can't control or influence what our government or that of New Earth does. I have to say I think the pacifists here have it right. If they allow water here, this colony burgeons and they lose control of the planet. If that happens out here it could be another trigger for renewed war."

"New Earth doesn't have the ship fleet to fight that war. They lack titanium."

"How about this, we scan this planet and the other truce worlds for titanium. If the deposits are weak we can at least put that rumor to bed."

Harris crossed his arms. "Where is it we crossed the line from being traders to trying to solve all man's problems? We came out here to check on plasma weapons. It looks like there aren't any here. Maybe it's time we head back and get on with our own business."

Commotion filled the hallway outside the room as word of the damaged condenser spread. Aside from the water purchases, it was a primary water source as part of the recycling system each settler maintained.

Harris stood in the doorway looking down the hall at several settlers who were riled up and arguing. Gandy stood just behind.

Harris turned back. "I'm calling our ride back out here. We don't need to be in the middle of this."

Gandy tapped him on the shoulder. "That guy said they didn't have weapons... I just saw a plasma rifle walk by."

Tawn asked, "You sure?"

Gandy nodded as he stepped back from the door with his hands raised. "I'm sure."

Daniel Falburn walked into the doorway with his weapon raised. "So new people show up and our equipment is damaged. I don't suppose the four of you had anything to do with that."

Harris replied. "We just got here. We don't have a beef with anyone on this planet."

Daniel pointed his plasma rifle at Harris. "A slug and a stump show up asking about titanium. Am I supposed to think that's a coincidence? Kind of stupid of the Domers to send you out here."

Tawn stood. "Hey, we're on your side. The Domers screwed us. Built us for war and then there's no war. The rest of them hate us. That plasma rifle... how you think it got out here? That's a repeater. Military issue. Look at the stock. If the serial number begins with an M5, it's one we sold on Bella III that was then transferred to here."

Daniel scowled as he turned the weapon down to check on Tawn's revelation. "Doesn't prove a thi—"

The flying chair impacted the New Earth settler before he had a chance to react. In a flash of insane speed, Tawn Freely was across the room, stripping the unsuspecting commissioner of his weapon. Two plasma rounds found their way into the chests of a pair of settlers that were moving down their way. A hard punch saw Daniel Falburn knocked cold. Tawn dragged him into the room.

Harris shook his head. "No going back from that."

Gandy and Trish stood staring with their mouths open.

Tawn replied, "He wasn't planning a welcome party for us."

A plasma round charged down the hall outside the door, striking a wall at the end.

Tawn checked the charger on her weapon. "This one only has thirteen rounds left. If we're to live, we need more weapons. That means going out in this hall and taking them, or heading back to our ships. We go down that way to get outside. I don't fancy the blast furnace out there with no water supply."

Harris asked, "What do you see?"

Tawn glanced down the hall, pulling her head back as another plasma round skimmed past. "At least two. Cowered around the corners. Only saw one rifle exposed."

Harris turned to look around the room. "We can't stay here. They'll be coming through that outside door any minute. We can't defend both doors."

Tawn aimed her weapon at Gandy.

"What'd I do? What's happening?"

Tawn gestured with the rifle. "You move you ass away from that wall unless you want to be knocked through it."

Gandy hurried over to behind her. A plasma round entered the hollow wall construction, exploding backward, leaving a two meter hole that could be walked through.

Tawn moved forward toward the new exit. "Let's go. Two more walls and we've got the angle on those shooters."

Another blast had the foursome walking into a new room. Before hitting the last wall, the Biomarine briefly stepped into the hallway, unleashing another round at the corner before returning to the current mission. A final round saw a wide hole opened into the cross-hall.

Tawn looked at Harris. "Which one you want?"

"What are you suggesting?"

"I'm suggesting you stick your head out one door to draw fire while I pop out the other and put an end to this."

Harris chuckled at the suggestion. "So I'm bait?"

"You have a problem with that?"

Harris grinned. "No. Just wanted to be clear."

Positions were taken and a nod exchanged. The stump made the first move, charging into the hall, pushing off the far wall and falling to roll backward into the door he had come from. As the Earther's attention was grabbed, Tawn Freely slid into the hallway through the blast hole, unleashing three rounds into the startled inhabitants standing before her. All three exploded, coating the walls, floor and ceiling with their blood and guts.

Tawn walked up to the remains of the first victim, removing a Fox-40 from a hand on the end of a severed arm. Harris was quickly beside her, pulling a plasma rifle from the body parts and fluids of the second victim.

Tawn gestured to a terrified Gandy. "Get that other weapon."

Trish pushed him aside to dig through the pile of exploded meat that had once been a human. "Got it. Ew."

Tawn turned to Gandy. "You ever fired a repeater?"

A still stunned Gandy slowly shook his head. "No."

"Let me dumb it down for you. You aim this end, you pull the trigger. It shoots. Got that?"

Gandy nodded. "I got it."

As he reached for the weapon, Tawn pulled it back. "Hold on. We have about six full power shots left in this charge. I'm dialing you down to a quarter power. Should push you up to a couple dozen. Not as deadly, but they should do the job. Now, I need the two of you to go back and retrieve our friend Daniel. Smack him around, wake him up. Bring him here."

Harris said, "We're flying blind in here. Would be nice to know the layout."

Tawn flipped her head back toward the others. "That's why they're bringing the Earther up here. He's gonna tell us where we need to go."

A groggy Daniel Falburn was soon standing behind them.

Harris asked, "Tell us the layout of this building. And if you lie don't think I won't hesitate to fill you with plasma. You're only useful to us for your knowledge. You cooperate and we might just let you out of here alive."

Daniel wiped the blood from below his nose with his sleeve. "These two halls fold back around into each other with a layout the same as on this end of the building coming after."

"And what's behind this wall?" Tawn asked.

"That would be the fusion reactor we use to keep these buildings cool. The ceilings are lined with thermoelectric cooling panels. Please don't blast through that wall. You take out that reactor and this building as well as the others will be an oven in about a half hour. That reactor powers this entire complex."

Harris stepped in, taking the Earther by the neck. "What kind of vehicles you have out here?"

Daniel slowly shook his head. "We don't. Only the pacies have transports. Another way they keep us in our box."

"How'd the Fletchers or whoever it was your friends mentioned... how'd they get here?"

Daniel frowned. "Walked two kilometers under a sunshield. Which is why they were practically dead when they arrived."

Tawn stepped close. "How many of you are there in this building? And how's it connected to the others?"

Daniel pointed. "Around that corner is a door leading down to the tunnels. But look, just call your people and have them come pick you up. Leave us be. We don't care about the titanium. We were forced to come here and told to look for it. The pacies have mostly kept us pinned in."

"You saying you don't know where the titanium is?"

Daniel again wiped his nose. "We don't even know if there is any. We came here to look, but we've been under their thumb since we got here. No weapons, no vehicles, and no water."

Tawn looked down at her hand. "No weapons? Then what am I holding?"

"Those showed up outside the compound three weeks ago. The pacies claimed we were smuggling water. We had nothing to do with it, they just showed up. And before you ask, yes, we were happy to have them."

Harris said, "So the reports of pacifists dying were true."

Daniel shook his head. "We didn't know who they were. Only that they were attacking our compound and they were armed. We fought back, they lost, we took their weapons. Can't say for certain if they were pacies or not, but they attacked. The bodies are stored down in our morgue. The pacies wouldn't come to claim them."

Tawn looked up at Gandy and Trish. "Keep an eye on this one. We're gonna circle this building."

Harris asked, "How many exits in this building?"

"Two. One at each end. Three if you count the stairs going down."

"Tawn, when you get to the exterior door, see if you can block it off."

Daniel said, "You'll find a slide bar on each of those. They lock from the inside."

The building was cleared with an additional six inhabitants being captured and confined. The exterior doors were sealed and locked with the slides. The Biomarines returned to the door leading down to the tunnels below.

Tawn sighed. "We open that door and we're likely to have a mess on our hands."

Harris chuckled, "Not sure what you call that back there in the hall then. Give it a few more hours and it's gonna begin to ripen up in here. I've tried opening a comm to the pacies, they keep rejecting me. I have to wonder if they think we're out here taking care of business for them."

Tawn shook her head. "I don't think so. They seemed adamant about no violence. Most likely this is part of their 'just don't respond' campaign. They know what we are and our presence has to irk them to no end."

Harris glanced back down the hall. I'm guessing at least some of them are waiting behind that door. What do you say we give them something to think about. A few of those body parts tossed down may work in our favor."

Tawn grimaced. "That's pretty gruesome... I like it."

Harris took a step toward the remains. "Hang on. I'd like to talk to Daniel again. He was some sort of commissioner. Maybe we can negotiate our way out of this."

"Have at it."

The seven captured Earthers lay huddled in a corner. Trish and Gandy sat in chairs with their weapons trained on the group.

Harris walked in, grabbing Daniel by the arm and pulling him to his feet. "You're coming with me. I have a few demands I want to deliver to your people."

Harris released his arm when they reached the door heading down. "You're gonna poke your head in there and tell them to lay down their arms."

Daniel replied, "Why would they comply?"

Tawn said, "Because you're the commissioner. That has to hold some sway. And because you want to keep them alive. So you're gonna tell them to stack all their arms at the bottom of those steps. We're gonna collect them. And then we're gonna figure out a way off this planet. After that you people can settle your arguments as you will."

Daniel looked at the time on his wristband. "You're too late."

Chapter 21

Harris asked. "Too late for what?"

"Too late to save the pacies. Two days ago we received another drop of mystery equipment in a large container. Once brought inside and opened, we found it contained biosuits. We tested them for a day and determined our people could last a full week out there in the heat. A force of more than two hundred left for the pacie colony just after you arrived.

"By tomorrow they'll be descending on that colony. Without transports, or one of those suits, you have no way to make it there to stop them. Tomorrow the colony of Eden becomes an unofficial New Earth colony.

"And the reason they aren't responding to comms is because our operatives took them down. No calls for help will be going out today. Probably best that you just turn yourselves over to me. I'll see to it you're treated fairly."

Harris turned a half frown toward Tawn. "You know what this means?"

Tawn nodded. "We have to go out there to stop them."

Daniel huffed. "Outside these walls is death. You heard what the twenty minute walk did to our two people this morning."

Tawn replied, "Well we're not your people. Show us these sunshields your people used. And we're gonna need a supply of water and a half dozen of your people to carry it."

Daniel returned an angered look. "You can't be serious. You take anyone out there with you and they're dead."

Harris shook his head. They'll have excess water and sunshields. We'll only be dragging them along for another forty-five minutes. Your sun will start setting about then. I'd have to believe the temperature moderates at night."

Daniel scowled. "None of us can make it out there for forty-five minutes. Wait the forty-five and I'll help carry."

Harris patted the Earther on the back. "We go now, and you're going with us. So tell your people at the bottom of the steps to stack their weapons. Otherwise we come down there blasting and we'll take them ourselves."

Tawn leaned in. "And before you start thinking about it, keep in mind what he and I are capable of. You have to have heard stories. And I can assure you the reality of those stories is far worse than what you heard. So open that door and send down the message."

The New Earth colony leader yelled down to his followers. A stack of a dozen repeating rifles and Fox-40s were soon at the bottom of the steps. One of the other captors was used to carry them up.

Harris yelled down. "Listen up the lot of you. I don't care how many of you there are, but if anyone tries to enter this building we'll blow your fusion reactor. We have the means and we have the will. Understood?"

A voice echoed up the steps. "Understood."

Tawn yelled down. "One more thing. If we find you're holding out on weapons, we're blowing that reactor. Understand? You have anything you'd like to add to that pile?"

The voice came back. "Three more rifles and a handgun. We're putting them at the stairs now."

Tawn looked at Harris with a smirk. "Some people need extra incentive. Mr. Falburn, if you'd care to take us to a supply of water and some sunshields, we'll get this operation underway."

"I'm begging you to please wait another forty minutes."

The threesome walked into the room with the captors.

Harris gestured to the people lying on the floor. "The lot of you get up. And you come with me."

The smallest among them was taken to the hall where the remains of his comrades lay. "Grab that arm and the rest of that leg."

The man replied, "What?"

Harris pushed his shoulder. "Pick them up, moron. And hurry."

The man complied, reluctantly. His eyes averting from the massacre before him.

"Now we go to the steps. This is your lucky day."

Harris opened the door. "Down."

The man looked up. "What do you want me to do with these?"

Harris sighed. "You take them down with you. Show all your friends. Remind them of what will happen if any of them come up these steps. You'll all want to go back to your other buildings and stay there.

"If your forces come back, well, you're obviously free. If you see my face, one of two things will happen. I'll be feeling generous and leave you as you are, or I won't be feeling generous, and you can guess the outcome. I'm giving you the option of setting how I feel by how you behave while I'm gone."

The door to the stairs was closed as the lone captor descended carrying a severed arm and leg. A supply of water was gathered along with eight sunshields.

Harris stood in front of Trish Boleman and her twin brother Gandy. "Here's what we need you to do. You'll be staying in the reactor room. If you hear anyone out in the hall and it's not Tawn or myself, you fire a couple rounds into that reactor. And yes, that probably means you're dead."

Tawn added, "And before you ask, if you have to ask, you're doing this for your planet. This is for all Domicile. We stop this here and we stop the war from returning. Consider yourselves soldiers now. Millions are counting on you to protect them. Are you willing to sacrifice it all should the time come?"

Gandy stood, bracing his rifle. "We are!"

Trish frowned. "Not what I thought I was signing up for, but I'll do my part. Just make sure you do yours and you come back."

Harris placed his hand on her shoulder. "We'll be back before you know it. Just remember, you hear a voice that's not mine or hers, you take down that reactor."

The Boleman twins nodded.

The sunshields were little more than reflective robes. Vents allowed building up heat to escape while allowing outside air to circulate in. The robes topped out to an umbrella like hood that spanned just over a meter outward in each direction.

The water supply was frozen before being stuffed into insulating containers. Those were loaded on two fat-wheeled carts. The captives would pull the carts behind them until a third of the water supply had been consumed. At that point, Tawn and Harris would each don packs with another four liters of the life-sustaining substance. The captives would be sent back with the rest.

The door to outside was opened. The heat immediately let itself be known. Groans from the captives told of their trepidation.

Harris turned to Daniel. "I know the direction. You know which path was taken by your people. Point me toward them. And keep in mind, lies are not tolerated. And that goes for the rest of you as well."

Daniel pointed. "They went this way. It's twenty kilometers further, but the terrain along the last half is easier. This way and we get you to Barner's Ridge at about the halfway point. You'll have to make your way up and over that on your own. We can't pull this water up those rocks."

Harris nodded. "We go this way then. And when we hit that ridge, the rest of you can come back. Just keep in mind, the quicker we get there, the sooner you're coming home. The two we left behind will let you go through the door and down the steps. You go near that room and you lose your reactor. Got it?"

Daniel nodded. "Got it."

Tawn waved her hand. "Let's hustle up, then. We have a lot of ground to cover."

Tawn and Harris broke into a slow jog as the others complained, attempting to keep up. The repeated promise of sunshields being taken and their roasting bodies discarded added incentive. Seventy-three kilometers were covered before the ridge was reached. The sun had long set.

Daniel pointed after taking a large swig of water. "Path goes up through there and then over. If you survive you should join up with the other trail about three kilometers from the colony. In about four standard hours the sun will be coming up. We're on eighteen hour days here."

Tawn said, "That leaves you in the sun for a couple hours on the way back. I'd say you'll want to get a move on."

Daniel nodded as he took another drink. "It's early sun, which is far better than late sun. Still, our chances are not good."

Tawn waved her hand as she pulled a pack of water up under her reflective robe. "I'd wish you luck but I'd just be lying."

The Biomarines turned toward the ridge, leaving the Earthers to fend for themselves.

"That looks like a decent climb. You think they'll make it back?"

Harris nodded. "I'm sure he was padding the amount of water they needed. They'll have more than enough. I'd be more worried if I was one of the others with him. They start running short and there won't be any drawing straws to see who gets dumped."

Tawn glanced back at the six men who were hurrying away. "They'll make it. They've been out here long enough to know what they can and can't do. I'm more worried about our first mates when they do get back. That guy will be trying something. He's not gonna sit and wait to see what happens."

The trek up onto the ridge was difficult, but manageable by the two genetically engineered humans. The total transit took less than two hours, putting them back on somewhat flat terrain for the remainder of their hike. The previous slow jog turned into a marathon-like pace.

Tawn asked as they ran, "How you holding up?"

"Good. This night heat isn't as bad as I thought it would be."

Tawn smirked. "Not the heat that'll get ya. It's the lack of humidity. I know we were climbing back there, but I've used almost half my water. Not gonna get cooler when that sun comes up."

"I'm down a liter. Getting close to loading up though."

Tawn looked around. "All this desolation... who in their right mind would want to live down here?"

Harris laughed. "Not me. I'd much rather be hanging out at the Luxus. And I could use a trip to the Emporium about now. Steaks and eggs for breakfast. A big pile of 'em. That would hit the spot."

Tawn frowned. "Thanks. Now I'm hungry."

Harris pointed to the side of the trail. Plenty of rocks down there... you could get your iron intake for the week."

Tawn half smiled. "Actually I was thinking about the nice fat calf of a fellow Biomarine. You'd cook up pretty quick out here."

Harris laughed. "Never took you for a cannibal."

"Probably would never have considered it until you told your Helm story with the blood drinking. When it comes down to it I guess it's all about survival, isn't it? And when you're desperate, you'll eat just about anything, no matter how disgusting."

Harris chuckled. "You implying I'm disgusting?"

Tawn shrugged. "Don't know... yet, but I would have to assume."

Harris looked his business partner up and down. "You might not be a bad eat. Got a few extra pounds on you. That added fat adds flavor, you know."

Tawn shook her head. "How about a new subject before you start thinking about this too much."

Harris laughed as he reached back, pulling a liter bottle from his pack. "Fair enough. Although, you know what would be great right now? A big dip in a cool bath in one of those Luxus soaker tubs. And a bucket of chicken. I could get into that."

Tawn did her best to hold in a laugh, instead releasing a sigh. "At least you keep it entertaining. I can't tell you how many stumps I was assigned with who had the conversational ability of a dead bogler. You'd have made a good squad partner back in the day."

Harris shook his head. "You might want another sip of that water. You're starting to sound delirious."

The morning sun was soon peeking over the horizon. A flap had to be lowered to prevent the heavy infrared rays from baking the skin on their faces and damaging their eyes.

Tawn gave status. "Ninety minutes to go. How's your water?"

"Half a liter. How about you?"

"The same. Lips are getting crusty from the dry and the dust. Could have really made use of some lip balm."

Harris nodded. "Same here. Feels like I stuck them on a grill beside a nice T-Bone."

Tawn winced. "Uh. Why'd you have to mention food again? I'm starving... what kind of sauce you put on that steak?"

Harris pulled back. "What? You'd ruin a good steak with sauce? Not me. I like the natural charred flavor of a nice rare cut. Slap it on a hot grill for a minute a side then drop it on a plate. And get out of my way because that knife and fork will be flying. Add a big stack of fresh mashed potatoes... and some asparagus. Now we're talking about a meal."

Tawn slowly shook her head. "Should have figured you for asparagus. I know that's an original Earth food along with the potato, but bleh, what an awful texture and taste."

Harris replied with a half scowl. "You don't like asparagus? What are you... a New Earther?"

"Now, let's not be insulting. If you're gonna talk food, at least make it something good. Maybe a nice hot loaf of camber bread, butter, and honey."

Harris nodded. "I could get behind that. Tack on a six pack of Amber ales and we're... loafing, I guess. What would you call eating that for a meal?"

Tawn smiled to a cracking lip. "Mmm. Loafing would be good."

Harris asked, "How are your eyes doing?"

"Not bad. I've been squinting for the last couple hours. That seems to help."

Harris reached for his remaining water, pulling his hand back to his side. "Sorry. I meant to mention that to you back when we started. One of our tricks from back on Helm. Don't know if it actually helped, but we lived."

"Nice of you to mention it about ten hours too late. And if your body is telling you to drink that water you should have at it. It's not doing you any good in that bottle. Drinking it down now doesn't mean you'll be worse off later. If you need it, you need it."

Harris pulled the bottle, downing his last half liter with several big gulps. The bottle was placed back in the pack.

Tawn giggled. "I can't believe you fell for that."

Harris glared. "You saying that was a mistake?"

Tawn burst into a laugh. "Relax. I'm just jerking you around. Call it a payback for talking about food. If you needed the water you needed it."

Harris asked, "You gonna drink yours?"

Tawn shook her head. "Don't need it yet."

Harris scowled. "Yeah, right. You need it just as much as I did."

"Not yet. I'm stubborn like that. We should be on our last fifteen kilometers in ten minutes. I'll down it then."

The time came and passed with the remaining water being consumed. The morning sun, now well off the horizon, was beating down hard. The two less than optimally conditioned Biomarines kept up their pace. The final hour was grueling, with both accepting that their bodies were no longer suited for such a mission. The trail ended as it merged back into the one coming from the north.

Tawn checked the ground. "No sign of two hundred soldiers coming through here."

Harris looked down the trail. "Three kilometers... we can be there in a few minutes. They have water."

Tawn frowned as she looked down the trail the other way. "See that dust rising? That would be our assault force."

Harris pointed toward a close hill. "Over here. Gives us a view of this whole area. They move this way it's into our firing zone. This is where you prove out those Level 4 sniper stripes."

The two person team moved up the hill, taking position behind a group of protruding rocks.

Tawn took a deep breath. "Aw, that is just scorching. I sure could have used an extra liter of water."

"Let's hope this fight doesn't drag on."

Tawn scowled. "Two hundred of them. It's not gonna go fast. And I know we have a couple thousand rounds between us, but we need to use them sparingly."

The first of the soldiers came into view. Reflective silver biosuits glistened in the bright sun. They ran in unison to a medium paced jog.

Tawn huffed as she looked over the troops through the scope on her repeater. "Those suits keep in all the moisture. They're probably as hydrated as the minute they left."

Harris grinned. "Makes them an easy target, though. All we have to do is hit or damage those suits and they're toast. Literally."

Tawn glared. "Says the man with a big fat shiny umbrella on his head."

"I guess we're gonna have to lose these, aren't we."

Tawn pulled hers from its mount. "See if you can position it on the rocks. That sun is behind us. At least that's one advantage."

Harris grimaced as the reflected heat from his surroundings began to cook the skin on his otherwise bald head.

Tawn laughed. "Don't be an idiot, at least pull your hood on."

Two minutes later, the front of the jogging column was easily within range.

Tawn took aim. "I've always found these weapons to hit a bit low at this distance. Aim for just above their heads. Once they reach that rock, you can aim for whatever you normally would."

Harris chuckled. "I have shot these a time or two you know."

Tawn smiled as she squeezed off the first round. "Not at level 4 you haven't."

The head of the lead soldier exploded. Damaging the biosuit of the soldier beside him. Harris was next, catching his victim square in the chest. Another dozen rounds exited their rifles as the New Earth invaders scrambled for what little cover the sandy desert had to offer.

A second dozen hits followed the first before their position was located. A hundred plasma rounds at once dug into the front of the hill or passed over their heads. Tawn Freely and Harris Gruberg continued their relentless and deadly accurate barrage of plasma fire. The attackers were soon in retreat.

Harris held back from a shot as Tawn took another three, all striking their victims and ending their potential raid of the nearby community.

Harris shook his head. "That is uncanny."

Tawn shrugged. "After the first few shots I have a good feel for where the round will go. See that last guy who's slowed to a walk?"

Harris chuckled. "That's eighteen hundred meters if not more. These weapons aren't meant to be that accurate."

Tawn took careful aim, squeezing off a round. A blue bolt of plasma moved across the expanse with a slight arc, striking the soldier center back, the result being his chest exploding out onto the ground in front of him.

Harris's mouth remained open. "That was an impossible shot. How'd you do that?"

Tawn grinned. "That was actually luck. Didn't think I'd actually hit him from here. Was hoping to get close so I could grumble about what a crappy weapon the repeater is for sniping."

"You still feeling lucky?"

"Not lucky like that."

Harris sighed. "Now's when it gets hard for us."

"Why?"

"Why? Because we're sitting in this oven with no water while they're down there dickering about what their next move will be. We could be sitting here for an hour before that happens. Not sure I have an hour left in me."

Tawn looked through her scope. "You know what I'm thinking about right now?"

"How would I know that?"

"I'm thinking about the *Kingfisher* and all the cool water she has aboard. She's just the other side of that colony. About five clicks from here. We could probably make that in fifteen minutes if we sprinted. Too bad that stupid dog of yours couldn't bring us some water."

Harris replied, "That may not be an impossibility. Although I don't know how his chassis would hold up in this heat. Tell you what, I'll send him the command and we'll see what happens. If we die out here anyway, it's not like it will matter."

Tawn said, "There's an alternative."

"What's that?"

"You walk into town and bring us back water."

Harris winced. "Not leaving you out here. That's still a hundred fifty soldiers down there. They charge this hill and you're dead. Probably making plans as we speak to do just that. Besides, what are the chances any of them will open the door for me when I get there?"

Harris lifted his arm. "Farker, this is your master. I need you to bring two cold liters of water to the following coordinates. And bring them in an insulated bag."

Tawn chuckled. "You think that dog can figure that out?"

Harris replied, "Depends on how smart his programming is. What I'm more worried about is did he even receive it. We're at the max distance for this signal bracelet I use to comm with him, and the Earthers said they were jamming. It's on a different frequency than our comms, so maybe we get lucky. Remind me to upgrade it to something decent when we make it out of here."

Chapter 22

The attackers split into four groups, three of which began to move parallel to the position on the hill.

Tawn scowled. "Don't like this. They get in behind us and we lose most of our cover."

"Options?" Harris replied.

"We could run. Going into town would be bad. What are the odds we could lead them around the outskirts and back to our ships? You have that railgun. Pop out a few rounds from that and we mop up the whole group."

Harris glanced back at the desert behind them. "You think they'd follow?"

Tawn shook her head. "Not a chance. They would split with half that crew heading in to complete their mission in town. At least that's what I would do if I was commanding."

Harris took careful aim, squeezing off a round at a group moving at just over two kilometers away. The round impacted the sand a hundred meters short of their position.

Tawn laughed. "Level 4 you aren't. Want me to show you how it's done?"

"You feeling lucky?"

Tawn took aim, raising her sights slightly above the intended targets. A plasma round zipped out, blowing a stream of hot sand up near the middle of the running group.

"Bah. Crappy weapons."

Harris laughed. "Still impressive."

The four groups of New Earth invaders came to a stop at the same time.

Harris said, "Here we go."

"I'll take these two groups behind us. You take the two in front."

Harris nodded. "Consider them dead."

The attack began from all four groups at once. The soldiers spread out, zig-zagging in random patterns as they fired the occasional round at the hill. Tawn and Harris opened up when they had reached twelve hundred meters. Every fifth shot was finding its mark.

Thirty members of the assault force had fallen before the others reached the base of the small hill. Plasma rounds from the opposing weapons gained accuracy as they closed in, with several striking the rocks next to where Harris held his firing position. Shrapnel punched a number of holes into his sunshield.

"Getting hot up here!"

Tawn replied, "Just keep shooting. We have them pinned down at the moment."

Harris said, "We can't outlast them. My shield is getting shredded."

"You suggesting we charge down?"

Harris thought for a moment. "They may not be expecting that. We head down your side we have fifty meters of cover. That's most of the way."

Tawn said, "You move, I'll follow."

Harris stood. Crouching over, he sprinted for a line of rocks leading three quarters of the way down the hill. Tawn ran after, all the while firing her repeating plasma rifle into the group gathered at the base below them.

The short run saw multiple plasma strikes on the terrain surrounding the runners. After diving and rolling the final twenty meters as plasma bolts slipped over their heads, the two came to rest behind a large boulder.

Harris glanced over at the heavily breathing Tawn. "Burns the lungs doesn't it. I say we put an end to these pukes and get our asses off this insanely hot planet."

Tawn nodded. "Lead the way."

A mad dash had the duo closing in on the thirty-four New Earth soldiers who inhabited their side of the hill. Harris stayed low as Tawn moved her way up the hill slightly to give her a better firing position.

In the course of the few minutes that followed, sixteen of the thirty-eight invaders found their lives at an end. The aim of the Biomarines made them deadly. The continuous movement made them near impossible targets. The New Earth squad commander called for a retreat.

Tawn yelled, "Make your move now! We've got them!"

Half of the retreating men fell silent before the others joined with the next group.

Harris gestured back toward where they had come from. "We make those rocks or we're dead. Those other groups will be reaching the hilltop any second now."

After another short run, the team found themselves huddled between two rocks.

Tawn said as she took heavy breaths. "That was one heckuva charge back there. Worthy of having a story told to the hillbillies back on Farmingdale."

"Squat down. Take advantage of this shade for a minute."

Harris stood, running ten meters to the dead body of an Earther, dragging it back to beside Tawn.

Tawn chuckled. "You planning to pull a vampire on him?"

Harris shook his head. "Don't have the filter here for that. What I want to do is see if he has any kind of water supply."

Tawn nodded. "You check for that while I look for a comm. Maybe we can work up a truce."

Harris laughed. "Good one. We're badly outnumbered and outpositioned. They rush us again and we're goners."

Harris growled. "Nothing. Looks like the suit keeps that all internal. The open sections are already completely drying up. What's it been, three or four minutes of exposure?"

Plasma rounds began to dot the grounds going out from their position. Harris looked out from behind the rock where they had taken refuge. A medium-size gray mechanical dog darted back and forth across the sands as they exploded upward. The robotic pet named Farker carried a satchel in his mouth.

Harris shook his head. "You believing this?"

The dog dodged a final few rounds as it entered the rock formation surrounding them.

Harris took the satchel as the loyal pet sat, wagging its mechanical nub of a tail. The satchel was practically ripped open, revealing two liters of cold water. Both Biomarines turned the containers up, swigging down the precious liquid with large gulps.

Harris grinned as he reached out to pet his friend and savior. He pulled his hand back with a frown as the synthetic fur coat began to come off in his hand. A brush of the side of the dog left it with the appearance of mange. Harris gestured for the dog to move into the shade.

"He's gonna look hideous by the time we're done here."

Tawn chuckled. "Kind of like us?"

Harris looked at his dog. "We'll heal. He'll have to be repaired."

Tawn flipped up the visor on the helmet she had removed from the fallen Earther. "I can hear their comm, but there's no way I can use it. Can't get that little helmet over my big head. Same for you."

Harris held out his hand. "Let me see it."

The helmet was flipped over repeatedly as Harris took stock of its structure. Placing the headpiece between two rocks, the heavy Biomarine stood. A jump up and a hard kick by his boots saw the biosuit helmet split into three pieces.

Harris handed them back. "There. Let's see how your negotiating skills are."

Tawn looked over the three sections. "Won't make a difference now. You killed it. It's dead."

Harris shrugged. "Not like we could have used it otherwise. You willing to attempt your sniping on those above us?"

Tawn scowled. "Problem is, at this distance they can do the same. With that many rifles they're likely to get in at least one good shot."

Harris grinned. "I'd say that leaves us with three options. We stay here and take a beating. We charge up that hill and try to take it back. Or we head out the way Farker just came in, hoping to dodge everything they throw at us."

"Option two."

Harris raised an eyebrow. "Hilltop charge? I'd place that at our lowest probability of success. That's about thirty people up there. And the ones to the right and left of us will be firing at our backs the whole way up. And we have twenty meters of open to cross before we have any semblance of cover."

Tawn looked at Farker. "All we need for that is a distraction. Three or four seconds and we're on our way."

Harris frowned. "You want to send my dog out to draw fire? After he just saved our lives by bringing water?"

Tawn shook her head. "It's not alive. It's mechanical. And yes, I want to send your dog out there to draw fire. We make it to those rocks and we have a shot at charging all the way up. And I tell you what... we make it out because of this he can hump my leg as long as his robotic heart desires."

Harris turned to face his pet. "You up for this, boy?"

Three farks were returned.

"When I give the word, I want you to race back out across that sand. You're objective is to get shot at, but not hit. You got that?"

Three farks were again returned.

Harris laughed. "I almost believe he understood that."

"Yeah, well get your ass together because we're going in five. That group to the left is starting to move this way."

Harris gave the order. "Go get 'em, boy."

The dog ran out into the open. Turned as sharply as it could in the sand. Multiple plasma rounds rained in from all three positions.

214

Tawn yelled, "Move it!"

The Biomarines jumped into the exposed area together, each racing up the twenty meters to the next set of rocks. A flood of plasma rounds came their way. Tawn lay prone, poking her plasma weapon around a low corner of the rock to her left as she quickly ripped off three rounds, ending the lives of three soldiers who decided it was time to rush forward.

Harris continued his climb as shrapnel from the rocks around them ricocheted and bounced. Down on the sand, Farker turned and darted, continuing to draw fire before a round exploded in the sand under him. The robotic canine rose five meters into the air before falling back and going silent.

Harris glanced back with a scowl before turning his wrath toward the occupiers atop the hill. A relentless assault of two shots fired followed by a quick move, propelled him up the slope as Tawn continued her sniping of the two groups who remained at the hill's base.

As the upward charge continued, a plasma round entered a rock beside the stump. Shrapnel blasted outward, shredding the sunshield on the right side of his body. The intense heat of the Eden sun began to sink into his skin. Harris pushed his shoulder into the one spot that offered a moment's shade, before popping up to continue his assault.

One by one the occupiers were picked off as the genetically-engineered warrior showed his worth. When the count on top had dropped to two dozen remaining, the squad commander ordered a retreat. Harris raced forward, reclaiming his prior position.

Round after round of plasma bolts found the backs of the retreating force with the last falling before reaching the base of the hill. With the top retaken and the retreating group finished, Harris turned his fight toward the lower groups. From his new position, many were exposed and began to pay the price.

The lower groups signaled retreat. Tawn Freely stood with her weapon, firing into their backs as they ran. As the fleeing men streaked back across the expanse toward the trail from whence they had originally come. Harris lowered his rifle.

214

"Tawn? You OK down there?"

"I am," Tawn yelled back. You?"

Harris glanced down at his reddening shoulder. "Shield is half gone. Gotta get out of this sun... and fast."

Tawn climbed the final few feet to his position. "How many we got left?"

Harris replied as he looked back down at the sands where his pet lay motionless. "I count close to fifty."

Tawn nodded. "Impressive charge. That's one for the history books for sure. Looks like they're heading back out on the trail."

Tawn turned to look at her partner. "Wow. You shoulder is already blistering. We need to get you some cover."

Harris reached down, picking up the upper torso of a fallen Earther. The arms were snapped off and the suit split open. One half was used as a shield against the merciless sun.

"Let's go collect my dog."

As they walked toward the downed animal, Tawn said. "We should hustle over to the ships, come back and collect the weapons, and then catch the rest of those troops on their way back. If they surrender their weapons we'll let them go. After that we pick up Trish and Gandy."

Harris sighed as he leaned down to collect his defunct pet. "Hope they're OK. Wasn't exactly a good situation to leave them in. They aren't trained to deal with conflict like that. I thought Gandy would faint when he saw the first dead body."

The sprint back to the ships took twenty-five minutes. The two retired, Zwicker Class warships lifted into the hot Eden air, setting down beside the hill several minutes later. The area was scanned and the weapons collected. The bodies of the fallen were left to bake in the extreme sun.

A second run was made to catch the retreating troops. A single blast from the railgun of the *Bangor* was followed by a complete surrender. Again the weapons were collected. The captives were sent on their way. The two ships landed only meters from the Boxton compound.

Tawn and Harris entered the building to an immediate call for their surrender.

A call came from the first hall. "We have your people. Give up your weapons."

Harris stood just outside the door exiting the welcome room. "Not gonna happen. And we have news for you about your assault. It failed. The last of your people are headed back this way. You turn over our people and your weapons and we'll leave you alone. Otherwise you all die here."

The voice replied, "How you figure? We have you outnumbered and we have your people!"

Tawn shook her head. "If you'd like we can go collect the fifty of your people who are still alive out there and bring them back here for an exchange. Hows that sound."

"Sounds like you're in the weak position. Our demand stands as it is."

Harris replied, "Fine then. Be stubborn. I would suggest you move away from your reactor room though. It will be open to the sun in a couple minutes. My ship has a weapon aboard. A powerful weapon. I take out that reactor and you're all dead. How's that sound?"

The voice laughed. "Your ships are no longer yours! We have them surrounded!"

Tawn sighed. "Bad move on your part."

She turned to face Harris. "You want the inside or the out?"

Harris thought. "As much as I'd rather stay in the cool. I'll take the ships. I'll signal you when I'm in the air. Maybe a well placed tungsten round or two will convince them they're the ones with the weak hand."

Harris cracked the door going out only to be greeted with several plasma rounds impacting the walls beside the door.

He stepped back. "Looks like another rush job. When I fling this open, expect a few rounds to come through."

Tawn grinned. "Won't much care. I'll be moving in three to four seconds."

The Biomarine slug dove into the hall, firing as she rolled toward the far wall. At the same moment, Harris yanked the door going out wide open. Two additional plasma rounds struck the exterior concrete wall as a third came through the door. With a short run, Harris made his own dive out into sand. Two plasma rounds found their targets as he pushed himself to his feet with his left hand while firing with his right.

Two of the eight men guarding the ships lay dead, their chests blown out through the back of their rib cages. Harris stood against the near hull of the *Bangor*.

Tawn came over the comm. "How's it going out there?"

Harris replied, "I'm out. I just need to push them around a corner so I can get in the ship. How about you?"

"I took out three. Have them pushed back to the main hall. They have the angles on me from here. I'm kinda stuck."

Harris chuckled. "Well unstick yourself. We need control of that reactor room. You can threaten to shut it down, even if only temporarily. Let that temperature rise in there and they'll be begging to give up Trish and Gandy. This fight comes down to life and death. And my guess is they all want to live."

Harris ran, dove, and rolled up into a shooting stance, taking out the stunned Earther who was guarding that particular corner. Two additional steps had the back side of the ship cleared as the men attempting to hold it scampered around a far corner. The hatch slid open and Harris hopped inside.

The *Bangor* lifted, tilting down to take aim at an adjacent building. "Tawn. I have the ship."

Several seconds passed before Tawn replied, "They got the drop on me. Came through a hidden door."

Harris replied, "Tell whomever is in command I have one of their buildings in my sight. They have fifteen seconds or it gets destroyed."

Tawn again gave a delayed reply. "Guess you have to destroy it. They said no."

Harris pressed the trigger. A thunderous explosion shook the compound. The building that had once housed a supply room, now showed as a five meter deep crater. The hallway beneath it collapsed.

Chapter 23

Harris opened a comm. "They have another dozen buildings and I have plenty of rounds. The choice is they surrender the three of you or I destroy these buildings one by one. And if any of you are injured or killed by their hand during that process, they will all die. Including the fifty still out on the trail."

The comm was silent for almost thirty seconds.

Tawn said, "They want to know what assurance they have that you won't kill them all if they release us."

Harris laughed. "None. What they have is my word. A word that already spared the lives of fifty of their friends. That's all the assurance I can offer. That next building goes in about twenty seconds."

After another moment of silence, Tawn replied, "We're coming out. Trish and Gandy are OK."

Harris asked, "With the weapons?"

"With the weapons."

"Tell them to signal their team outside to lay their arms down in front of your hatch door. We'll leave once they are disarmed. And I would advise them to all make their way back to the spaceport for a ride home. And tell them we're willing to provide that ride should they accept."

Seconds later, Tawn stepped aboard the *Kingfisher*. "How we gonna do that?"

"We have a thirty-two passenger shuttle do we not?"

Tawn scowled. "We don't. The Retreat does."

Harris replied, "We'll I'm sure the foundation wouldn't mind us borrowing it for a worthy cause."

Trish stepped in from the heat. "That is insane out there. What happened to you? You look like you came out of a deep-fryer."

Harris nodded. "Got caught out in the sun a bit longer than I was hoping. But it looks like we accomplished what we came here to do. We have the weapons and the threat to Eden is diminished. They treat you OK in there?"

Trish returned a half scowl. "They did, but I've decided being a hostage is not my thing."

"How'd they get control of you?"

Trish sat in the copilot's chair. "They turned off our lights and told us the oxygen and cooling were next. I tried to bluff about destroying the reactor, but they wouldn't bite."

Harris nodded. "A bluff during war is only as good as your willingness to see it through."

Trish half smiled, "Yeah well, I'm new to this war thing."

Tawn stepped back into the cabin of the *Bangor*. "I offered the ride. They declined. Gandy performed a scan for plasma charges. Looks like we have them all. Might be best if we just leave."

Trish added. "I like the sound of that."

Harris replied, "See you up top for a jump back to our space."

Tawn hopped out into the blazing heat of the midday sun, hurrying over to the *Kingfisher*. The two ships began to lift from the compound.

A comm came in from the pacifists at Dove. "*Bangor* and *Kingfisher*. This is the port director at Dove, speaking for the government of the planet of Eden. Your violent methods are not welcome here. You have chosen to violate our covenants, and from that a unanimous ruling by our council has been passed down. Both ships and their registered crews are hereby banned from Eden proper and Eden space.

"Any further intrusions into Eden space will be met with a stern warning, a citation and a fine. And please recognize that while pacifists, we are not above incarceration. We ask that you immediately comply with this ruling and as always... that you go in peace."

Harris chuckled. "Well there go my dreams of being a pacifist."

Trish replied, "You act like you enjoyed all that. Even your crusty smile says so."

"It's not that Tawn and I love war. Heck, we'd both prefer to not have to fight just as much as anyone. But if someone is insistent on bringing it to us, well, it's what we were made to do. We're warriors and we fight wars. We trained our whole lives to do so. I'd much rather be gorging myself at the buffet than having my skin roasted off in some extreme climate while hostiles are trying to kill me."

A wormhole opened and the two centuries-old ships passed through.

***

Harris sat in his soaker-tub, with bubbles covering the surface and a cigar in his mouth. A half eaten bucket of chicken sat at the tub's edge.

Tawn walked in. "Figured I'd find you here."

"Man's gotta recover from the stresses of war. And thanks for knocking. Chicken?"

Tawn chuckled. "The door was unlocked. And thanks, I'll have a drumstick."

Harris nodded as he passed the bucket. "Yeah, I just leave it that way. The staff is in and out of here so much, I just decided not to bother locking it anymore. Not like I have visitors... usually. What's happening in slug-ville?"

Tawn looked around, taking the only seat available, on the toilet. "I'm guessing you haven't been watching the news."

"I do my best to avoid it. I think we'd all be happier without listening to all the negative things that go on. Something special happen?"

Tawn took in and let out a deep breath as she studied the ornate crown molding of the luxury suite's bathroom. "I checked those weapons we confiscated from Eden. As we suspected, they were ours. The serial numbers matched up to our manifests."

Harris sat up. "Please tell me you haven't been holding on to those. That's hard evidence against us should you get searched."

"I have. Not sure why, but something told me I should. Anyway, I'm certain Baxter held onto her copies. If she wants something at some future date, she'll come demanding our help."

"I knew that one was bad from the start, but I was desperate."

Tawn chuckled. "We both were."

Harris puffed on his cigar. "Well, you came in here for a reason. Spit it out. What's our trouble?"

Tawn set down her drumstick after stripping it of meat. "Eden. Reports are all over the news that the pacifists slaughtered a group of settlers. New Earth is demanding to send in a delegation to check the facts."

Harris threw up a hand, splattering bubbles across the floor. "So let them look. Any investigation will find the truth as to why we went in there. The Earthers had weapons and we stopped an invasion and takeover."

"You seriously think that's what will be reported? First, there's no evidence of the Earthers having weapons. We took them. Second, there's no evidence of an invasion of Dove. What there is evidence of is an attack on the Earther colony, by us. And there's evidence that a railgun was used to destroy a building. A railgun fired from a ship owned by us."

"So what are you proposing we do?"

Tawn shook her head. "Not proposing anything. I just think we've been running around like a couple wild boglers leaving our hoofprints everywhere. I almost wonder if we shouldn't burn those two ships and get a couple fake identities. Something that would let us disappear."

Harris flipped on the display hanging on his bathroom wall. "There. They're discussing a three colony trade deal. Our news has probably seen its fifteen minutes of fame."

The next reporter came onscreen with a *Breaking News* banner scrolling above her head. "We're receiving reports of violence at the Retison colony. It appears a town populated by Domicile citizens has been overrun and demolished by an angry hoard of Earthers. Earthers who were out for revenge for the supposed Eden massacre."

Tawn looked over. "I'm betting if we go to Retison we find a cache of weapons out there that went through our company to the outer colonies. Bax played us. We're the cause of this."

"Let me guess, Retison is another of the truce colonies? And we're not the cause of this, but we might be the trigger that made those people take action."

"I think you should disable that railgun and sell the *Bangor*. Maybe even scrap her."

Harris huffed. "That's not gonna happen. You need a different plan."

Tawn stood and began to pace. "OK, how about we jump the *Bangor* into the sun out there... and I'll sell you the *Kingfisher*. She's got a clean record. She's even registered to Gandy Boleman still. No tie-in to either you or me. It's the same ship, only in better shape."

Harris stood, grabbing a towel from a rack. "Not selling or destroying the *Bangor*. That's the only real home Farker knows."

Tawn returned a frustrated chuckle. "How is Farker?"

"He gets out of the shop tomorrow. His parts are ancient and they've been having trouble finding equivalent replacements. The techs are all stunned that such a machine even exists, and that it's somebody's pet."

Harris pulled on a pair of skivvies followed by military issue, surplus trousers. A tight t-shirt sporting the name and emblem of the Emporium Buffet was pulled over his barrel chest.

Tawn laughed. "Where'd you get that from? I thought they banned you."

224

"I agreed to mind my manners next time I was there, and to wear this shirt as advertisement when I'm walking around the promenade."

Tawn shook her head. "Half your face and neck are covered with blisters and scabs from Eden. Not sure you walking around with an emporium shirt is the best of advertising. You're sort of extra-hideous right now."

Harris smiled. "Thank you for the kind words. And I'm heading over there right now. Trish will be joining us if you want to come."

Tawn scowled, but the thought of the buffet brought her back to the reality that was hers. She was a slug and she liked to eat.

"Let me comm Gandy. He can meet us there."

Tawn took one final glance at the news feed on the display. "This is gonna blow up on us. I know it."

"Not before we eat. Let's go."

***

Harris sat down with his fourth plate. Trish looked at him with disgust. The young manager stood not far away with a scowl on his face as the image of the ghastly-looking stump kept the tables around him empty.

"These ribs are just delicious. Trish, have another rib. Put some meat on those skinny bones."

The young woman slowly shook her head. "No thanks, Mr. G. You're having more than enough for both of us."

Tawn set the bone from a turkey leg down on her plate. "That's not good."

Gandy asked, "What?"

Tawn pointed. "The news feed says the military is threatening to send a fleet to Eden if the New Earthers send a delegation. This whole thing could erupt into a new war."

224

Harris licked barbecue sauce from his bulbous fingers. "Not before we finish eating. I'm paying for this, so let's get my money's worth."

Trish said, "If there is war, wouldn't you two get reactivated?"

Harris stopped mid chew, setting an unfinished rib gently on his plate. "We signed agreements that we were out. There weren't any clauses about recall or reactivation. At least none that I saw."

Trish replied, "So if we go to war with New Earth, you aren't willing to fight?"

Harris turned. "I didn't say that. All I said was they can't just recall me."

Tawn rubbed the back of her neck as she sat back. "Out processing papers only said you were out. Was nothing there saying they couldn't call us back. I would bet there's a document we blindly signed way back that states they own us during time of war. Not that I want to fight either, but if needed, I'll go."

Harris dug into his rib.

Trish laughed. "You're not done, I take it?"

Harris shook his head as he chewed. "Not if this might be my last meal as a free man. Gonna be tough going back to that slop on the chow lines."

Tawn gave an odd grin. "I actually find myself missing that sometimes."

Harris looked up. "That's because you're defective."

When the meal was finished the group headed for the exit, escorted by the young manager. "What happened to you? Did you fall in a blender?"

Harris shook his head. "Nah. Stayed too long in a blast furnace. Almost got cooked to death. What happened to you?"

The manager turned away with a huff as he pulled his tie straight.

The foursome stood out on the promenade sidewalk as two men in military uniforms hurriedly approached their location.

Harris frowned. "This doesn't look good."

One of the men nodded as he passed. "Excuse me, sir."

Seconds later they interrupted a woman coming out of a shop, causing her to drop a package. One of the men picked it up as the woman stared.

The other said, "Sorry, ma'am. We just got called up. Looks like it may be war for Eden."

Harris said, "Trish, I may be joining you on the ship tonight."

Tawn added, "Same here, Gandy. I think we stay close if for some reason we need to move."

Trish asked, "And what are we going to do if war is declared?"

Harris shrugged. "Don't know, but I'd like to be on the *Bangor* if that happens. Gives me options."

Tawn nodded. "Same here. *Kingfisher* gives us options as well."

When the foursome arrived at the adjoining slips, Baxter Rumford was waiting. "You two had to go and screw things up. Not sure what force you took down there, but that Eden operation would have been over and no one the wiser without your interference. Now you've got both sides riled up."

Tawn said, "I should snap your neck for getting us involved in this. Traitor is exactly what you are."

Bax laughed. "As are the two of you. Living your fat lives by arming the outer colonies? And don't tell me you didn't have suspicions about where those weapons were going."

Harris crossed his arms. "How do we stop this?"

Bax smirked. "Don't know that it can be stopped. The Earthers want control of Eden. We both know why. Them and the Domers both know why. And your Domers have no stomach for war. And what on New Earth happened to your face? Somebody hit you with a flamethrower?"

"Just a mild sunburn. And you called us Domers, that mean you're actually from New Earth?"

Bax huffed. "Not that dump. Was born here, but I consider myself more of a galactic citizen than one of either of these two backward operations."

Tawn said, "You're a galactic ass is what you are. People are dying as a direct result of your actions."

Bax smirked. "And you two are the ones killing them."

Harris asked, "You here for a reason?"

"Here to tell you two to sit tight. My people had a team move in behind you on Eden and your issues of showing up in their logs or being seen at all have been taken care of."

Tawn sighed. "You saying the pacifists are dead?"

"The pacifists are now living off in their extra-planetary nirvana or wherever it is they believed their afterlife would take them. The New Earth settlers are now in control of Eden and the planet is about to see a titanium mining boom.

"Just this morning I bought options for shares in the Earther mining company that will be receiving the contract. Within a year, there will be a hundred thousand New Earth miners out there scratching out a living. And I'll be sitting atop a huge pile of credits.

"Have you ever been to New Earth? It's kind of a pit overall, but there are a handful of nice places. And as a galactic citizen, I can jump between both sides at will. I see exciting things coming up for Baxter Rumford."

Tawn glared. "More likely you'll see the outside of an airlock. And no one will care."

Bax returned a phony hurt gaze as she clutched her chest. "You just crush my tender heart, slug. You should be grateful I gave you the opportunity to make some credits. And just so you know, if it hadn't been the two of you, it would have been two other morons. There are plenty of broke people out there willing to do whatever is asked for a little pay."

Baxter Rumford turned with a laugh and a flick of her hair as she strode off.

Tawn shook her head. "That woman is just evil."

Chapter 24

Harris rubbed his forehead as he sat on a bench in the cabin of the *Bangor*. "We can't let this happen."

Tawn said, "We have to go back out there. We have to liberate Eden."

Harris laughed. "And how do you propose we do that? I bet every Earther down there is armed to the hilt. We might be able to get lucky against a couple hundred numskulls in the desert, but we're talking more than a thousand armed soldiers now. We would need an army."

Tawn thought for a moment before standing abruptly.

"You going somewhere?"

"You said we'd need an army. I just happen to know where we might find one."

Harris winced. "You plan on hitting up the Retreat for fighters?"

Tawn nodded. "Who better to protect our world? And we're not currently attached to any military. We're free citizens that can move wherever we want among the truce worlds. If I can manage a hundred or so, we could kick the crap out of the Earthers and start up our own colony."

Harris scratched the back of his head. "You're not suggesting we move out there to that furnace are you?"

"If we have to, temporarily. Look, it will take sacrifice, I know, but at least it will be on our terms. If we let the Earthers rebuild their fleet, nothing will be on our terms. Not even control of our own lives. We'll be back as part of the war machine."

Harris growled. "Sit down. I'll fly us. Trish, take us out and jump us to the Retreat."

Trish returned a snarky expression. "You'll fly us out? Sounds more like Trish will fly us out."

Harris turned toward the cockpit. "You unhappy with our pay arrangement?"

"No."

"Then zip it up and zip us out. We have an army to raise and a world to conquer."

Gandy sat on the bench, his eyes starting to tear up.

Harris asked, "Now what's wrong with you?"

"Nothing. It's just... this is like everything I used to dream of as a kid, all rolled into one fantasy. Fighting the good fight, saving the world from the Earthers. That's exactly what we're doing, right?"

"You're weird kid."

Tawn chuckled. "Says the stump who a few short days ago was storming an impossible hill. Tell me you didn't get a thrill from that."

Harris slowly shook his head. "No. Not really."

Tawn laughed. "You were pulling that trigger like a madman as you charged that hilltop, all the while with your skin blistering and burning. You loved it."

"OK... maybe... a little."

***

Colonel Robert Thomas met the *Bangor* as it landed at the Retreat. "Miss Freely, welcome back. I have great news. We now have more than four thousand residents with more coming every day. And all are pitching in on the homebuilding. Just yesterday we managed the completion of seventeen new dwellings. We'd love to show them off."

Tawn replied, "That's great news, Colonel. Unfortunately, we won't have time. Don't know if you've been keeping up with the news or not, but there's big trouble brewing."

"You're talking about the massacres on Eden?"

Tawn nodded. "The news outlets are only covering part of the story. Eden is rich in titanium ore. The Earthers want it. And with it they will have the ability to rebuild their fleets."

"That is troubling. How is it that it involves you?"

"We have some confessions to make, Colonel. Confessions that will give you every reason to kick us off this planet."

Robert Thomas laughed. "Not certain you could tell me anything at the moment that would rise to a request of such."

"We're responsible for the mess on Eden. Our wealth... it came over the last year by selling illegal arms to the outer colonies. And when I say arms I mean a lot of arms. Thousands of repeating rifles even.

"Anyway, some of those arms were sent to Eden to outfit a contingent of New Earth soldiers who were posing as settlers. We went in and stopped an assault on the main colony there. The Earthers claimed their peaceful settlers were attacked and used that excuse to stage an attack on another of the truce worlds. Supposedly an unsanctioned or unauthorized retaliation of sorts.

"When the media turned their attention to that and to blustery talk from New Earth, the soldiers on Eden conducted their raid, wiping out the governing colony there. The new government will be opening the planet to titanium mining where the old government refused. In a year the Earthers will have the beginnings of a new and powerful fleet."

Robert gestured around them. "So all this, the donations, your efforts, it all came from selling arms?"

"It did." Tawn nodded. "We were used by New Earth agents whose purpose was to move arms from here to Eden. The weapons are all traceable to Domicile and back to us should the authorities know where to dig for info. We inadvertently enabled the takeover of the titanium on Eden.

"And the Earthers have managed to do this with all the blame pointing toward us. Discoverable evidence will show that the truce was not violated because New Earth was in no way involved. They got us to do their dirty work for them."

The colonel crossed his arms. "Supposing all this is true, why have you come here? For sanctuary? You wanting us to hide you away?"

Tawn shook her head. "We've come here to raise an army, Colonel. We need fighters. We plan on going back to Eden to regain control. We need fighters who are willing to lay their lives on the line one more time for Domicile, and who are also willing to stay, at least for a short while. We plan on establishing a new colony with a government that will once again deny titanium to the Earthers."

The colonel stood, turned, and began to pace back and forth as he rubbed his chin. "That's quite the story you've got going. And quite the request."

"Had we known any of this could possibly happen, we'd have never gotten involved. We believe many of the arms we delivered out here have since been smuggled to the other truce worlds. The Earthers revealed plans of taking control of most of those worlds through unofficial uprisings, with Eden being their primary target."

The colonel stopped his pacing, placing his hands on his hips. "I'll have to run this by our community council."

Harris stepped forward. "Colonel, we aren't doing this for ourselves. We're trying to prevent the Great War from returning. The Earthers came to the truce table begrudgingly. Having this titanium source would allow them to pick up with the war where they left off. They want control of all the colonies. Including Domicile."

The colonel left to arrange a meeting. Tawn took the opportunity to inspect a newly constructed home beside the spaceport field. Harris sat in the *Bangor*'s cabin with Trish and Gandy.

Gandy asked, "I've heard you say there are about ten thousand slugs and stumps. And you all look to be the same age. Why aren't there any younger?"

Harris replied, "We've asked that question repeatedly. Best answer we got was they were scared of making too many of us. At some point there was also a rumor that the lab where we were created was sabotaged and destroyed, and the scientists involved were killed. From that they weren't able to replicate the prior breakthroughs that made us possible. Whatever the reason, we're all that remain of probably thirty thousand who were made."

"You ever want to dig into those stories and find out?"

Harris shook his head. "I am who I am. No evidence of this or that is gonna change what happened and how I came about. It's the same for all the slugs and stumps out here. That part of our past is irrelevant. All that matters is what we do from here forward."

Trish asked, "You think we'll get help from the others?"

Harris shrugged. "Can't say. But I will say the Biomarines are a patriotic lot. If you're gonna find a group to drop what they're doing to fight for Domicile, it would be here."

Tawn and Harris were called to a community meeting with the colonel. The situation was revealed and the request for assistance made. As an incentive, the colonel promised to turn over full ownership of any leased properties to any slug or stump who join up. Two hundred forty volunteers raised their hands.

With their army staffed, the two Biomarines returned to the *Bangor*.

Tawn said, "We can use the shuttle we purchased to move everyone from here. And we have some of the weapons we confiscated from the Earthers on Eden, but we need more. And I'd like to see if we could get biosuits for each of them. That environment is too hostile to just drop into."

Harris replied, "We'll want to make a few scouting runs while we're at it. An assault plan needs to be put together."

"Maybe the colonel could help you with that. He did volunteer his services. And I'd rather not put him in the fighting as I think they need him here."

Harris rubbed his forehead. "So we need more weapons and biosuits. We're also gonna need standard supplies like food and water. And we'll have to check our volunteers for any other skills they might have. If we take control, we'll have to do whatever maintenance it takes to keep the place running. That's mechanics, cooks... and just about everything else."

Trish said, "Sounded a lot easier when you just said raise an army."

Harris turned to face Tawn. "I think we should pay a visit to Bella III. Reacquiring weapons might be our toughest activity."

Tawn nodded. "Take Gandy and me back to Chicago. I'll look into the biosuits while you two work on getting some rifles."

A jump was made with Tawn and Gandy dropped at the *Kingfisher*. The *Bangor* returned to Bella III. After a full day of purchasing every weapon that was for sale, an ad was posted at the sporting goods store and a message was sent out to the advertising channels that a premium would be paid for personal plasma weapons.

By the following afternoon, close to a hundred fifty rifles had been purchased. Combined with what they already had, they remained twenty short. No other rifles were offered, even at five times the original price.

Trish piloted the *Bangor* back to Chicago port station.

Harris opened the hatch. "I'll be back in a few."

Trish asked, "Where you going?"

"Time to pick up my dog."

A short walk had the anxious pet owner standing in line at the pickup desk.

"You Gruberg?"

Harris nodded. "I am."

"How much you want for your... pet?"

"Not for sale."

"Hang on a minute." The attendant signaled a manager.

The shop owner hurried to the front. "You the owner of the robotic dog?"

"I am."

If you're ever interested in selling him, I would like first opportunity."

"Not interested. Is he ready to go?"

"First, I'd like to say, we did our best. He's very old. And those parts just aren't available. And probably haven't been so for centuries. He seems to be in good shape mechanically, but he doesn't seem to want to respond in the manner you said he should. Almost like he's running slow.

"Anyway, the bill may be a shocker. Sixteen thousand two hundred credits. I even gave you a preferred rate given the hours we had to put into him. And I'm sorry about his appearance. We weren't able to replicate his coat with any materials we have available, so we left it as is."

Harris sighed. "Well, can you bring him out?"

The owner turned, signaling a tech to bring the dog from the back. "I've worked electrical and mechanical gadgets my whole life, Mr. Gruberg. Farker is a first. Would like to have met whoever designed him."

The mechanical pet was brought through the door on a leash. As it looked up to see its master, its tail began to wiggle and the unusual grin appeared on its otherwise mangy face. A short burst of energy saw the dog standing on its hind feet as it attempted to lick its master.

"Whoa, boy. I'm not a Popsicle." Harris looked over his pet. "Other than looking like a junkyard mutt, he seems OK."

The owner shook his head. "That's more movement than we've seen from him since he's been here. The other robots we've had in here never acted like that."

Harris winked. "He's special. Now if we could I'd like to get checked out. I have urgent business to attend to."

The owner gestured for the attendant to conduct the transfer. "Say. I have a few professor friends down at the main university planetside. Would you be willing to bring him by for them to check out? I'm sure we could compensate you for it."

Harris declined. "Sorry. Not interested. And thanks for the work you did. I'll have my mechanics check him over."

The owner looked on anxiously as Farker left the store by his owner's side. As they proceeded down the promenade, two men emerged from the shop and began to yell and to wave. Harris took to a run, moving off the main path as he made his way back to the *Bangor*.

Once through the hatch he pointed at Trish. "Take us out and down to the surface."

Trish replied as she slipped into the copilot's chair. "What's wrong?"

Harris kept an eye on the door leading into the docking bay. "I think someone is interested in Farker and I'd rather not get tangled up with them right now."

The dog moved over to greet Trish, offering up his impish grin. Trish responded with a rubbing of the only spot of fur left on his head.

"They couldn't fix him up on the outside?"

"Said they couldn't find anything to replicate that fur. It wouldn't have lasted for centuries like that so it must get replaced at some point. After we catch up with Tawn I want to make a run out to Midelon to see if that structure that housed him can do anything. Those recordings inside him said the maintenance there was autonomous, maybe that includes for him too."

Tawn was raised on the comm. "How goes the look for biosuits?"

"Not well. The sizes we need would have to be custom made. The salesman said at least six weeks minimum. They might be able to pull that into five for a premium."

"We can't wait that long. And I'm not gonna ask anyone else to go down there without protection. There has to be an alternative."

Tawn said, "I have the sunshield I was wearing. I'm wondering if we could make a few mods to optimize it for use out there. Certainly wouldn't be perfect, but it kept us alive. And it was completely nonrestrictive of our movement."

"Have you asked about it?"

"Give me a sec."

Harris turned and held up a hand. "Hold on, Trish. Don't take us down yet."

Tawn came back over the comm. "Three hundred suits in three days. And they claim their material should offer slightly better thermal protection."

Harris nodded. "Good work. Order them up. And see what you can do about water-packs. We're gonna need to stay hydrated."

Tawn replied, "You could help with this, you know."

"I would, but we need to make a run out to Midelon for Farker. I want to make sure the repairs they did to him are OK. And I think that facility out there will let us know. I should have done that from the start, but it didn't occur to me until I just picked him up."

"Last time he went in there we had to wait hours for him to come out. He goes inside and you're stuck there until that door opens again. And how'd the weapons run go?"

"We came up 20 short on rifles. I left an ad running so I hope to be able to purchase more. Too bad we can't call on Bax for some additionals."

Tawn sighed. "If we did that, she'd have us snuffed. Which she might do if she finds out we're taking back Eden."

Harris reached for the comm button. "When we get back, I promise to go all in on putting this raid together. This dog saved us last time. I want that option available again. And at the moment I don't trust the repairs."

The comm was closed to an unhappy Tawn Freely. A jump was made to the Midelon system and a run made down to the surface. The *Bangor* landed in the grassy field beside the mystery structure.

Harris stood. "Wait here. We have plenty of food."

"You going in?"

"I'm gonna try. The door opened for the dog. Maybe it will open for me at the same time."

Harris hopped out of the *Bangor* as Farker followed. As they stood in front of the large heavy door. The dog let out a single fark. Nothing happened.

Harris banged on the door. "Hello?"

All was silent. The impatient Biomarine turned to walk back to the ship. Trish was standing in the open hatch.

"Nothing. Not opening." Harris said.

"Trish pointed as he reached the ship. "Opening now."

Harris turned and sprinted as his mechanical pet trotted through. The door to the structure closed before he reached it.

"Well that's not fair."

Trish smirked. "Maybe they don't like you."

Harris stopped with one foot up in the *Bangor*. "There is no they. It's a program."

"Then maybe *it* doesn't like you."

Harris glared. "You're not helping with those comments."

"They're helping me."

"Gonna help you out of a job."

Trish shook her head. "I don't think so. You like having a lackey to order around."

Harris stepped up into the ship. "Maybe."

Chapter 25

Two days later, the door to the structure opened and a renewed Farker bolted out. Harris was sitting in the hatch with a smile when the mechanical dog ran up to him acting all excited. Its external coat had been replaced.

Harris reached down, taking the dog's head in his hands and scratching the sides of its face. "Aw, you look good, boy!"

Harris and his pet hopped up into the ship and the hatch was closed. An hour later Trish had them back on Domicile. A comm was opened to Tawn and Gandy.

"How are the supplies looking?"

Gandy replied, "She's working on foodstocks. We're sitting outside a company that makes MREs. They've fallen on hard times since the truce, but still make replacement stock for the aging supplies in the military storehouses."

"Has she said anything about how we're gonna get all this to Eden? Just using that shuttle doesn't meet our needs. Maybe I should lease a larger transport."

"She's coming in now, you can ask her yourself."

Tawn stepped up into the cabin of the *Kingfisher*. "I just bought two months of MREs for two hundred people."

Harris chuckled. "I hope you ordered for slugs and stumps and not regulars."

Tawn nodded. "I did. Triple ration. We can stretch it if needed."

"Do we have a way to get it there?"

"Took care of that this morning. We leased the *Biarritz*. Big enough to accommodate everyone and our supplies. Tomorrow we'll have the suits and the food. How'd it go with the mutt?"

Harris smiled as he adjusted the camera to include the dog. "Good as new."

Tawn returned a guilty look. "I ordered a sunshield for him."

Harris laughed. "So you do actually like him?"

"I want to hate him but I just can't. If he would ditch the leg-humping, he'd be ideal."

"No. If he did that he would no longer be special to you. That's your bond. You secretly like the humping."

Tawn scowled. "This conversation is done. Glad your dog is back to normal. Now if you'll excuse me, I have to buy every type of tool we think we'll need out there to sustain a colony. I want to hit that place ready to go from day one. And I don't see it taking more than a day to take control."

"We'll make a run back the Bella III for the rifles. It's been a few days, maybe a few more will be available."

***

Trish piloted the *Bangor* down through the atmosphere of the Bella colony planet.

Harris commented. "You sure are getting good at that. Hardly felt a bump."

"You were right about letting the feedback guide you. Once you get that reaction set in your brain it all seems natural. Watch this landing..."

The *Bangor* dove toward the ground at an increasing speed. Harris gripped the edge of the console in front of him. Trish pulled back on the throttle, righting the ship at the last moment as they came in hard. It touched down with only the slighted sound reverberation through the hull as a cloud of dirt and grass spread out in every direction.

Harris nodded. "Impressive. Scary, but impressive."

Trish frowned. "Actually I botched that one. Cut it too close. Glad I didn't pick the tarmac to land on. I guess there's always next time, huh?"

A taxi was called and the duo made their way to the sports store where the posting had been made. Another sixteen rifles

240

were available. Premiums were paid and the weapons collected. When they returned to the *Bangor*, another ship was parked in the grass beside it.

Baxter Rumford was standing with her hands on her hips. "Hope the two of you aren't up to no good."

Harris said, "Just picking up a few rifles."

Bax crossed her arms. "You wouldn't be planning an assault on Eden would you?"

"I've had enough of that fire-pit. Why would I be going out there?"

Bax shrugged. "Maybe feeling guilty about it falling to the Earthers?"

Harris shook his head. "I'm sure you know about the Retreat. Well, slugs and stumps like having rifles. I'm just picking up a few to help out some friends."

"Some friends? That why you bought up a couple hundred a few days ago?"

"We have over four thousand of us at that colony now. I could actually use more if you have them for sale."

Bax held up a hand. "Not happening. And I can't say I like you digging into this out here. Paying that much for those rifles draws attention. I've done my best to cover your tracks from our dealings. Don't need you exposing them again. Make this your last buy."

Harris chuckled. "Or what?"

"Or the people I work for will see you as a liability they don't care to have." Bax pointed at Trish. "And that goes for your friend there. They won't hesitate to take out anyone they feel is a threat."

Farker growled at the red haired woman. "And get that beast away from me. Shouldn't he be humping someone's leg or something?"

Harris signaled for the dog to go back inside the ship. "He's just a good judge of character. Can't fault him for that."

240

Bax looked at the ground under the *Bangor*. "Who landed that thing? If you're making craters when you land you need a new pilot."

Trish began to step forward with a balled fist. Harris held her back.

"Looks like you need leashes for both your pets. Anyway, I warned you about your dealings. If they decide they're done with you there won't be a warning. Just a swift and sure end."

Baxter Rumford turned and boarded the *Fargo*. Seconds later the air surrounding it was rushing inward as it rocketed up through the atmosphere.

Trish said, "Please, just let me punch her next time."

Harris chuckled. "I don't know, she looks kind of scrappy herself. You sure you'd want to tangle with that?"

"Hmm. She may have the looks but I have the fists of wonder."

Harris laughed. "The what?"

"The fists of wonder. I boxed in grade school, and that's what my coach called me. Never lost a match, even in the weight class above me."

Harris sighed. "Big difference in a coached match and a fight out here. She won't play by any rules and wouldn't hesitate to stick a blade in your gut."

Trish slowly shook her head. "Wouldn't give her the chance."

Harris gestured toward the hatch. "OK, Warrior. Let's see if we can make it back to Domicile before you unleash your fury on someone else."

$$***$$

The reflective sunshields were collected along with the large supply of MREs. Drills, wrenches, welders and metal-formers were picked up and loaded on the *Biarritz*. A flight was made out to the Retreat where the two hundred forty slug and stump volunteers waited. A further jump had the ship in orbit over

Eden. The *Bangor* and the *Kingfisher* sat parked in a docking bay.

Colonel Robert Thomas stood in front of the recruits. "Men and women of the retreat, honored veterans, slugs and stumps. You volunteered today to fight against the oppression of the New Earth Empire, against the taking of your freedoms and rights, and against the domination of your beloved world... the free planet of Domicile.

"Long ago we all swore an oath to protect and defend our world. It was an oath intended to shield our citizens, our form of government, and our inalienable rights, from those who would do them harm or take them away. Today you are called upon to hold true to that oath and all it stands for.

"On the planet below is a complex of buildings with connecting underground tunnels. Those buildings once housed the colony of Dove, a pacifist community that came out here to live in peace. That community was overrun and butchered by Earthers who are bent on controlling this planet.

"Eden is not for the weak or faint of heart. It's a desert planet with scorching surface temperatures. Its Domer inhabitants rarely came out into the light of day. Earthers have seen to it they never will.

"Eden is also rich in titanium, titanium New Earth wants and needs if it's to rebuild its fleets. Those fleets, if brought up to the levels of their desires, would be used for conquest against all the colonies of Domicile. We all swore an oath to stop that from happening.

"Shortly we will be down on the surface. I've drawn up plans for the assault of the complex. Our goal is to disarm or dislodge the invaders and to establish a sustainable colony that will deny the titanium ores to New Earth. We may be here for months or possibly years. Your commitment has shown your loyalty to your world. That commitment will one day be revered and celebrated by all.

"If any of you have doubts about the operation we're undertaking here, please feel free to make it known. You will be returned to the Retreat without question or comment. As we have said before, your duties here are voluntary."

The recruits sat in stern silence.

The colonel let out a long breath. "You have each been assigned to squads and those squads have each been given missions. When those have been accomplished you will move on to secondary tasks. If all goes well, I expect the fighting to be over within the hour.

"The force below is estimated to be as many as fifteen hundred strong. They butchered twenty thousand of our peaceful citizens. I expect that kindness to be returned, not through acts of revenge or torture, but through acts of overwhelming and decisive force. When our goals have been accomplished, all surviving prisoners will be dealt with in our standard, humane ways."

The colonel looked over the room. "Some of you I've fought beside before. Others... I look forward to doing so today. As your commander, I'll be going in with you."

Tawn frowned as she whispered to Harris. "I was hoping he wouldn't do that. The Retreat needs him. They can't afford the loss."

"He'll be fine. Just like us, he's done this before. Besides, he's got more than two hundred Biomarines backing him up. I doubt this will take the hour he's planned on."

The speech was wrapped up and the order to prepare was given. Water packs were distributed and put on, followed by the sunshield suits. Plasma rifles were handed out with spare charges. The cargo hold of the *Biarritz* was soon echoing with the whining sound of plasma rifle charging circuits as they were put through the standard pre-fight testing.

In addition to the water-packs, a hundred cooled water-stations would be dropped between the buildings along with spare sunshield suits and food rations. When the preparations had been checked and rechecked, the order for the assault was given. The *Biarritz* dropped into the atmosphere of Eden.

Harris made his way toward the *Bangor*.

Tawn asked, "You not fighting?"

Harris laughed. "I am. I'm just taking in my ship. I want her at the scene in case we need the railgun. And I want her close

244

to the ground in case I want Farker. He might be useful when clearing these buildings. You going in with the others?"

Tawn nodded. "I am. Gandy will be staying here with the *Kingfisher*. If I need him he's only a comm away."

Harris stepped up into the cabin of the *Bangor*.

Trish asked, "We going?"

Harris sat in the pilot seat. "I want you to drop me at the designated building. From there you go back up to fifty meters to wait for my command. I might want Farker, or I might want a pickup, or I might need you to fire that railgun. You have issue with any of those?"

"No sir. I'll be waiting."

Harris nodded. "Good. Take us out and let's get this done."

The *Bangor* shot out of the docking bay as the *Biarritz* reached ten kilometers. A short buffet saw Trish Boleman take control. After a nose-over maneuver, the *Bangor* raced toward the ground as a second fireball. Trish pulled the ship to a stop a half-meter above the sand.

A cloud of sand blasted the building beside which they had landed. The hatch opened and Harris Gruberg jumped out. The door of the building he targeted was checked. It was open. Harris pulled back hard, diving forward into a roll and coming up into a shooting stance. The room was empty.

A comm opened from the colony of Dove. "Unidentified ships. This is the colony port for Eden. Please identify yourselves."

A short jog down a hall brought the sound of voices. Again the Biomarine dove, sliding to a stop in front of a doorway with his plasma rifle at the ready. Four, robe and sandal wearing pacifists, sat on several couches.

"Hello?"

Harris asked, "Where are the Earthers?"

"The Earthers? Is that a weapon? Those aren't allowed here!"

Harris rolled over, coming up on his feet with his weapon still raised. "New Earthers took this colony. Where are they?"

244

The respondent hesitated. "After the incident, we allowed a ship to land at their outpost. They all went home."

The confused Biomarine slowly lowered his weapon. "They didn't attack here?"

A comm came in from the colonel. "Anyone seeing any resistance? We're hitting nothing but Domers so far."

As Harris went to respond, Trish came over the comm. "We have visitors! It's... a New Earth destroyer! Just came through a wormhole! And the guy at the port desk... he's a Domer."

A hail came in from the Destroyer. "Assaulting vessel. This is the New Earth Destroyer *Ernst*. You are in violation of the Truce of Beckland and the constitution of the colony of Eden. You will cease all hostilities and submit to our authority."

Harris scowled as he looked out under the hood of his sunshield suit. "Played by Baxter Rumford... again."

He turned and sprinted back toward the door. "Trish, I need an immediate pickup!"

The door was flung open to a blast of hot sand as the *Bangor* settled just above the ground. Harris dove into an opening hatch, ordering it to immediately shut.

Trish asked. "What are we doing?"

A second wormhole opened. A second New Earth destroyer slipped through. Harris flipped off the sunshield and hopped into the pilot's chair, his lap belt was fastened and pulled tight.

"We're running. Nothing good will come from our capture."

The *Bangor* lifted up and began to race away across the desert as the bulky destroyer dropped through the atmosphere.

Trish said, "The *Kingfisher* just came out of the *Biarritz*!"

Harris opened a comm. "Gandy? What are you doing?"

"I'm following you!"

Two plasma bursts from the *Ernst* rumbled on the hull of the *Kingfisher*. Gandy Boleman did his best to evade the shots that followed. Two additional hits saw smoke starting to fill the cabin.

246

Gandy yelled, "They're pounding me here!"

Harris growled. "Should have stayed put. Hang on!"

The *Bangor* circled hard back, stretching the limits of the inertial dampener system. "Bring the railgun up."

Trish replied, "Against that? A destroyer? Are you serious?"

"Just do it! And set the feed to auto!"

Harris dodged the first rounds that came their way as the *Bangor* closed on the daunting New Earth destroyer.

Gandy said, "I'm putting her down! Can't see in here!"

Harris yelled into the comm. "I'll be right there. Swooping in fast. You be ready to dive in the hatch!"

A hesitant Gandy replied as the *Kingfisher* slowed and descended, "OK."

Two plasma rounds found their mark on the front of the approaching *Bangor*. The ancient warship jerked violently. Harris pushed the stick from side to side as he kept on the close. Another round struck the hull as two others missed.

The trigger for the railgun was pressed. Vibrations reverberated through the ship as a series of supersonic cracking sounds were heard through the hull. The nose of the attacking destroyer caved in as its armor was perforated and its superstructure failed.

Explosions followed, with the immense ship diving straight for the desert surface. Sand flew in every direction as the forward bulkheads of the destroyer buckled and folded on impact. As the ship came to a stop, the back half slowly rolled over, slamming to the surface with another blizzard of sand and dust being kicked up.

Trish sat with her jaw dropped as Harris stared in disbelief at his display. The control stick of the *Bangor* was turned and the craft raced back toward the ground. The second destroyer began firing from high altitude as it entered the atmosphere of Eden.

Harris guided the heavily armored, Zwicker Class ship in low, pulling to a stop just short of the downed *Kingfisher*. A wave of sand and dust passed Gandy Boleman as he made his way

246

toward the open hatch. A dive into the cabin had the *Bangor* swiftly moving away as plasma rounds began to impact the ground around the *Kingfisher*.

The centuries-old ship exploded, shattering into thousands of pieces as the New Earth Destroyer opened up with all cannons. A small crater of debris, billowing with smoke, was all that remained.

A new general comm came in. "Hostile vessel. This is the New Earth Destroyer *Kabalat*. Cease all activity and prepare to be boarded."

Harris pulled back on the control stick, turning the *Bangor* into a fireball as it raced up through the atmosphere. Repeated plasma rounds sizzled the air around the departing ship as it rocketed upward.

As the blackness of space began to fill the display, Gandy asked, "What about Miss Freely?"

Harris shook his head. "Can't help her now."

Once out into free space, a wormhole opened. The *Bangor* slipped through.

Chapter 26

The ship drifted in the dead space between two star systems. Harris Gruberg paced back and forth on the cabin deck.

Trish sat with her arms crossed and a dejected look on her face. "You couldn't have known."

Harris shook his head. "She played us like sock puppets. Her hand was in all this. She knew we wouldn't let Eden fall to the Earthers like that. And who knows what our government has been doing in all this? Where are they? There are New Earth destroyers out there. That has to be a violation of the Beckland Truce."

Gandy insisted. "We have to go back for her."

Harris glared. "And do what? That destroyer will keep its distance. We got lucky that first one was sloppy. They won't make that mistake again."

Trish said, "We should at least go back and see what's happening. We can keep our distance and jump away if we have to."

Harris thought for a moment and nodded. "Let's do that. We can't go back to Chicago Port. The DDI will be waiting there for us."

Gandy said, "Maybe not. What if we go to the Retreat and take the shuttle to the station?"

Harris rubbed the back of his neck. "And do what? Even if we make it on the station, what is there to do? They'll just come get us. Cameras are everywhere. If they want to find us, they will."

After several paces Harris gestured toward the cockpit and Trish. "OK. Take us back to Eden. For the moment we do as you suggest. We observe. But bring us in far enough out that they won't detect the wormhole opening. We'll sit and watch and decide what to do from there."

Trish piloted the ship to within sensor range. A third New Earth warship had come on the scene, parking in orbit. The second hovered just above the *Biarritz*, which had settled on the sand beside the colony of Dove. Three wormholes opened with Domicile warships coming through.

Instead of a confrontation, the Domicile cruisers pulled to a stop beside the New Earth Destroyer. Several minutes of inaction passed before one of the ships turned toward the *Bangor*.

Harris sighed. "That's our signal to go."

A wormhole opened and the *Bangor* slipped through.

Trish said, "If we can't go back to Chicago, can we at least go to the Retreat?"

"And what would we do there?" Harris replied.

"Hide out? Or load up on supplies? And what are we gonna do about jump fuel? At some point we'll have to visit Chicago."

Harris sat in the pilot's chair. "We jump to the Retreat. And we take the shuttle and siphon the fuel. We can raid the storehouse there as well. Won't be long before those Domer ships are heading out there to question everyone. I still can't believe we were such suckers."

A jump had the ship in orbit above the Retreat. Minutes later she rested on the grass of the spaceport. Harris opened a comm to the second in charge.

"This is Captain Huat. How can I help you, Mr. Gruberg?"

"I'll try to be brief. Big trouble is coming. Our raid on Eden was a setup. The colony had not been overrun by Earthers. Now it has both New Earth and Domicile warships in orbit. Our people have been captured. We need food and fuel and we need it fast. I would expect Domicile ships to be here shortly. So we're gonna need to grab and run.

"Can you send a few hands over to the supply warehouse? And I need someone with equipment who can transfer fuel from the shuttle into our ship."

The captain nodded. "Give me a few minutes to get organized. What do you need from the supplies?"

"We've got about 50 Cubic meters of cargo space. I'd like to load half with food and half with containers for fuel."

The captain replied, "We have the food. In fact, we just took shipment of about fifty thousand MREs. Miss Freely sent them along because she had heard a number of comments from some of us that missed them. I can load you up with as many of those as you need.

Harris asked, "And the fuel?"

"The fuel canisters, and any fuel, might be a problem. The shuttle should be back in a few hours. I can send a ship making sure they top off before coming back, but you'll have to wait for them. We do have the fuel transfer equipment in the storehouse. I can give you a set to take with you."

Harris frowned. "I don't know if we have a few hours. The Domer ships could be jumping this way any minute. Bring us the food. If we have to we'll camp out somewhere for a month and come back when the furor has died down."

"Sorry to hear about the mission. Who has control of Eden?"

"The Pacifists for the moment. But I have a suspicion that might be changing soon. Oh, and you'll probably appreciate this one. I managed to down a New Earth Destroyer with the *Bangor*."

"How would you have done that?"

Harris grinned. "We got one of her railguns working. Shredded the nose of the destroyer, sending into the ground. Crashed hard. If there were any survivors, luck was with them."

The captain smiled. "I'll be sure to pass that news around. Even with this going bad, that little fact will make you popular."

Harris shook his head. "I don't need popular right now. I need a new identity."

The captain leaned into the comm. "We do have several slugs who were in intelligence. That might be something we could work up for you. I'll see what I can do."

The captain turned away for several seconds before looking back into the comm. "You should have your MREs in about fifteen minutes. And for the fuel, if the Dreambus isn't back before you go, I can always have it meet you somewhere. And I'll have it make a couple jumps so we know it's not being followed."

Harris nodded. "Excellent suggestions, Captain. I'll send you a set of coordinates. You can have her meet us there."

The supplies were loaded. Harris Gruberg pushed their stay out for an additional hour before deciding it was time to go. Six hours later, the Dreambus, which had been named the *Warlift*, popped into the same space.

Harris opened a comm. "Happy to see you, *Warlift*."

The pilot replied, "Major Divos, sir. Happy to help."

"Any word on the news channel back at Chicago?"

The major replied, "Very little. There was news that something has happened on Eden, but no one knows what that is. The military did up its alert level another notch. They're now at a three. First time since after the truce."

Harris frowned. "I hope we haven't fouled things up enough to bring back war."

The major smiled. "I don't think we're near that level yet, sir. Oh, and I have a data message for you. Some hot redhead at Chicago Port asked that I give it to you if I saw you. And don't worry, I had one of our intel guys scan it. It's clean. I'll send it over."

An additional hour was spent transferring fuel to the *Bangor*. The equipment provided, along with a short spacewalk, had the ship's main tank topped off. Instructions were given for obtaining additional fuel as well as for spare storage canisters for the hold.

Gandy suggested a tanker ship be purchased instead. His prior shipyard had one such used ship that would hold enough fuel to keep them supplied for months. Credits were transferred to the major for the purchase and filling of the tanker, if it was still available. Coordinates for an alternate jump point were given as well.

The *Warlift* departed, leaving the *Bangor* and her crew to wait. Harris tapped into the data message, sending it to the console and cabin speakers. An image of a smiling Baxter Rumford appeared.

"Hi Goober. You two losers are the biggest suckers around. I warned you to keep your noses out of the business of Eden, but you just couldn't do it. Now look what's happened. You were caught assaulting a peaceful colony! Hahaha! What rubes!

"I can't tell you how much enjoyment I'm getting out of this. And the downing of that destroyer? Kudos to you for coming up with that. It was like icing on the cake. We were hoping to use this incident as leverage to force the pacies to allow our people back, with some water rights.

"Now, with a warship down, the Domers are squirming. And guess what? They're pressing for their own wellhead at the Earther colony, and your government is going to back it.

"And with that well, that colony will burgeon and surpass the size of Dove within six months. After that the pacies own charter will work against them as every resident gets an equal vote in their government where a simple majority rules. Soon they will be out of office and no longer in control of the planet. But they won't complain because they'll be left alone, which is all they really want."

The image of Bax leaned forward, close to the camera. "You know, I thought I was going to be releasing the data showing how you and I were involved in gun running and interference with the truce colonies. With the downing of that destroyer that all went away. Now Baxter Rumford is completely in the clear. And when those mines kick in, she will be ultra-wealthy. Ta-ta."

The message ended.

Gandy frowned. "She is just evil."

Harris shook his head. "She's smart. Dumb but smart. She found patsies to pin her doings on while she goes off to become some mining queen. She's a red menace. And I will snap that twig of a neck next time I see her."

Thirty hours passed before the *Warlift* showed up with a long thin tanker ship following close behind.

The major was on the comm and smiling. "We did it. And she's full. Half with regular fuel and half with jump juice. And I got the canisters you requested. When we dock we can turn off the grav system and float them over. They're full also."

Harris nodded. "We can't thank you enough, Major. We should be good out here for at least three months. Any more news from Eden?"

The major replied, "Yes. The Earthers are being credited with saving the colony from invasion. They claimed to have a ship in orbit that sent word of the invasion to their military, who in turn sent those destroyers. And if you were wondering, the truce states that a military force can be used to provide aid if it is to be immediately withdrawn after such aid is given.

"The Earthers are the ones who requested Domer assistance after the downing of their destroyer. Preliminary talks are underway to resolve this crisis, with the initial word being the Earthers will get their colony on Eden back, with water rights."

Harris sighed. "So it looks like we delivered Eden into their hands. I can't say that bodes well for the future. Any repercussions at the Retreat?"

"None so far. I have a few buddies who are active military who told me the government wants to keep us in the bag should war ever break out again. There's even word of the captured slugs and stumps being returned with only a hand slap. Supposed to get that decision tomorrow. So far, they seem to be buying the story that we thought the colony had been overrun and the pacies slaughtered seeing as that's what the news was reporting just before the attack."

Harris half smiled. "Thank you for that information, Major. Let's hope that happens. And if you go back to Chicago or Domicile, see what information you can find out about Miss Freely."

The *Warlift* moved away through a wormhole. Trish and Gandy Boleman stood staring at Harris Gruberg.

"What?"

Trish said, "Exactly. What. As in what do we do now?"

Harris scratched the back of his neck before looking at the nav display. "Mr. Boleman, you think you can fly that tanker?"

Gandy nodded. "Should be standard controls. Where we going?"

"I think we take it to Midelon. And I think we build ourselves a little warehouse there and stock it with as much food as we can. We're the only ones who can get there, so we'll make it our hideaway."

Trish frowned. "So I'll be trapped on a remote planet on an island with my brother and a stump for the rest of my life? Is that where this is going?"

Harris guided the *Bangor* next to the tanker, extending the docking tube. "I guess that's not really fair to you, is it? To either of you. Your names aren't on any of this, I suppose you could just go home. I can scrub any record of you from the ship's logs."

Gandy shook his head. "Not me. The *Kingfisher* was registered to me. I paid for it."

Harris leaned back in his chair. "There is that. OK, Trish, We can drop you at the Retreat. They can take you back to Domicile from there."

Trish sighed. "I'll just stay. Would rather not be stuck on that planet waiting for a ride. That gravity is crushing."

Harris smiled. "Good, then. Get your ass back in the seat and prep us for a jump to Midelon. And Gandy, we'll hold the wormhole open long enough for you to come through. After that we set down on the surface and start planning out how we survive."

***

The fuel tanker was parked on the surface. Several jumps were made back to the Retreat where building materials were obtained. A ten meter square hut soon contained the food supply, a supply which quickly tripled in size.

Harris laid back on the grass with his fingers locked behind his head. Farker lay beside him. Gandy poked around the exterior of the boson field structure while Trish sat in the hatch of the *Bangor* with her feet swinging back and forth.

"How long we gonna stay here?" Trish asked.

Harris rolled over on his side to face her. "I think we give it another week. We'll go back then and check the news. Now that the Earthers have our own government's backing on Eden, I don't see where we can stop the titanium mines. I still find the shortsightedness of those in charge astounding."

Trish hopped out onto the grass. "We need to be doing something. Otherwise I'll die of boredom before the week is up."

"If we got the parts, would you want to work on that other railgun?"

"That would at least keep me busy for a day."

"What parts do you need?"

"Just that auto-feeder. The rest of the parts I can fabricate. Might not be a bad idea to have more equipment for a real shop out here. Too bad we can't get the stuff Tawn bought for Eden."

Harris replied, "Who says we can't? Most of it's still stored at the Retreat. We can have our friends buy us a hauler, load the equipment and park out at our pick-up point."

"Can we do that now?"

Harris sat up. "Sure. Not like we're busy. Gandy! Get over here!"

***

Eighteen hours later, the shop equipment was sitting in the newly constructed warehouse. Trish was excited at the prospect of putting it together. A request had been given for an additional auto-feeder to be purchased from Domicile. The news from home was that nothing had changed. The negotiations for Eden, and the fate of the slugs and stumps involved, were yet to be determined.

Gandy stood beside Harris at he looked at the door to the boson field structure. "What do you think is in there?"

Harris frowned. "Don't know. Wouldn't mind finding out, though. We just have to get past this door."

Harris looked down at Farker and then back at the door. "What I don't understand is how Cletus Dodger got a hold of this dog. There's no evidence of him having been here."

Gandy replied, "I've walked about a third of the island. I did see some cave openings on a rocky hill to the south, but nothing that looks man-made."

"Well, you up for an adventure? If so, go tell your sister where we're headed. Maybe there's something to see out there."

A fifteen minute walk had the pair staring up a hillside. A short climb brought them to one of two cave entrances. It was shallow, going back only five meters. The second cave offered a more inviting prospect. After extending back fifteen meters, the cave passage turned to the right. Further exploration was required.

As the two entered the front passage, Farker sat on his hinds.

Gandy looked back. "He won't come in. What do you suppose that means?"

"I don't suppose anything. Maybe his programming doesn't allow it."

The corner was passed and the passage opened into a broad room. A handful of items were stacked against one wall.

Harris walked over to inspect. "Food containers and such. Not too old, either. Could be Mr. Dodger sheltered in here or something. Although I don't know why, if he had his ship."

Gandy turned, stumbled and fell, disappearing into a wall as it crumbled.

"Gandy?"

"I'm here. Banged my head, though. I think it's bleeding."

Gandy Boleman walked back into the chamber. "There's a door back there. No handle."

Harris said, "Hang on. I'll get the dog."

He returned carrying the mechanical pet in his arms. It offered no resistance. The fake wall was stepped through and the dog set on the passage floor. Nothing happened. Harris banged on the door. There was no answer.

Five minutes were spent inspecting the mystery door before Farker bolted back out into the daylight. He sat waiting for his master. Harris and Gandy emerged several minutes later.

"Definitely from that structure. Which tells me half this island might be whatever that boson field device is."

Gandy replied, "That door didn't sound as thick as the one back at the ship. Maybe we could cut through it?"

Harris chuckled as he climbed down the hill. "Not risking knocking out all wormhole travel. If that structure let's us in I'll go in, but I'm not breaking in."

An additional day was spent assisting Trish with setting up her shop. When the task was complete, a jump was made to the pick-up point to check for collection of the auto-feeder. The major was waiting in the *Warlift*.

Chapter 27

Harris said, "Thanks for getting this for us. What's the latest news?"

The major frowned. "There have been a number of DDI agents sniffing around the Retreat in the last few days. Our captured people have been turned over to our military. A determination as to what to do with them has yet to be made. The news reports stated the New Earth colony on Eden would be reopened, and with unrestricted water rights."

A wormhole opened only a few kilometers from the two docked ships. Harris sprinted across the docking tube, slapping the airlock button as he came aboard the *Bangor*. The tube retracted as the small ship attempted to flee.

A hail came over the general comm. "This the Domicile Cruiser *Beckwith*. Cease all maneuvers."

Harris cinched his lap belt tight. "Gandy! Strap yourself in! Gonna get turbulent!"

The *Bangor* zigged and zagged as it began to gain speed. The *Beckwith* stayed with it.

Trish said as she gripped the console in expectation of plasma rounds striking the hull. "We can't outrun that!"

Harris huffed. "Well I'm not giving up. We have a live railgun on this ship. Way illegal. I have no interest in either going to prison or being turned over to the Earthers. So we run if we can or we turn and fight."

Trish returned an uneasy look. "That's a full cruiser out there. They can take us out with one salvo."

Harris nodded. "I'm aware of that. Powering up for a jump. We'll see if we can shake them."

A wormhole opened to Midelon. The *Bangor* raced to pass through it. The *Beckwith* opened a similar portal. Both ships slipped to the other side, still one behind the other.

Harris gave a confused look. "How'd they do that? How'd they follow?"

Gandy replied, "They were probably close enough to us and Farker to allow it."

Harris growled, "We'll I can't take them down to the surface. Hang on, I'll go for that moon."

Five minutes of hard course corrections and continuing ignored hails saw the two ships approaching the surface of Midelon's lone moon. Another ten minutes of chase followed as the two ships raced across the surface, rising over peaks and ducking into valleys. The cruiser pilot held the much larger ship in close proximity to the *Bangor*.

Harris shook his head. "That pilot is good. I can't shake them. Maybe it's time I gave them something to think about."

Harris enabled the railgun circuit.

Trish protested. "You can't! They aren't the enemy! Those are our people! Our soldiers!"

Harris turned with a sour look as he flipped the enable to the off position. The ship was turned up and away from the moon and another wormhole opened. This one leading to Chicago Port Station.

Harris looked at Trish. "If we're giving ourselves up, we might as well do it on camera."

Again the *Beckwith* followed with a wormhole of its own.

Harris accepted the comm hail. "Fine. You got us."

The captain of the *Beckwith* replied. "Mr. Gruberg. You are not under arrest. However, we would like to bring you in for a debrief. The crew of the *Biarritz*, minus the weapons they carried of course, are in the process of returning to the Rabid system. I've been sent by Admiral Warmoth to bring you back, should you wish to cooperate."

Harris crossed his arms. "So no arrest? And what about Miss Freely?"

"I don't have specifics, Mr. Gruberg, other than to say they are all being released. Along with the ship they came in on."

Trish was grinning. "No more running? That sounds like a win to me."

Harris looked into the comm camera. "Open us a bay door, Captain. I'll come aboard. My friends here will return to Chicago."

The captain nodded. "Bay four will be welcoming you, Mr. Gruberg."

Trish piloted the *Bangor* to the open docking bay, settling on the deck. Harris stood with an unhappy look.

Trish asked, "You should be giddy right now. Everyone is free."

Harris shook his head. Somehow I don't feel free. I don't know anyone who has ever come back giddy after a discussion with the DDI."

The hatch opened. Harris hopped out onto the deck. "See if you can connect with Tawn, if they actually released her. Otherwise, I'll see you back on the station when they're done with me."

***

The *Beckwith* settled above the tarmac of Port Henry on the surface of Domicile. The port was well known as the primary location of the Domicile Defense Intelligence forces. Harris Gruberg was escorted through a number of layers of security checkpoints and scans before descending in an elevator for close to five minutes.

His two escorts turned him over to an attendant sitting behind a desk. "Have a seat over there, Mr. Gruberg. The admiral's aide should be here to collect you shortly."

The attendant came from behind the desk holding a steel ring in his hands.

"What's that?" Harris asked.

The attendant stood in front of him. "It's an electronic tracking collar. All guests to this facility have to wear them. And don't worry, it comes off when you leave."

Harris scowled. "Wasn't expecting to be treated like a dog."

"Sorry, sir. This is our highest security facility. Nothing is left to chance. Your escort has programmed the route you will be taking back to the admiral's offices. Should you deviate from that route, you can expect a swift visit from security."

The collar was fastened as the admiral's aide came into the room. "Mr. Gruberg, if you would follow me. The admiral is expecting you."

Harris followed the aide for almost ten minutes. The underground facility was enormous, stretching out for kilometers in every direction. A long door-less hall ended at another reception desk.

"This is Mr. Gruberg. He has an appointment with the admiral."

The desk attendant stood with a scanning device. Almost every item of Harris' being was scanned and logged. The attendant returned to his desk as a door opened to an office. Harris was escorted In and the door closed behind him.

What appeared to be a stump was sitting behind a polished black desk. An equally stumpish cigar jutted from his mouth. "You made quite the mess, Gruberg."

Harris frowned. "Sorry, sir."

The admiral stood. "Call me Dirk.. or Warmoth... whichever you prefer. Never liked the title of Admiral. Anyway, do you know why you're here, Mr. Gruberg?"

"No Dirk. I do not."

The admiral placed his oversize fists on the desktop as he leaned forward. "Robert Thomas. He's a personal friend of mine. He recommended I talk with you."

Harris asked, "The colonel is a good man. And I had no idea there were any stumps in the DDI."

The admiral scowled. "Some of us got too many brains for the battlefront. So they shoved us in here. Three slugs and two stumps. Robert and I go back to bootcamp. Came out of training two years after you. You and Freely are two of the originals. She's a firecat, that one."

"I'm familiar with her."

The admiral nodded. "Well, I'm here to tell you that I'd like that relationship to continue. I'd like you to be her partner."

Harris returned a confused look. "I am her partner, sir."

The admiral huffed. "Not her business partner, you moron. Although we do want that cover to continue. We want you to be her DDI partner. We want the two of you as a team. The truce worlds are falling under the influence of the Earthers, and we need to the two of you out there working on our behalf."

Harris fiddled with the steel collar around his neck. "Wait. I'm confused. You want me and Tawn to be agents?"

Dirk smiled. "You catch on quick, don't you. Yes. We want you both as agents. You've shown you have initiative. You make things happen. And right now there are things happening in the truce sector that we have lost control over. Our leaders are eager to regain that control. I've been given the go-ahead to bring you and Miss Freely aboard as undercover operatives."

Harris crossed his arms. "Me... a DDI agent? And you think that's a good idea?"

The admiral moved the cigar from one side of his mouth to the other with his tongue. "I think it's a great idea. So great in fact that I came up with it myself. Listen, Gruberg, that sector is going nuts. Those weapons you sold in the outer colonies -- and yes we knew about them -- well, we weren't expecting them to find their way to the truce worlds so easily.

"The DDI has been wanting to arm the outer colonies for years. With the truce and our boundaries well defined, we were willing to turn a blind eye to your efforts and the efforts of one Miss Baxter Rumford. We even supplied the weapons. The Earthers pulled a fast one with diverting those they did to the truce worlds. A few heads around here rolled because of that."

Harris asked, "What is it exactly you would want us to do... Dirk?"

The admiral sat back at his desk. "We want the two of you to set up a supply business out there. All legit, but backed by yours truly. From that supply network you'll gather intel, and possibly be called upon to perform various missions."

"Various missions?"

The admiral nodded. "You know what I mean. Missions. As in anything we ask. It will be dangerous. And you won't have many friends back here. The media has already begun vilifying you on the daily news feeds over this whole Eden affair. You can expect that to continue. And the more of a villain you are, the more legit your creds will be out in the truce worlds.

"The two of you will be greedy loners who are seen as doing business with both sides. Shouldn't be a difficult cover seeing as how that's exactly what you've been doing here."

Harris protested. "Now hold on... Dirk. We weren't doing that purposefully."

The admiral laughed. "Are you saying you're an idiot? A fool? Easily duped?"

Harris sat back. "Well... no. I wouldn't say that. Just unlucky, I guess."

The admiral winked. "Unlucky. Precisely why we want you out there. The two of you manage to get yourselves in the thick of it without managing to get yourselves killed. That's the kind of agents we need. Agents that will get results and return hard intel."

The admiral pressed a button on his desk. "Send in Miss Freely."

The door opened and Tawn strutted in.

The admiral grinned. "Agent Freely. We're attempting to recruit Mr. Gruberg into our operation. Your first mission is to convince him it's the right thing to do."

Tawn sat with a smile and a snort. "This is great. DDI agents. Who'd have thought?"

Harris shook his head. "Not me."

Tawn grabbed his forearm as she looked at his face. "You can't tell me you're thinking of not doing this."

"Tell me why I should."

Tawn raised a finger. "Unlimited account credits."

A second finger was raised. "You can stay at any luxury hotel you want while here. And eat what you want."

A third finger popped up. "A get out of jail free card."

She raised a fourth finger. "You'd be doing a great service for your homeworld."

A thumb was held up. "The admiral has promised to help us track down Baxter Rumford. And I was having the thought of seeing to it that her mining investments go south. But that's just my own personal motivation."

Harris scratched the back of his head. "And what about our first mates? Where does that leave them?"

The admiral tapped his fingers on his desk. "You can use them if you like. Or we can assign you first mates from our freelance pool. What do you say?"

Harris replied, "I'm thinking."

Dirk Warmoth brought an image up on his desk display, flipping it around. "The *Bangor*. A fine ship. And one that has surprised us with its survivability. We'd like to bring her in for a few upgrades.

"Those railguns are about a third as powerful as the final models were before they were retired. You virtually have no electronic shielding against plasma weapons. And your sensor tech is far behind what we have available."

"Any way to squeeze a plasma cannon on there?"

The admiral frowned. "I'm afraid not. Not one with any significant power anyway. You saw what you did to that Earther destroyer at Eden. The updated railguns will do worse. And we have a few stealthy techs we can apply that will help you sit at a distance and spy with less chance of detection. In fact, that ship design, with these upgrades, is being evaluated as a new agent vessel."

Harris shrugged. "Sure. I'll do it."

Tawn grinned.

Harris said, "What else do I have to do now that my partner has become a DDI agent?"

Tawn stood, shoving her fist in the air. "Yes! Where do I get my badge?"

The admiral shook his head. "There won't be any badge, Miss Freely. In fact, contact with any DDI personnel or any mention of DDI is a show stopper. You'll have contracted handlers that will make contact with orders. Other contacts will return information or log requests. And they will only answer to me. You will have no direct connection to the DDI itself. And your visit here today will be nonexistent come tomorrow."

Harris winced. "That makes me a bit uncomfortable, Dirk."

The admiral sighed. "That's the only way this works. You'll be causing trouble out in the truce worlds. Our government can't be connected to that. You'll essentially be freelancers out there doing whatever it is you decide you want to do, with my slant on the intended results, of course."

Tawn squeezed his forearm. "Come on, stump. We were made for this assignment. And we get a shot at taking down that red witch."

Harris looked at the admiral. "Trish and Gandy Boleman... how do we do this and keep them safe? I'm assuming they can't be in the know about this arrangement?"

"Keeping them safe and alive will be your responsibility if you choose to have them aboard."

Harris took a deep breath. "And if we keep our crews, how exactly do we explain the new equipment we have aboard?"

The admiral once again shifted his cigar. "You have millions of credits in your accounts. Not too tough to figure out. Just tell them you went on a buying spree for the newest tech because the truce worlds are getting dangerous. And you see those worlds as a great business opportunity. Something to help grow and build your tiny empire."

Harris looked at a smiling Tawn. "I guess we're in, then. Where do we sign?"

The admiral shook his head. "Nothing necessary but your word. And I will add this before you go, this is not an on-and-off type deal. You walk out that door and you're in it for the long haul. Once I get this ball rolling, there's no easy out or turning back. We go so long as the truce worlds are an issue. I'll need that one final yes before you go."

Each returned a simple nod.

The admiral stood with his hand out for a shake. "Patriots, both of you. Our citizens may not know of your individual sacrifices, but they'll know they were made by someone. You'll be contacted by your first handler shortly."

As they turned for the door, the admiral held up a finger. "One more thing. You jumped through a wormhole to the planet Midelon. You been there before?"

Harris shook his head. "I was just trying to get away. Thought I was jumping to the Rabid system. Something special about Midelon?"

The admiral stood with his hands on his hips. "Yes. We've never been able to jump there before. Every attempt we've made resulted in the wormhole not opening. And the probes and ships we've sent in at normal speeds, they came back after about a week. The logs and the crews showed a wormhole opening in front of them that sent them back. We've not once been able to get near that place until that chase with you."

Harris replied, "That's strange. Could it be where we jumped from or our speed or something?"

The admiral looked on suspiciously. "I'm told you headed for a moon instead of the planet itself. Why?"

Harris chuckled. "Was just trying to get away. Thought I might be able to slingshot around that moon or something. The pilot of that cruiser should get a medal. He stuck right with me through every turn."

The admiral stood, looking for a nervous reaction of any kind. "Yeah, well, probably had a lock on you with the auto-nav enabled."

Harris rolled his eyes. "Hadn't occurred to me."

The slug and the stump made their way out of the office.

The admiral followed them to the doorway. "Jonas, no calls this afternoon. I'll be busy."

The aide replied, "Yes, sir. Ma'am, sir, if you follow me I'll lead you back to the elevator."

***

Tawn and Harris stepped up into the cabin of the *Bangor*.

Gandy smiled. "They let you go!"

Tawn nodded. "All charges dropped. We're in the clear. Free to do whatever we want."

"This is exciting." Gandy replied. "What do we do now?"

Harris said, "We've been talking. We think there's an opportunity to build a supply business in the truce worlds. They've been getting a lot of settlers. And we'll be out from under the thumb of the DDI."

Gandy returned a confused look. "I thought you just said we're in the clear?"

Tawn nodded. "We are. But that doesn't mean we aren't being watched. Out there we can just be people."

Trish asked, "Aren't the truce worlds dangerous? What about the Retreat?"

Harris grinned. "Bigger risk, bigger reward. We'll still be servicing the Retreat. Think of this as an expansion. And the colonists out there will be willing to pay a premium. We've already decided that's where we're going. You two in or you out?"

"Are we getting a replacement for the *Kingfisher*?"

Tawn replied, "Not yet. But we will."

Harris said, "I'm expecting a mechanic that specializes in high-end upgrades to be visiting in the next day or so. I've ordered parts for the *Bangor* that will take her up a notch or two. Again, I ask, are you two in or out? Will be all four us on the *Bangor* until we get established."

Gandy raised his hand. "Count me in."

Trish sighed. "I've got more credits to my name than I've ever had, and now I'm heading to the truce colonies... sure, why not."

Tawn patted her on the back. "Hey, if it works out and we start making a killing, the two of you are gonna do well. I'll see to it even if he won't."

Harris laughed. "You trying to make me the bad guy? I tell you what. For every million credits I make, I'll cut each of you in for 5 percent."

Harris sat on one of the benches with a smile. "Can't say I ever imagined doing business out in the truce worlds. I'm apprehensive and excited at the same time."

Tawn added, "We also plan on going after Baxter Rumford wherever we can. She'll be wanting to do business on Eden. We'll be there to see to it she fails. I think our lives are about to change... again."

Harris said, "I do have one thing to ask of you two, though."

Trish broke the silence after a long pause. "Well?"

"Are you hungry?"

Trish chuckled. "Why did I know that was coming."

The foursome hopped out onto the deck with Farker following close behind. The truce worlds would come soon enough. This day... the Emporium Buffet was about to be raided.

~~~~~

What's Next?

(Preview)

ARMS

(Vol. 2)

Harris' Revenge

This Human is asking for your help! In return for that help I have a free science fiction eBook short story, titled "THE SQUAD", waiting for anyone who joins my email list. Also, find out when the next exciting release is available by joining the email list at comments@arsenex.com. If you enjoyed this book, please leave a review on the site where it was purchased. Visit the author's website at www.arsenex.com for links to this series and other works.

The following preview is the first chapter of the next book in the series and is provided for your reading pleasure.

Stephen

Chapter 2.1

Trish and Gandy were given six weeks off, paid, as the *Bangor* was taken away for her upgrades. The two caught shuttles back to Domicile to visit family and flaunt some of their newfound credits.

Tawn and Harris spent several weeks of the downtime with their first DDI contact. The meetings were all about the organization of the supply business, analysis of the truce colony needs, and where they should establish supply routes. The colonies of Eden and an Earther colony on Jebwa would be the highest priorities. Their first order of business was to make contact with a list of suppliers on Domicile.

Harris belched as he emerged from an all-you-can eat diner in Juniper City. A manufacturer of nuts, bolts, washers and other fasteners was eager to do business with the partners.

Tawn asked, "Who's next?"

"Metal fabrication machines. There's a company here that makes a complete shop setup to turn out steel bars that can be formed to whatever shape is needed. They take raw materials through smelting all the way to finished product. If you have the ores, one of these units can produce enough steel in a year to build out a standard fifty thousand settler colony."

"I saw another ad for a colony company this morning," Tawn replied. "They're offering transportation, housing for a year, and a job if you move out to their settlements. No education or experience required."

Harris nodded. "They're following what New Earth is offering settlers. This is a race for having colonies that favor one side or the other."

Tawn sighed. "And what are the chances these colonists will get along with each other and the whole plan backfires?"

Harris laughed. "No way. Will take a couple generations before loyalties are no longer strongly tied to where they came from. This will all come to a head long before that. And that first well on Eden will be complete and functional, probably in a few weeks. By the time we get the *Bangor* back, the New Earth colonists could be streaming in there."

Tawn stopped in front of the next building. "Life sure has its twists and turns. A slug and a stump... first gun runners and now spies. I have to wonder what comes next."

Harris shook his head as he chuckled. "Probably fugitives."

***

The hull of the *Bangor* was chrome in color and texture. A multitude of small protruding additions had been added to her exterior.

Tawn remarked, "For a box, she doesn't look half bad."

Harris frowned. "Gonna draw attention looking like that."

The mechanic handler stood behind them. "The skin is active. It can be changed to whatever color or simulated texture you desire. You can add numbers or company logos or whatever you like, all electronically. You enter a pattern, press a button and the ship is covered with it. You should have several exterior images already entered for you to select from."

The mechanic began to walk the outside as he talked. "Those antennae gather electronic emissions, sending out canceling signals to anything they find when turned on. On planet, the best sensors out there will have to be within a half kilometer to detect you. Out in space that jumps up to fifty kilometers."

He stopped at one of a number of small boxes dotting the hull. "These are your new plasma absorbers. They wrap the ship in an ion field and they'll knock a full power plasma round down by about half. Given your hull thickness, you should be able to handle a dozen rounds without taking major damage. That's not a foolproof system, by the way, just estimates."

272

The hatch was opened. "The active surface can also be used as camouflage. You have a selection that will mimic your surroundings. Not perfect, but it will make you much harder to see."

The mechanic stepped up into the cabin. "Your bunkroom has been updated to hold the four of you. As requested, mil-grade mattresses were installed. Most of the cabin, except for your benches, was left untouched. In the cockpit you'll find most of the modifications."

The mechanic pointed. "Displays have been upgraded to the latest hi-res units. Your ship's computer as well, including a redundant unit buried back in the bunkroom. There's also a virtual console back there where the entire ship can be controlled from if necessary. You also have copies of the latest nav-maps, and your sensor displays are now state-of-the-art."

The mechanic stopped. "Who's responsible for the auto-feeder on the railgun?"

Harris replied, "That would be my first mate, Trish."

The mechanic smiled. "Nice work. We only changed a few of the mountings. Both rails are now active. I saw a practice firing. You get within a couple kilometers of any ship and you can open her up. We don't have armor thick enough on anything in the fleet to stop even one of those rounds. New Earth will be the same."

Harris chuckled. "Yeah, who wants to be within a few kilometers of one of those warship monsters?"

The mechanic shook his head. "That's in atmosphere. In space it's more like the fifty to a hundred kilometer range. Depends on the reaction time of the ship or her pilot. Anything over that distance and we're getting in the seconds range for reactions."

"When can we take it out?"

The mechanic headed to the hatch. "It's yours. Oh, and I have a bracelet for each of you. Press this button if you're in comm range and the ship will come to you. When it arrives, press it again and the hatch will open. If your second attempt

272

is a press and hold, the cabin will evacuate and the airlock will open instead."

Tawn nodded. "That could come in handy. Could have used that our first time on Eden."

The mechanic replied as he hopped out onto the tarmac where the ship sat. "It's an untested feature, so you'll want to get in a few practice runs to see how well it works... or doesn't. I'd suggest your first move before taking off should be to set the outer skin color. Try out the samples and see what you like."

The mechanic hopped out and began to walk away.

Harris called after him, "Where do we bring it for problems or repairs?"

The man yelled back as he continued to walk: "Don't care! You're on your own from here on out!"

The mechanic disappeared behind another ship on the tarmac.

Tawn moved to the cockpit. "I guess that's it, then. We begin here and now. Hello, fellow spy."

Harris shook his head as he moved to the hatch and hopped out to look at the exterior. "Are you a slug or a nerd? Pick us a color scheme and I'll tell you what works."

Tawn selected *Newly Abandoned*.

Harris frowned. "Looks like too much of a junker. That would draw attention on its own."

Corporate Shuttle was set.

Harris laughed. "Dripping with credits. Too posh looking."

Aid Ship was next in line. "Not for traveling. Could come in useful at some point though. What else?"

Tawn made the next selection.

Harris laughed. "Looks just like the old *Bangor*. What'd they call that one?"

"Slug and Stump Gunrunning Spy Ship," Tawn replied.

274

Harris smiled. "At least they had a sense of humor. Let's go with that for starters."

The skin was set and the updated ship taken to Belmont, the city where Trish and Gandy were waiting.

Gandy hopped into the cabin looking around. "New benches, that it?"

Harris pointed at the control consoles. "Mostly here. New sensors. And we have exterior shielding that should ward off plasma strikes for a bit longer. Railgun two is also operational."

Gandy shook his head. "I still can't believe the government didn't find that and then arrest us after you took down that Earther ship."

Harris shrugged. "Who could say. They know it's there now."

Trish asked, "So what's the plan?"

Tawn replied, "We're heading out to Eden. The Earther colony there will be looking to retool and expand. In six months that might be the capital. If we hustle, we could be a major supplier."

Trish scowled. "We're helping the Earthers?"

Tawn sighed. "They're expanding whether we sell them supplies or not. If we take control of that effort, not only will it be profitable for us, but we could cause timely material delays if need be. If we can stall that well coming fully online for a few weeks to a month, it gives us time to come up with a better plan."

"So we haven't given up on Eden?"

Tawn half smiled. "If we're not successful slowing the colony growth, maybe we can slow the opening of the mines, should it come to that. So no, we're not giving up yet. But we'll want to play nice in the meantime. One of our goals is to build trust with the Earthers."

Gandy sat in the cabin. "None of this makes sense. We killed a hundred fifty of their colonists. We shot down a destroyer. Why would they let us anywhere near that colony?"

Harris crossed his arms as he sat back in his chair. "Maybe they still don't know or believe we shot it down. The latest

274

news reports have been saying it crashed on its own. And that the crash was planned as a way to get leverage in the Eden talks.

"We invaded. They lost a ship while stopping that invasion. As to the hundred fifty Earther soldiers, we'll find out if that's an issue. If so, we focus our efforts elsewhere. One thing we have to remember is Eden is a truce world. Domicile and New Earth are not supposed to interfere."

Tawn said, "We've been busy while you two were vacationing. We've been lining up legitimate suppliers and cutting deals. If they allow us, we're hoping to be the major supplier on that planet. Maybe even delivering the well drilling equipment ourselves."

***

The *Bangor* landed in the intense daytime heat of Eden at the colony of Boxton. A handful of other ships were parked on the newly poured concrete tarmac.

The administrator working in the welcome room greeted the new arrivals. "Welcome to Boxton. Are you settling? I wasn't expecting anyone today."

Harris replied, "No. We're here to do business. I have word you require well drilling equipment?"

The man nodded. "We do. The funding for that is being lined up now. Once that comes through, we'll be putting out for bids. You suppliers?"

Harris smiled. "We are. And I can provide financing for the equipment if needed. We want your business and are willing to take it on at cost to get ourselves established."

"Wow," the man replied. "If you'll excuse me for a moment, I need to fetch my boss. He'll be making the actual decision."

As the man left, Tawn turned to face Harris. "I thought we were going to slow this effort down?"

Harris nodded. "We will. But first we have to earn the job."

The boss walked into the room several minutes later. "I'm Garp Huukov. I'm told you can supply water-well equipment?"

Harris held out a powerful hand for a shake. "Harris Gruberg. My associates and I are suppliers. I see this colony as a tremendous opportunity to grow our business. And I was telling your administrator here we'd be willing to finance the drilling equipment as well as supply it at cost. We would consider it an investment in our future for doing business here."

Garp gestured toward the door. "Come to my office where we can sit. Have you eaten?"

Tawn grasped his shoulder, as a reminder to stick to business.

"We have, but I can have an appetite at times. Let's discuss our options first. Afterward we can eat if you like."

Garp nodded as they walked. "Wholly acceptable."

The five turned into the office of Garp Huukov and were seated.

Garp leaned forward on his desk. "This equipment... what size well head are we talking?"

Harris scratched the back of his neck. "We can go from a thousand liters an hour up to about four million. I have the suppliers back home already lined up."

"You're Domers, aren't you?"

Harris nodded. "We are."

"And aren't you against the expansion of New Earth colonies out here? You know there's been violence, right? We lost a bunch of colonists just a short time ago."

Harris sat forward. "We heard. Our government is against any Earther expansion, that's no secret. But the rest of us don't care. We're not at war. And we all have to earn a living."

Garp sat back in his chair. "Technically, we are still at war. That was a truce they signed, an armistice, a cessation of hostilities. The war never officially ended."

Harris smiled. "Our government is busy with its own problems. I can get that equipment out here in as few as three days. My government will be under the impression it's going to an outer colony, which it will be when the drilling is complete here. And you won't actually be purchasing the drilling equipment. Just leasing it."

"And what about the well head?"

Harris replied, "My government couldn't care less about the sale of a well head. They just don't want the well drilled. Besides, if we don't supply it I'm certain some company from New Earth will."

Garp tapped his fingers on his desktop. "This is interesting. It's the second offer I've had for drilling equipment in two days."

Tawn asked, "Who else has been out here, if you don't mind my asking? We like to keep tabs on our competitors."

Garp opened a desk drawer, pulling out a tablet. "Let's see. Rumford mining supplies. It was a tall, red-headed gal. She offered a full package, but nothing like yours."

Tawn nodded. "We know her. Have had a few shady business dealings out of her in the past. Our last venture didn't go so well for the customer."

Harris said, "Look, Mr. Huukov, we want this business. And I'm prepared to offer you a piece of the pie, so to speak. We plan on moving a tremendous amount of material out here in the coming months. We have the ships, we have the personnel to do it, and we may be willing to negotiate in a percentage for parties who assist us in growing this business."

"Is that a bribe?"

Harris leaned forward. "I like to call it a business investment. And for those involved... they may earn a few extra credits, but they'll get the job done out here faster and for less."

Garp rubbed his chin with his hand. "That's quite the interesting proposal, Mr. Gruberg. Getting that well up and running early might actually go a long way toward cementing my position here as the colony buyer. I have the buying authority, at least initially. That well would certainly increase any support given by my bosses."

Harris held out a hand. "We could have it here in three days."

"Are we talking the four million liter equipment?"

Harris smiled. "If that's what you want."

Garp walked out from behind his desk, taking Harris' hand and shaking it vigorously. "And before I give any go-ahead to you to begin this process, what can I be expecting as a cut?"

Harris released his hand as he sat back. "In the past we've paid consultants as much as 2 percent of cost. However, given that I'm feeling generous today, I'll bump that to 3 percent of cost and 2 percent of profits. That extra 2 percent gives you incentive to pay a fair price for our goods on future deals, thus ensuring a fair profit is made by us all."

Harris stood. "Can I see your credit store?"

Garp asked, "Why?"

"I'd like to pay you a consulting fee for today's session. How does a thousand credits sound?"

Garp was silent for several seconds before holding out his store with a big smile. "It sounds fair. Very fair. Does that include the conversion rate to New Earth credits?"

Harris smiled. "Certainly. You mentioned food earlier?"

Garp gestured toward the door. "I did. And I'm feeling generous today, so when we get there order whatever you like. It's on me."

Trish said, "That might be a mistake."

Garp turned. "Why?"

Trish pointed. "I've seen these two eat. They just might eat that thousand credits, or more."

The meal was consumed and the business crew walked back to the *Bangor*.

Trish asked. "How is it they don't seem to know who we are?"

Harris replied, "Bax did say all records and logs were scrubbed. And these are new people at the colony. Maybe that info just wasn't passed down."

"Either way," said Tawn, "we're snaking this from under Bax. She'll be pissed."

Harris nodded. "Couldn't have gone better. I actually want to have the first of that equipment out here tomorrow."

"You told him you'll be taking it to some other colony afterward," Gandy said. "Where would that be?"

Harris though for a moment. "How they set for water at the Retreat?"

Tawn replied, "The colonel was in the process of ordering an additional well if I recall."

"Perfect. Looks like the Retreat will soon be getting a four-million-liter-per-hour well drilled."

Tawn shook her head. "That's way more than they need."

Harris smiled. "Bigger is better. And since it won't be costing them anything, I'm sure the colonel won't refuse it."

They stepped up into the *Bangor*. Coordinates to free space were entered and the craft lifted up through the atmosphere.

Trish looked over the nav display. "We have another ship coming down. Transponder says... it's the *Fargo*."

~~~~~

Once again, this Human is asking for your help! If you enjoyed the book, please leave a review on the site where it was purchased. And by all means, please tell your friends! Any help with spreading the word is highly appreciated!

Also, I have a free science fiction eBook short story, titled "THE SQUAD", waiting for anyone who joins my email list! By joining, also find out when the next exciting release is available. Join at comments@arsenex.com. Visit the author's website at www.arsenex.com for links to this series and other works!

Take care and have a great day!

Stephen

Printed in Great Britain
by Amazon